CHAPTER 1

I live in a small town on the New Hampshire seacoast called Maplewood. There are lots of drug addicts here. Even my mom is a drug addict. Last year, I graduated from the DARE program. A police officer, Officer Sanchez, would come to our class once a week and tell us all about the awful things that would happen if you took drugs. I think the police in Maplewood should be talking to the people at Lake Street Park. There are so many needles and beer cans there that the kids in my class who live near Lake Street Park don't go there anymore.

Maybe you're thinking, New Hampshire, are you kidding? There are no drug addicts there. You should see what it's like in Newark, New Jersey, or Los Angeles, California. Well, I can only tell you about Maplewood. I've never been to Newark or Los Angeles. Maplewood isn't that bad, I guess. There are some great parks and lots of good places to find food. They're trying to make it all fancy now. They tore down all these gross old buildings by the waterfront and built beautiful condos and fancy restaurants. The people who lived in the gross buildings had to move to a poorer town.

Some people were pretty angry and started complaining there weren't places for kids or families. So, the next thing you know they put in this really awesome park. Of course, they had to tear down some more buildings, but the park is awesome. It has a great playground for little kids with a handful of climbing things. There's even a splash pad. I guess people wanted things for older kids too, so the city of Maplewood put a skate park in about five years ago. At first it was beautiful, but now there are lots of needles, beer cans, and other gross things scattered around. I tried being a skater for about three days because I had this crush on a skater dude. I just couldn't figure out how to skateboard. I looked like a total loser, so I never went back.

I know the skateboard dude, Nick, kind of liked me because my cousin Dom told me he did. I still have a crush on Nick. He's a year older than me and has long blonde hair and sweet blue eyes. He's so cool, I can't believe no one's going out with him.

My cousin Dom is two years older than me. He's going to Maplewood High next year which is a miracle because he's as smart as a dog turd. He looks like one, too. Dom has some major issues. His mom, my Aunt Susan, was drunk through her whole pregnancy with him I guess because Dom has fetal alcohol syndrome. He told some kids he has fetal alcohol syndrome, so this one kid, Corey, calls Dom FAS. Other kids call him a retard. He's really odd looking. His eyes are far apart, he has these gross buck teeth, and he's tiny. He can't really speak well, like how he pronounces my name "Joo why" Yeah. My name's really July, which explains a little bit about my mother.

Dom's a decent guy, but he's mentally challenged. I feel bad when the other kids torture him. It's tricky to know how to react to people calling each other retard because it isn't really a kid's fault that he's retarded, or mentally challenged or whatever you want to say. I try not to respond when someone calls him a name because I don't want to come across as a loser, but I hate when people make fun of Dom.

My sixth-grade homeroom, math, and science teacher, Mr. Winters, was a real freak about not using the "R" word. One day he had all these disabled kids come to our class and talk about what it was like to be mentally challenged and how awful it is to be called a retard. We had to sign this poster that said we'd never say the "R" word or something like that. I secretly think Mr. Winters was called a retard when he was a kid because he doesn't really know how geeky he is. For example, he referred to himself as "Mr. Win" and told us that all the kids in his class were "winners."

Again, her soft eyes plead. "I know there's something, but I can't help you if you don't want me to. Mrs. Masterson would be happy to meet with you. She's really good at helping kids with problems."

Wait, what? I think. Does she think I'm one of those kids who need to see the crazy guidance counselor? No way. Yeah, I'm poor, yeah, my mother stays home and waits for a check so she can buy more drugs, but I don't need anyone snooping around. What if those foster home people find out my mother's a druggie? My friend April had to go to a foster home for a while. It was awful—she had to clean the whole house herself and the father kept walking in on her when she was taking a shower.

If people find out my mother's a druggie, they'll take my brother Abe and put him somewhere, probably back with his dad. Then I'll end up with some perv foster father who'll watch me take a shower, no thank you.

I've been able to keep things together. I change and feed Abe before I leave for school and then put him safely in his room with a bunch of Cheerios until I get home. Sometimes Mom knows what's going on with him, sometimes not. It's working. I don't need anyone's help, and I don't want it either.

I say nothing to Ms. Paulson. Finally, she sighs and says, "July, you're a great writer. You don't have to submit this poem. You don't have to submit anything. Just think about it. That's all I ask."

CHAPTER 2

My best friend, Maddie Flynn, is the only person who knows about my life. She knows my mom's a druggie. She knows my mother can't take care of us, so I have to take care of my brother and me. She's the only person I let into my world.

Maddie lives with her dad. It's just the two of them. She doesn't really know anything about her mom. Maddie's dad said her mom looked a lot like her. They both have red curly hair, lots of freckles, hazel eyes, and they're both tall and thin. Maddie doesn't know anything else about her. Her dad won't tell her. When she asks, he just says, "I don't know where she is Maddie. She gave me you and that's enough."

Most days Maddie comes to my house after school. The thing I like best about Maddie is that she ignores my mom. She never says, "Hey, July, why is your mom passed out on the floor?" or "Aren't you afraid to leave Abe here?" She knows the answers without having to talk.

We can walk to my house from school. It isn't too far. We live in a two-bedroom apartment on the lower end of Appleton Street. It's important for you to understand the difference. The upper end of Appleton Street is pretty nice. There are all these big, beautiful old fancy houses surrounded by maple trees. Once you cross Summer Street you're on the lower end of Appleton Street. On the end of my street there are lots of three-decker houses close together. You can tell at one time it may have been nice, like maybe a hundred years ago. Crappy cars, old broken chairs, empty beer bottles, and used needles line the street. The lower your house number, the worse it is. We live in number three. Our apartment is on the second floor.

Maddie and I know how to navigate the stairs. If you step on the first or second step just the right way it might hit you in the side of the head. The best thing to do is to grab the railing and pull yourself up to the third step. You get used to seeing mice and cockroaches, they don't really bother me that much. Maddie sometimes screams if she sees a mouse, but she's cool with the cockroaches. Neither of them comes out that much in the daytime.

Climbing up the stairs to our apartment I can hear the blare of some awful band my mom likes. Yup, as I open the door the lyrics and the noise bombard us. It's the heavy bass that I really can't handle, the deep beat that keeps me awake knowing mom is deep into her drugs, reminding me I have to be aware in case something happens so I can protect Abe. Walking into my house is always pleasant (not).

I walk over to the CD player and turn it off. My mom seems to notice something's different and looks up in a drug-induced haze. "July, baby, come give Mommy a hug. Why did you turn my music off?"

I hate it when I get home and she isn't passed out and she acts all sappy and lovey. It really pisses me off. Maddie and I ignore her and sprint into Abe's room. I never know what goes on with him during the day. Because he's two, he can't really tell me. He was a preemie when he was born, so he's a little guy. I just pray he's safe until I get back. Of course, today he's naked. Sometimes I guess that's better than running around all day with a poop-filled diaper, but now I have to look around for puddles and stuff.

Abe's always so happy to see me. I think coming home to him is better than coming home to a dog or cat. "Sissy, Sissy," he shrieks in his little sing-song voice. "Maddie, Sissy hooray."

"Come on little guy," I tell Abe. "We're going out." I put a diaper and some clothes on him.

"Momma sleep?" Abe asks.

"I hope so, buddy, I hope so." I sigh. Maddie loves to pretend Abe really is our baby. I know he's really my baby—well, not really, but I sure feel like it.

"Hey, grab a couple of extra diapers, will you! "I shout to Maddie.

"Can I pack these in his diaper bag, or can he wear them now?" Maddie asks, holding up a pair of Carhartt overalls and a flannel shirt. "They're adorable."

Abe's grandmother bought those for him. In a way Abe's lucky. His dad, Roger, isn't a bad guy. At one time I really thought of him as my dad, but that was a while ago. Roger doesn't say anything about what's happening with mom. Mom tries to pretend she isn't stoned or anything when Roger comes to pick up Abe, but he knows she's a druggie. That's why he left. Sometimes I just want to say to him, "Wake up Roger, Jenny's using again," but I don't. I know he'd take Abe away and then what would happen to me?

Roger lives with his mom in Berwick, Maine, which is only about 20 minutes from here. He usually picks up Abe every Friday and keeps him for the weekend. Whenever Roger brings him back, he always has some new clothes. Roger also gives me twenty dollars in cash. He never says anything. He just puts it in my hand. I think Roger believes I spend the money on myself, but I usually spend it on diapers or food.

I'm not sure about my dad. I haven't seen him since I was three or so. I don't remember anything about him. He was dealing drugs and got caught. He's in jail somewhere. Mom never brought me to see him, so I guess that's it—no dad for me.

After we pack up the diaper bag, we walk by Mom who's now totally passed out on the couch. I can see the straw she used to snort the powdered whatever off her little mirror.

"Bye-bye Mama," Abe waves in his cute little way.

We walk downtown to the playground. I hold one of Abe's hands and Maddie holds the other. The weather isn't too bad for the end of March. We begin pushing Abe on the swing, Maddie on one side, me on the other. Abe loves this. Every time we push him, he laughs and yells, "Again." Again and again, we push. He's so cute that Maddie and I start laughing, too.

Across from the playground is the skatepark. I can see Dom skating. He isn't very good, but he tries to be cool. It must be hard to be him, I think. I catch his eye and he waves. I wave back. Maddie turns to see who I'm waving at.

"It's just Dom," I explain.

"Yuck, he gives me the creeps. I bet you a hundred bucks he'll be over here soon if he sees me with you. I think he has a crush on me or something. I know he's your cousin, but the kid's a retard," Maddie complains.

"Hey, didn't you sign the no "R" word pledge?" We both laugh at the thought of dumb Mr. Winters. I wish Maddie wouldn't call Dom a retard, but I know she doesn't say it to his face like some other kids.

"Oh, shoot, here he comes," Maddie says. "I can't even understand what he's saying." She looks ready to run, but it's too late.

"Joowhy, Mahee, good to theee you. I was skaten wif Nick." Dom tells us.

I understand perfectly. Maddie looks confused and keeps pushing Abe, ignoring Dom.

"So, Tony say you was cwying today," Dom says. "True or no?"

Now Maddie's interested. Maddie isn't in my class. She's in one of Ms. Paulson's other classes. I didn't tell her anything about the poetry thing. I was getting upset because I didn't think anyone noticed. Oh boy, this sucks.

"Shut up Dom," I tell him. "Tony's a loser." I grab Abe out of the swing and start running back towards home.

Maddie shouts behind me, "Wait, July, come on, it's me! Stop!"

I don't want to talk about my stupid poem and stupid Ms. Paulson. I just want to run. Maddie's so much faster than me. Plus, I'm carrying a toddler. It takes her no time to stop me.

"Really, July, what the hell? Are you really going to run from me?" Maddie's breathless. Her red curls are blowing in the wind, and her hazel eyes give me the I-have-your-back look, which I know is true.

"Oh, alright." I take a deep breath. "Today in Ms. Paulson's class, Ms. Paulson was telling us to find poems to put in some contest."

"Yeah, we had to do that, too," Maddie nods, encouraging me to go on.

"She called me to her desk all happy, telling me what a great writer I am and all this crap. Anyway, she wants me to put a poem into the contest that I wrote about my mother and how she isn't really there. Jesus, Maddie, I don't know what happened. I could just feel tears welling up and the next thing I know I'm crying. Ms. Paulson brings me into the hall and tells me she knows all this stuff like how I'm poor and have a tough life, blah blah blah. She starts telling me I can talk to Mrs. Masterson, that everyone wants to help. If people really know about my mom, the state will take Abe away and give him to Roger. They'll make me live with some perv like the guy April told us about, or worse. I just can't handle it." The next thing I know, I'm sobbing again.

Maddie puts her arm around me and doesn't say anything for a while. Then she says, "Hey Abe, want to get ice cream? My treat." Just like that Maddie makes things better.

On the way to get ice cream we just kind of walk and swing Abe between us saying this crazy rhyme we used to jump rope to in elementary school.

> *Miss Susie had a baby,*
> *She named him Tiny Tim.*
> *She put him in the bathtub,*
> *To see if he could swim.*
> *He drank up all the water,*
> *He ate up all the soap,*
> *He tried to eat the bathtub*
> *But it wouldn't go down his throat.*
> *Miss Susie called the doctor,*
> *Miss Susie called the nurse,*
> *Miss Susie called the lady,*
> *With the alligator purse.*
> *In came the doctor,*

In came the nurse,
In came the lady,
With the alligator purse.
Mumps said the doctor,
Measles said the nurse,
Hiccups said the lady
With the alligator purse.
Miss Susie punched the doctor,
Miss Susie kicked the nurse,
Miss Susie thanked the lady
With the alligator purse.

Now the three of us are laughing. We get to the ice cream place and order one chocolate ice cream with some gummy worms and sprinkles to share. Abe loves it. He puts some in his mouth and laughs. Maddie takes out her phone and takes really cute pictures of him. I don't have a phone, so it's nice to look at Instagram with Maddie.

"Wow look at this," Maddie says, handing me her phone.

There's a picture of Nate Green without his shirt. Let me tell you, Nate is something to look at. It's obvious that he knows he's something to look at, too. He's got this serious look on his face like he's posing for a model shoot.

"Yummy," I sigh. Maddie laughs and puts her phone away. "You know, July, you can always stay with me and my dad, no questions asked. My dad's pretty laid back."

"I can't leave Abe alone any longer than I have to, you know that," I explain, knowing she'll understand.

"Well, someday when Abe is with Roger, come over. It'll be fun. You've never slept over before. We could watch movies, do our nails, and look at more pictures of Nate on Insta." Maddie tells me all this in a sing-song voice like I'm just a normal twelve-year-old. She's the best. Then I feel my stupid eyes getting all watery again. What the hell, this stuff has got to stop. Being a normal twelve-year-old going to sleepovers, buying clothes with your mom at Old Navy or even Target—that would be amazing.

"I don't know why I keep getting all teary and emotional," I confess. "Maybe I'm getting my period?"

"Haven't you had it yet?" Maddie asks, kind of surprised. "I've had to deal with that awful thing since fifth grade. It sucks."

"Nah, not yet, but I'm guessing soon enough," I tell her. "Is it really that awful? On commercials they make it seem like you can do anything as long as you have an Always pad on." The thought of having to deal with a period along with my mom and taking care of Abe makes me tear up again. What the hell is going on?

Maddie smiles and hands me this little zippered case from her purse. "Keep it," she says.

I unzip the case and inside are three maxi pads. For some reason this makes me laugh my butt off. Maddie starts laughing, too. Even Abe starts to laugh.

Finally, Maddie asks, "Why are we laughing?"

"It's just so freakin' weird, I don't know." I hand her back the case.

"You keep this, but thanks anyway." I started thinking about Maddie having to deal with her period. She must tell her dad that she has her period and needs pads. That must suck. Then I think, who am I going to tell? My mother's too stoned most of the time. I usually do all the shopping. I'll just deal with it myself.

Abe starts running around the tables and the guy working behind the counter looks annoyed. "I guess we'd better go," I say. "Thanks, Maddie, for well—just thanks."

I feel the tears well up again. Tears again, really?

Maddie hugs me and says, "July, you really do write great poems." Then she smirks and runs out of the ice cream store.

CHAPTER 3

I pick up Abe and walk back to our lonely apartment on Appleton Street. I do write really great poems, but they're for me—no one else. When I was in fourth grade, we did this poetry unit with my teacher, Mrs. Jackson. She told us that sometimes writing can help if you're having a bad day, or to get your feelings out about something. She read us a poem some kid wrote about his parents' divorce. I don't remember the poem exactly, but I remember thinking, *Wow, I could do that.*

That was the year my mom was pregnant with Abe. It was a pretty good year, actually. Roger was living with us. We lived on Second Street in a way better apartment. Mom was really great then. I guess she was in love. Anyway, she was happy and doing her art. My mom used to be this amazing artist. We still have some of her paintings around our crappy place. The way she blended colors to create moods made you want to be part of her work. She has this one picture of New Castle Commons that I just want to jump into sometimes when things are super bad. You can see the old lighthouse and seagulls flying around, but the color of the water and the serenity of the scene is what pulls you in.

When she found out she was pregnant she painted this beautiful picture of Roger holding a little baby. I made a card for him. I remember the day we gave our gift to Roger he grabbed both of us and hugged us and cried because he was so happy. Mom was happy, too. I think it was the last time I felt safe like a normal kid.

Roger wanted to marry Mom, but she didn't want him to feel like he had to marry her because she was pregnant. Sometimes I wish they did get married because maybe, just maybe he would have adopted me. Now when he comes over, he's nice to me, but it's not the same. He takes Abe to his mother's house, but he never takes me. I don't think his mother ever really liked me. I know she didn't like Mom. We only went to her house a few times, but she certainly didn't seem like a grandmother type.

One Christmas we went to her house. Roger's nieces and nephews were there. His mom, Mrs. LaMarche, gave all those kids lots of gifts. It was awkward because there was nothing for me. Finally, Roger's sister, Stephanie, said in a loud voice, "I have something for you July. I can't believe you got her nothing, Ma. She's a little kid."

At that time, Mom was working at Dunkin Donuts early in the morning. Roger would wake me up in the morning by saying, "Rise and shine, Sleeping Beauty." He'd always have my breakfast ready and would even wait at the bus stop with me.

It was almost like having a normal family.

I guess it was March or April. I would come home from school and Mom would be sleeping, which wasn't too weird because she was pregnant. Then she just wouldn't get up. When Roger got home, he'd ask me, "Hey, has Jenny been asleep for a long time?" He always seemed sad. Sometimes he'd take just me out for dinner. He really liked pop musicians like Taylor Swift. He knew all the words to "Call Me Maybe." We'd listen to WERZ in his truck and sing along together. It was fun.

I could be myself with Roger. He really encouraged my poetry writing. He told me he was sure I'd grow up and write beautiful songs. He even gave me a cool diary and a set of ninety-six gel pens to write my poems with. He told me to write something every day.

Things with Mom started to get worse. She'd always be in bed. If I tried to talk to her, she'd get cranky and tell me to leave her alone. Roger would come home later and later. I felt like I was alone most of the time. It was really awful. I have many poems in my notebook about this time. Mrs. Jackson was right—it helped a little, but not enough.

In the middle of May, I guess, Roger couldn't take it anymore. The day he left Mom didn't even seem to care. She was seven months pregnant. Roger said, "If anything's wrong with the baby, so help me, I will take him from you, and you'll never see him again." He turned to me and said, "I'm sorry July, I never signed up for this."

I was really confused. What was he talking about? Why would something be wrong with the baby? I started crying. Mom just looked at me, and this is when I really noticed something was wrong. Her eyes were all weird. They were halfway shut, and it was like she didn't really see me. She talked in this slow, dreamy voice. "Come on baby, let's go upstairs," she said. Now I was really crying and scared. Mom didn't seem to notice. She'd just made me some mac 'n' cheese, and in the dreamy voice she said, "Eat up, buttercup." Then she laughed this crazy laugh like it was the funniest thing she'd ever heard. She just kept repeating, "Eat up, buttercup," over and over and laughing.

I remember throwing the mac 'n' cheese away and running outside while my mom was still laughing. I ran and ran. I didn't know where I was going.

I ended up at my Aunt Susan's house. I banged on the door. Dom opened the door and kind of looked at me like I was some kind of maniac. I was crying and stuff.

"Joowhy what da hell?" He opened the door and let me in. There were empty beer cans all over the place. The kitchen looked like it hadn't been cleaned in weeks. Dishes were overflowing in the sink. The trash in the trash barrel was full so the trash was spilled onto the floor. Clothes were piled on the floor in the living room. Aunt Susan was passed out on the couch. Her cigarette was still burning in the full ashtray. I sat on the floor and just cried and cried.

"Mom will be sweepin' it off for da west of da night," Dom told me. "Come on, wet's go out," he said in his Dom bad speech impediment way.

It was getting dark. Dom and I walked to Dunkin Donuts on Main Street. This was the place my mom worked. We went inside. My mom's friend Cindy was working so she gave Dom and me each a donut for free. "How's your mom, July?" she asked. I haven't seen her in a while."

"Haven't you seen her at work?" I asked, confused.

"No, honey, she hasn't been coming to work for a while. I figured she got a new job," Cindy told me.

Now I was really confused. Roger was still getting me up in the morning and making breakfast. He was even waiting at the bus stop. I just assumed Mom was at work. What was really happening?

We went outside and sat on the little bench, and I just started crying again.

"Did somefing happen to Aunt Jenny?" Dom asked.

"I don't know. She's all weird, Dom. Roger moved out. He said there better not be anything wrong with the baby. What did he mean? What is going on with Mom?"

Dom isn't the sharpest knife in the drawer, so I didn't expect him to have any answers. His eyes bulged a little further out of his head as he looked at me. His chocolate donut was stuck to his buck teeth. "Joowhy it thucks when your mom's a drunk, but Aunt Jenny, she's good. Don't wowwy." We finished our donuts, and he walked me back to my house.

"Caw if you need me." He high fived me and walked away.

As I walked up the stairs, I heard loud, really loud music coming from our apartment. I went inside and there was this dude I'd never seen before sitting on the couch with my mom. He was tall and skinny. He had tattoos everywhere, even on his face. He and my mom didn't even know I was there.

Now I was really scared. I went into my room, shut the door, and put a pillow over my head. I tried to fall asleep, but it just wasn't happening.

Around two in the morning my mom started screaming like she was being killed. I ran out of my room. The weird tattoo guy was gone. "Help, July!" my mom screamed. "Call 911. Something's wrong with me!"

No kidding, I think. I called 911 and the ambulance guys showed up in about five minutes. They asked me what happened, but I didn't really know. I brought them inside to where my mom was screaming on the floor. The ambulance guys told me to get some clean towels. One of them called into his radio thing and said, "Woman in active labor. We'll bring them both to the hospital as soon as the baby's here."

A few minutes later my mom started making all these weird noises I can't explain. The ambulance guys were talking to her, saying, "I see his head, you're doing great," and just like that Abe was born. He was a tiny guy. The ambulance guys told me he and my mom would be fine. They asked me where my dad was, and I told them he was in jail. They looked at each other and said to me, "Okay, honey, is there anyone you can stay with?" I wasn't really sure what they meant. I was looking at both of them kind of confused and began to cry.

They took me with them to the hospital. When we got there, they took my mom and Abe away and made me go talk to some older grandmother-type lady. She was pretty nice. She gave me a toasted bagel with cream cheese and some hot chocolate. Then she started asking me questions about my dad.

I told her I didn't know anything about him. He'd been in jail since I was three. She asked me who I thought the baby's father was and all this other weird stuff.

I didn't answer her. The way she was asking made me scared. "Is Mom, okay?" I asked. "Is the baby, okay? Can I see them?" The lady told me everything was fine. I asked her if I could call Aunt Susan. She seemed relieved that I had a grown-up to call.

"Of course. Now tell me about Aunt Susan."

What did she mean, tell me about Aunt Susan? Like I'm going to say she's a wicked drunk and has a retard for a son. Aunt Susan came to the hospital a little while later with a blue teddy bear and flowers. I almost didn't recognize her. She was wearing clean clothes and she obviously wasn't drunk. Her long, scraggly brown and gray hair was in a neat ponytail. Her blue eyes weren't even bloodshot. She was still incredibly skinny, but she looked like she had her act together. She met me in the old lady's office and gave me this big hug. "July, I am so proud of you. Why didn't you call me earlier? You know I would have rushed right over to help!"

She shook the old lady's hand and thanked her a bunch for taking care of me. "Where can we find Jenny and the new baby?" Aunt Susan asked, all concerned.

I could tell I was supposed to act like this is how Aunt Susan always is. She gave me this knowing look, like you'd better not have told this old lady anything that would get your mom in trouble or you into a foster home.

Soon Aunt Susan and I were in an elevator by ourselves going up to the maternity ward. "Listen July, you did a good job helping your mom, but just don't tell people our business. No one needs to know anything about our family. You know what I mean?" She asked me this knowing that I better know the answer. Don't tell anyone any of the dumb stuff grown-ups do. It's no one's business, and even nice ladies with bagels who act all concerned will send you away.

I nodded my head so she would understand I knew that what happens in the Crowley house stays in the Crowley house. My mom and Aunt Susan are both Crowleys. Neither of them was ever married. My last name is Krativitz because my father's last name is Krativitz. I don't know anyone else named Krativitz. I don't even know if my dad had any family. I never asked.

We walked into my mother's room. She was sound asleep. A nurse came in and told us my brother was down the hall. We could see him if we wanted. She told us he was hooked up to some machines because he was so little, and his lungs weren't fully developed. We had to put on these gowns and masks to go see him. She said he would be fine and that he was just little, but she could tell he was a fighter. That scared me a little.

As I walked into the nursery, I saw his special incubator. On the side, it said *Baby boy Crowley, born May 23rd, 3 pounds 6 ounces.* I put my finger inside his little crib. He grabbed it and really looked into my eyes. "Don't worry, little guy," I told him. "I will never let anything bad ever happen to you, no matter what. You're safe with me."

He sighed a contented sigh and closed his little eyes.

CHAPTER 4

The next day starts like every other except I wake up and realize what Maddie told me was true. I guess I got my period. It's nasty. I don't understand why this is supposed to be a good thing. My stomach is in a knot, my back hurts, my head hurts, and I'm tired. I have to throw away my underwear and throw my sheets in the wash. Really, I can already tell this was not going to be a good day.

I ran into the bathroom and look for pads. They aren't in the cabinet under the sink, and I can't find them in the linen closet. *Come on, please, Mom, tell me you have these somewhere.*

I walk into my mother's room and try to wake her up.

"Mom." I started shaking her. "Mom!" I yell.

My mother wipes her eyes and looks up at me in a sleepy fog. "What is it, baby?" she asks in that dreamy voice that I now hate. I hate that she calls me "baby." I hate her dreamy voice. I hate her dark room. I just hate everything.

"Where are your maxi pads? I can't find any in the bathroom," I complain.

"Oh, baby, did you finally get your period? That's great news. Now you can experience the joys of being a woman," Mom laughs sarcastically.

"Come on, Mom, it's late. Just help me out this one time." Again, I can feel the tears coming.

Mom gets all motherly. She has me come and sit on her bed. She rocks me a little and strokes my hair. Now I lost it. I just started bawling and I can't explain all the things I'm feeling. I think grief is the biggest feeling. I feel sad that this person who's holding me isn't my real mother anymore. There was a time when she was, but not anymore. The mother I have now could care less about me or Abe or even herself. She only cares about her drug. She lives for that drug. I'm not even really sure what she's taking or where she gets it. I only know that when I get home from school she's passed out and Abe is alone.

I suddenly remember that this woman hugging me isn't my mother anymore and I hate her. I push myself away and begin looking through her room for the maxi pads.

"Baby, baby, stop," she says.

But I don't stop. I open her closet and begin throwing everything out of it like I'm possessed or something. I walk over to her bureau and open the drawers and start pulling things out. In her drawer I find this little black box. I take it out and my mom jumps out of bed and starts to freak. "Leave that alone, July. Do you hear me? Give that to me right now!" She's screaming and crying and trying to rip the box away from me.

I look at her. She's pathetic. I'm as tall as she is, but she's so much smaller. She has no fat on her body. I notice the desperation in her sunken brown eyes. For the first time, the tiny pinpricks on her thin arms make sense to me. Track marks, I think they're called. I ran with the box into the bathroom and lock the door. Mom's pounding on the door, screaming. Now I hear Abe crying, too. I hear his little voice, "Sissy, Sissy."

I open the box knowing I'll find the key to my mother's drug problem. Sure enough, there's a little Ziplock bag with some kind of white powder. Under this is a syringe like the one the doctor uses to give you a shot. There's a little spoon and a cigarette lighter. I'm not really sure what they're all for, but I know I must get rid of them. The white powder is easy to flush. When my mom hears the toilet flush the pounding gets desperate.

"Open the door, you little bitch. I swear I will kill you if you don't open the door right this minute!" she cries as she pounds.

Abe is crying, too, but I don't care. It's like I'm obsessed or something. I think that if I flush the spoon or the syringe the toilet will overflow, but I do it anyway. The syringe goes right down, but the spoon gets kind of stuck a little. I take the toilet cleaner brush and turn it and flush again. Down it goes easy. I look at the lighter. For some reason, I don't flush this. I put it back in the little black box. I listen to the strange cries from my mom. I slink down on the bathroom floor and look at the shelf above the toilet. As a trickle of blood spills down my leg I notice the Always maxi pads.

CHAPTER 5

I take a shower while I listen to my mom and Abe cry, but I take my time trying to figure out what to do next. I have to go to school, but I can't leave Abe here with this crazy woman. Who knows what she'll do? She'd probably sell him for some new drugs. The drugs are so much more important than either of us. As I dry my hair and figure out how to wear the maxi pad, I have an idea. I don't think it's a good one, but it's my only choice.

I step over my mother as I come out of the bathroom. She's just sitting in front of the door crying, calling me all kinds of bad names. "Come on, little guy," I say to Abe. "I think you might be going to see Daddy." I picked up mom's cell and find Roger's number. I keep thinking, Roger's not a bad guy, he loves Abe, he would take him. I think this is a great idea, but then I remember Roger's threat: "I swear to God if anything is wrong with the baby, you'll never see him again."

I hang up quickly before the phone starts to dial, so there's no chance Roger will think anything's wrong and rescue Abe from his druggie mother. I pack a bag for Abe, grab him, and leave. Mom doesn't seem to care. It's obvious from the stoned look on her face and her silence that she probably got hold of some of her drug again.

At this point it's obvious I'm going to be late. School starts in twenty minutes, and I still have to figure out what to do with Abe.

Walking up Appleton Street toward Maplewood Middle School, I'm still not sure what I'm doing.

"Good morning, July," our neighbor Mrs. White says. "Oh, hello Abe, what a big boy you are. I just love him so much, July. Look at those big brown eyes. Where are you off to this fine morning?" Mrs. White is out in her yard trying to will daffodils to grow. She looks like she could be someone's grandmother. She has kind blue eyes, a few wrinkles on her always-smiling face, and that old lady short white curly haircut. She's always wearing old lady jeans with the elastic waist pulled up over her belly.

I really don't know what I'm thinking when the next words came out of my mouth, "I'm not sure, Mrs. White. My mother is so sick. I couldn't leave Abe with her. I have to go to school. I guess I'm taking Abe to school with me."

"Don't be silly, July," Mrs. White says. "Abe can't go to school. I'll take care of him. I'd love to. I don't have anything to do today anyhow. I'll just call your mom and let her know." She smiles as she takes Abe's little hand in hers.

"NO! "Don't call Mom," I say too quickly. I try to recover in time. "She's so sick. She hasn't been able to move from the toilet all morning. I'm sure she has that awful stomach bug. A lot of kids have it at school. I just don't think she can come to the phone. I'll just run home and let her know Abe is with you." I realize I'm talking really fast and hope Mrs. White won't notice my lie.

"All right, dear, that sounds fine. Come on Abe, say bye to July." Mrs. White picks up Abe and kisses his little cheek. Abe waves bye-bye, smiles happily, and pats Mrs. White on the back.

"You know, Abe, I have some warm blueberry muffins. I bet you'd like those. Come on inside and we'll say hello to my kitty, Annie." Abe cuddles onto Mrs. White's shoulder as she carries him into her comfy home.

"I'll be back by 2:45 to pick him up, Mrs. White. Thanks so much!" I yell. As I walk away, I have no intention of going back to tell my mother. She probably didn't even notice Abe was gone. I continue my walk trying not to think about home and focus on school. It's usually easy to do, but I know today will be different.

What was my mom pumping into her veins? I think I know the answer: heroin. I just don't want to believe it.

A lot of kids are talking about heroin now. It's easy to buy at the high school. Natasha Spinoza's brother died of an overdose a few weeks ago. When I got into homeroom the morning after he died, Mr. Winters told us to sit down in this really weird way.

"Mr. Win is really sad today, so have a seat," he said. "You notice Natasha's not here today. Her brother made a bad choice. He did drugs and now he's dead. Natasha's life has changed forever. Mr. Win can't even imagine how awful she feels." After his little speech, a bunch of Natasha's friends started bawling their eyes out. Mr. Win made Mrs. Masterson come in and talk to us. She read us this book about a kid whose cat died. She told us Natasha needed us to be her friend and treat her normally.

I look over at Will Martin's paper. He was drawing all these pictures of cats shooting heroin. For some reason this made me laugh really hard. I knew this was a bad idea, but I couldn't help it.

Mr. Winters was pissed. "July, go out in the hall. This isn't funny."

Mrs. Masterson came to my rescue because she told all of us that sometimes when you're dealing with an uncomfortable topic you laugh because you're not sure how to handle your emotions.

I think about this as I'm walking into school just as the bell rings. I certainly don't want Mrs. Masterson to read my class a story about a dead cat if my mother dies. Oh wow, I think my mother might die. This heroin stuff is scary. Part of me hopes my mother does die because I hate her for everything she's doing and not doing for us. But there's a bigger part of me that's terrified. If my mom dies, what's going to happen to me, and to Abe?

I sit in my homeroom seat next to Will. After a while he gives me a little kick and I look up and realize that Mr. Win's been talking to me. I have no idea what he was saying or how long he's been waiting for me to answer.

"Well, July, how was your night on a scale of one to ten," he says. "One is awful, and ten is the best day of your life."

I don't know if I should laugh or cry. I just say, "Five," like I usually do. Five is a safe number. You never get extra questions for five.

Annabelle Peters is another story. She's usually either a two or a ten. Today was a two day. "Don't do it, Mr. Win, don't do it," I hear Will pleading in a whisper, but it's too late.

"Why the two, Annabelle? Mr. Win is concerned."

Will sighs. I roll my eyes at him. Most of the other kids shift around in their seats.

"When I woke up this morning, I couldn't find my pink shirt. I told Bethany that I would wear my pink shirt, but I couldn't find it, so I had to settle for this red one. Bethany was really upset when I met her at the bus stop...."

As Annabelle shares, I try to imagine what she'd do if she discovered her mother was a heroin addict before leaving for school. Her missing pink shirt would go from a two to a six.

The morning goes by slowly. I'm totally off my game. I miss two wicked easy math questions, and Mr. Win says, "Careless, July. Come on, you're a winner. Take your time.

" He says this like that's all it'll take for my brain to forget what's happening at home.

I'm glad to finally see Maddie at lunch. Because we're "honor students" we get to eat outside if it's nice out. It's a beautiful, perfect day weather-wise. Maddie meets me at the outside door. I try to give her a normal smile, but she knows me, so she knows something's up. I can't tell her about my mom. Even though Maddie's been to my house, I've never told her anything about my mom. I know she gets that there's something wrong—she's not stupid. She's seen my mom passed out on the floor while Abe was crawling on her. She's noticed her slurred speech. She gets the don't-ask-because-I-won't-tell part of me.

"Yup, you were right, I got my period," I share, hoping this will be enough. "It sucks. When is my back going to feel better?"

"You can have my little zippered case if you want," Maddie laughs. "Hey, I know you have Ms. Paulson next. She's really pushing us to hand over poetry for the contest by Friday. I just wanted to let you know so you're prepared when you get there."

After lunch I go to Ms. Paulson's class. I'm ready to keep the poem she loves to myself. I can give her some other poem that won't win any contest. That's all I need right now: "Shoot up, Mom, we have to go get an award I won." Not going to happen.

At the end of class I hand Ms. Paulson a lame poem about sleeping.

Sleep

Darkness masks the color of my room
Soft snores fill the air from my fluffy dog
Flannel PJs feel cozy on my cold skin
As I put my head on my pillow, I wait
Breathe, don't think, just sleep

She accepts my choice, but you can tell this isn't the poem she was hoping for.

CHAPTER 6

I hurry to Mrs. White's house. I don't have time to wait for Maddie. The truth is I need to be alone today since I don't know what to expect from Mom.

I get to Mrs. White's house at exactly 2:40. I must have been running because as I reach her front steps, I'm trying to catch my breath. I ran up her steps and knocked on her door.

Even though Mrs. White lives on lower Appleton Street, her house is pretty nice. It's one of the few houses here that's single-family. It's also old, but it's homey. There are no signs of mice or roaches. Walking into her bright yellow kitchen I smell homemade cookies …bread? I'm not sure, but my stomach starts making those growling sounds.

"Sissy, Sissy!" I hear Abe before I see him.

"I bet it is Sissy," Mrs. White assures him. She's wearing an old Maplewood sweatshirt and some mom jeans.

"Oh, July, we had the most wonderful day. Abe is so smart. He knows all his colors. I found my son Jason's toys in a bedroom closet, and we played and played. Oh my, it was so fun. I can't believe the day's flown by so quickly."

Abe grabs my hand and pulls me down a little hallway. "Come see, toys."

I walk with Abe into a bedroom that looks as though it hasn't been touched since 1980. There are Winnie the Pooh bedspreads on each bunk bed and a poster of Winnie and Piglet on the wall. Abe walks to a closet and pulls open the door. It's a little boy's dream. There are lots of old toys, boxes of Legos, old Star Wars figures, and a big box of cars and trucks. You can tell the toys are from a long time ago because the cars and trucks don't look anything like the ones you see today. The Star Wars figures are cool, but totally old school.

"Look Sissy, trucks." Abe grabs a truck from the box and starts zooming it around the room.

I look up and see tears in the corners of Mrs. White's eyes. She notices me looking and wipes them quickly. "It's been such a long time since anyone used these toys," she confesses. "Once Jason was gone, I couldn't bear to come in here. The next thing you know thirty years have passed." Mrs. White has a faraway look in her eye. Then she smiles, "I know Jason would be happy to know a little boy was finally getting to play with all his toys."

I didn't know Mrs. White had a kid who died. I don't really know what to say about this, so I just say, "Thank you, Mrs. White. You have no idea how much you helped us today."

"It was my pleasure. I know your mother isn't feeling well, so I made you some bread, soup, and cookies for dinner. Do you have a microwave? You just have to heat the soup for a few minutes."

I don't know what to do—I wanted to kiss Mrs. White. All of a sudden, I thought this must be what it was like to have a grandmother. I could feel my stupid tears falling again.

"Mrs. White, you've been so nice to Abe. I'm not really sure why I'm crying. It seems like that's all I do lately. It must be that girl thing. At least I hope it is."

Mrs. White wraps me in her long, grandmotherly arms and kisses the top of my head. "Oh July, no need to worry about me. Your emotions get so mixed up at your age. I see what a great big sister you are. You can come over any time. Never hesitate to visit or let me watch your brother if your mom is sick. He is so like my Jason."

"Thank you," is all I can say.

Mrs. White hands me the bag with our delicious-looking dinner, then picks up Abe and kisses his head. "Thank you, Abe. Today was just what I needed."

It's difficult to walk away from Mrs. White's house. I'm not sure what I'll find back at home. Will Mom let us in? Did she find more heroin? Is she dead? How will I handle this?

I have my backpack on my back, Abe in one hand, and the dinner in the other. I have to put Abe on the third step and then boost myself up.

"Mommy home, Mommy sleeping. Shhh," Abe says as we walk up to our apartment. No one's there. Mom isn't passed out on the couch or her bed. She's nowhere to be found. "Looks like Mommy went out, Abe," I tell him, relieved. I secretly wish she'd never come back.

After spending time in Mrs. White's house, I really want to clean ours. I make a game out of cleaning with Abe. I start in the kitchen, putting Abe on the counter next to the sink while I wash the dishes. He plays in the water while I move on to sweeping and washing the floor. I used some bleach I find under the sink and wash all the counters, the table, and the fridge.

As I walk into the bathroom, I remember that my sheets are in the washing machine. Our bathroom is pretty big. Against one wall there's a stackable washer and dryer. I take the sheets off Abe's bed and wash his sheets, too. I then scrub and scrub our big, old tub. As I'm scrubbing, I imagine Mom in all sorts of places. I have to stop. I finish cleaning the bathroom and work my way into the living room.

I take out the vacuum. I hand Abe a dust rag and show him how to dust. He actually does a pretty good job rubbing the cloth across one end table over and over. For some reason, I decide I need to vacuum the couch. I take the cushions off and under the middle cushion, I find lots of little bags of that white powder. I take them all down to the bathroom and began flushing, one bag at a time. As I'm flushing, I become so angry. What if Abe had gotten into that stuff? Oh, if my mother was here….

Our apartment is really clean: I've cleaned everywhere except my mother's room. I open her door. She isn't in there, and nothing 's been picked up from her little tantrum this morning. I know I can't go back there. I've found enough of her trash, and I don't want or need to find anything else.

I feed Abe the dinner Mrs. White's made. It's incredible. I don't think I've ever had homemade soup. There are lots of cut-up pieces of chicken, carrots, onions, and some other things, but the thing that I like the most are these little round bread-like balls. Wow, those are amazing. The bread is squishy soft and dunking it in the broth makes me feel like maybe there really is a heaven.

Abe just laughs as he eats, asking for more. "Here you go buddy," I tell him. "A nice change from mac 'n' cheese or cereal."

After we finish the soup and bread, I look at the plate of cookies. I want to save them until after Abe goes to bed, but I don't know if I can handle the wait. Finally, I decide Abe and I will split one, but when I bite into the chewy scrumptiousness, I know I can't save them. The hint of vanilla and the melty chocolate chips taste like heaven. If I don't put them away now, I'll eat the whole plate. I'm not very good around food. It's not like I'm fat, but whenever there's more than one cookie or a container of ice cream, I have to eat the whole thing, like I don't believe there will ever be more. After I put Abe to bed, I could eat the rest of the cookies by myself.

"Bath time, little man," I say, scooping up my baby brother and tickling him all over. He's laughing and laughing. He loves taking a bath, so that's not a problem. As he's splashing in the tub, I realize how truly clean the bathroom is now. I don't think it's ever been so clean.

I open the door to the linen closet, which is kind of messy. I now decide it's my mission to straighten it out. I pull out sheets, towels, toilet paper, and lots of weird random stuff. On the very bottom shelf under the towels, I find two paintings. One is of a beautiful little girl with dark curls, a little dimple, and a really happy smile. Something about the picture is familiar. The dimple, maybe the curls, definitely the eyes. I turn the picture over. In my mother's fancy curly writing it says, "July in her second August." I turn the painting over again. I guess it is me. I hold the picture up to the mirror to compare it to my face today. I've changed a lot since my second August, though I have the same dark hair. My curls have been replaced by waves, I guess, but the dimple's still there. The eyes are mine, but I realize they're also Abe's and my mother's before she became a druggie. The smile, no way. I don't have a carefree smile anymore. I guess I know too much.

Abe's playing and splashing in the tub. I look at the other picture. This one's also familiar. It's a guy of about twenty-five. He has a similar dimple and lots of dark curls. I have a feeling that it's my dad. I don't remember too much about him. There's nothing written on the back of the picture.

I look around the bathroom and see that there's a perfect place for both pictures on the wall next to the sink. I find a couple of nails in the linen closet, get a hammer from the kitchen, and hang them up. They look great. If nothing else, my mom is a good artist—or, at least she was.

I glance down in the tub and realize Abe is turning into a prune. "Okay, all done," I tell him. I wrap him in a newly washed towel and get him ready for bed. Abe's crib is in my room. He can easily climb in and out of it and should probably have a little bed. I'm not sure where to get one of those.

"What should we read tonight?" I look through the pile of books we got from our last trip to the library. Abe cuddles his little blue blankie that he got from his grandmother. I wonder what it would be like to have a grandmother of our own.

I begin reading Abe, a story about a llama and his mother. As I read, I'm anxious that our own crazy mama will burst into this calm moment. I don't know what she'll do to me when she finds out I flushed her drugs. The thought creeps me out.

As I continue reading, I can't help but think that even the llama had a better relationship with his mama than Abe or I have with ours. There aren't any good books about drug addicts putting their babies to bed. "Goodnight moon, goodnight bed, goodnight drugs that get to mom's head," I guess no one would want to read that.

When Abe's sleeping soundly, I tiptoe out of his room and anxiously run to the cookies in the kitchen.

I eat the first cookie like I've haven't had any food in months. I just shove it in my mouth, chew, and swallow. I want all of them, I need all of them. I slow down for the second one: I can taste the melty chocolate perfection, perfectly yummy. I decide to take the rest of them into the living room and try studying for my math test. The more I think the faster I shove the cookies into my mouth. In no time at all they're gone. Ten cookies devoured in less than five minutes. I bring the plate back to the kitchen and try to focus on the ratio paper again, but I'm too wired and it doesn't make sense. I guess I'm not going to be a "winner" tonight.

CHAPTER 7

I grab my Percy Jackson book and jump under my covers. Yeah, I like Percy. He has a messed-up life, too. At least his father is a god. My father is a prisoner. I guess we don't have as much in common as I like to think.

At some point I must have fallen asleep because the next thing I know Abe is climbing into bed with me. I look at my clock: 5:22. I have eight more minutes of sleep, I think, then I wake up and realize I never heard Mom come back. I look into her room: she's not there. She's also not in the bathroom or on the couch. "Shit, Abe, now what do I do?"

"Shit Sissy," Abe imitates.

I want to laugh but know I need to be careful with my language around him. I decide to say nothing. I give Abe some Cheerios and jump in the shower. I'm really nervous about Mom. She's probably just somewhere getting high or whatever. She'll be back. But what if she isn't back? What am I supposed to do with Abe? "I'm twelve, dammit!!" I scream loudly and just let the tears flow.

As I'm getting dressed, I think maybe I should bring Abe to Aunt Susan's and tell her about Mom. I know he had a great day with Mrs. White, but I can't help thinking that if Mrs. White knows what's really going on with Mom, she might start asking a lot of questions and even call the police. I can't risk that. Besides, Aunt Susan may know where Mom is. It's early, she shouldn't be too drunk yet.

"Hey Abe, we're going to Auntie's house," I say all cheery.

Abe's such an easy kid, he starts dancing all around—I don't know why. He puts his blankie in his bag, and I put some extra clothes and diapers in there that he'll need. I decided Aunt Susan will have food—or I hope so. We have to leave because Aunt Susan's house is about fifteen minutes out of the way.

Dom and Aunt Susan live in the projects. The projects are where the poor people live. Well, I guess only some of the poor people live there because we aren't exactly rich. There are about a hundred apartments in the projects. The projects are on these three streets in Maplewood with fancy names, so you don't automatically think of them as the projects where the poor people live. Aunt Susan lives on Pleasant Valley Way, and the other two streets are Sunshine Lane and Morning View Circle. If she cleaned her place up it wouldn't be too bad.

It's only 6:30 when I reach Pleasant Valley Way. The old junk cars litter the street. Many backyards have clothes already hanging on the clotheslines. The cement duplexes are fairly close to each other. Aunt Susan and Dom live at number 37. By this point I'm carrying Abe along with his bag and my backpack, and it's getting heavy. He's also getting a little whiny. If I bring him to Aunt Susan like this there's no telling what might happen.

As I get closer to Aunt Susan's house, I start to doubt my decision. Aunt Susan is like two different people. Sometimes she's sweet and loving, but there's another side to her, the side that's scary—the one that comes out after a long day of drinking. It's early, so hopefully she won't be drinking.

I walk past the empty beer cans strewn on the steps, take a deep breath, and knock on the door. I put Abe down while we waited, and he starts throwing beer cans down the stairs and laughing. "No, no Abe, stop," I scolded him quietly, at the same time understanding that if I leave him here, this is what his day will be like, playing with beer cans. But what choice do I have?

Finally, Dom comes to the door wearing just his boxers. Man is he skinny. I think I have a good thirty pounds on him. "Joowhy, Abe, wat da heck?" Dom stares at us confused.

"Dom, can we come in? Mom has been gone since yesterday and I don't know what to do." The stupid tears again. Man, this emotional thing sucks. I hate being a woman.

Dom opens the door all the way and we step into the apartment. It reminds me of one of those creepy reality shows, like *Hoarders*. Trash is everywhere: old food, cigarettes overflowing in ashtrays and beer bottles, dirty dishes taking over the kitchen, and I'm afraid to even look in the bathroom. *This is where I'm leaving my brother?* I think to myself. *What's wrong with me?*

I start to compare Aunt Susan's mess to Mrs. White's immaculate, baked cookie-smelling house, but it's too late to go back.

"Mom's still sweepin," Dom says. "I don't know if I should wake hur. She didn't go to bed til pewty wate." He scratches his chest like he really doesn't know what to do. He's drinking Pepsi and burps loudly, maybe hoping this will wake his mom.

Abe starts laughing at Dom's burp. Then Dom starts laughing too. He burps again, sending both him and Abe into gales of laughter. "Want some, Abe?"

Dom hands Abe the Pepsi, and Abe takes a sip and pretends to burp like Dom did. For some reason this makes me laugh. Now all of us are laughing. Abe thinks this is the best game ever. He sips and pretends to burp, sips and pretend to burp, then looks at us for approval.

"What the hell's going on out there?!" Aunt Susan yells in a not-so-pleasant voice. "Can't a person get some sleep? Jesus, Dom, what the hell are you doing having a party at this hour?"

"Joowhy and Abe is here. Aunt Jenny's gone! "Dom yells back.

Aunt Susan comes out of her room. She's wearing a giant New England Patriots shirt and that's it. She looks like hell. Her eyes are all bloodshot and she has mascara smeared down her cheeks. Her hair looks like her apartment, dirty and unkept. She looks at us, lights a cigarette, and orders Dom to make her some strong, black coffee.

"Jesus, July, let me have some coffee to clear out the cobwebs, then we can talk. Come here, Abe, come see Auntie." Aunt Susan picks up Abe and kisses his cheek.

"Yuck," Abe says, and wipes her sloppy kiss off his cheek as he squirms to get down. He picks up the Pepsi can and slowly pours it onto the floor.

I grab the can from Abe, and he begins having a two-year-old temper tantrum. This really sucks. I have a math test in an hour. I really can't handle this right now.

"Give him the goddam Pepsi to shut him up, for God's sake, July. " Aunt Susan doesn't yell, but she's kind of whining like Abe.

I can feel myself starting to get angry. I want to scream at her: *I don't know what to do and you, dear Aunt Susan, are my only hope. You're the grown up—you're supposed to know what to do.* Instead, I say, "Mom didn't come home yesterday. I have a math test in an hour, and I can't leave Abe alone. I didn't know what else to do." I start crying again.

"Dry up, July. I'll take Abe just for today. I'm sure your mother will be home later. She probably just needed a break. Go to school but come right back here after. Got it "Aunt Susan tries to sound reassuring, then yells, "Dom, get your butt out to the bus, and take your cousin with you!"

Dom shows up in the living room wearing his usual gray hoodie. I started to wonder if he has any other clothes. "Come on Joowhy. Bye Ma., Abe, high five."

Abe runs to give Dom a high five. I pick him up, looking around at all the dangers awaiting a two-year-old in this dump. Now I'm really worried about my decision.

"Be safe, little man," I say, hugging Abe tightly. "Thanks, Aunt Susan," I say, trying to hide what I'm really feeling.

The kids at Dom's bus stop are horrible to him. I guess I already know that because I hear what kids call him at school, but this is a whole new level. A kid in my class, Corey Rice, gives Dom the most grief. He starts mimicking him, "Hey, FATH is thith whore your girlfriend?" Dom looks down and says nothing.

"Shut the hell up Corey, you big loser," I yell.

"I'm a loser? You're the one hanging with FAS. What is it you like about him, his handsome looks or his brilliant personality?" Corey starts laughing.

Fortunately, the bus comes. Dom gets on first and sits in the very first row trying to pretend no one else is there. I never realized how hard his life really is. Corey walks by and hits him on the head with a textbook.

"F you," Dom says.

I can't believe what happens next: the bus driver starts yelling at Dom. She says nothing to Corey. "Language, Dom! Do I have to report your behavior to the dean of students? If I report, you again you'll be kicked off the bus."

Now I'm pissed, "Hey, didn't you see that other kid hit him with a book?"

The bus driver looks at me confused. "Are you a new kid?" she asks. "I don't have you on my bus."

"I'm staying with my cousin," I tell her.

"Well, you better get a pass for the ride home. This is the only time you'll get on this bus without a pass," she says as she shuts the door.

I sit next to Dom, neither of us saying anything. Dom pulls his hoodie tight around his face. I think he's hoping to hide. Fortunately, there aren't more stops and we get to school in about ten minutes. Unfortunately, we have to wait on the bus for five long minutes because we get there too early. The horrible taunting and teasing begin again. The bus driver pretends not to notice as she looks at her cell phone. I guess writing kids up is too much work. Kids start throwing trash at Dom, yelling "Think fast, FAS!" Dom sinks lower in the seat and looks out the window. I can tell he's embarrassed that I'm there. I'm not sure what to do, so I do nothing.

Finally, we're allowed to get off the bus and go into school. "Have a good day Joowhy. Don't wowwy about Abe, Mom will be fine with him. I know Aunt Jenny will be home when you get there." Dom tells me this like he wasn't just humiliated on the school bus. I want to hug him, but I just smile and say, "Thanks."

"Hey what's it like having a retard for a boyfriend?" Corey asks as we walk to our lockers.

Now I can't control my anger. "At least he's not a fat, ugly loser," I say. I stick out my foot and he trips, causing a domino effect in the crowded hallway.

"You bitch!" Corey yells!

From across the hall Mrs. Chamberlain yells, "Language, Corey. Get up and come to my office."

I smile as I walk to my locker. There's Mr. Winters in his locker monitor costume. I can't believe he's still doing that. Cameron is standing next to him; they're chatting about ratios. Cameron's no longer the locker monitor, but he keeps acting like he is. He follows Mr. Winters around telling him which students are doing their best and which ones Mr. Winters needs to check.

Watching Mr. Winters and Cameron, I begin to think that Mr. Winters was a lot like Cameron when he was a kid. Mr. Winters doesn't really know how to blend in or get along with his peers. As he's doing the locker monitoring you can tell the other teachers are laughing at him, like us kids do to Cameron. I wonder if it ever changes, people making fun of other people because they're different, awkward, or geeky.

As I walk into homeroom, I hope Will is there so he can show me how to do these ratio problems before the test. There he is slumped over, drawing something. I like Will, but not in that Nate Green kind of way. He's one of those kids that you're relieved is in your class. He's easy to talk to, but he never asks a lot of questions. He's not all weird about talking to girls like some guys are. I guess Will's just this average kid. He's not complicated and he's wicked smart, he just doesn't like people to know it.

"Will, can you help me with this ratio stuff?" I ask him. "I know we have a test today, but I just don't understand the way Mr. Winters teaches it to us."

"What's the matter, July, aren't you a winner?" A big smile crosses Will's face as I hit him with my homework paper. "Give that to me," he says, and grabs my paper. "Hmm, eating some chocolate I see. That may be why you didn't get it," he jokes. "You were on a sugar high."

I pretend to laugh. "Come on, Will, we only have a few more minutes before the patrolling Mr. Win walks in. I'm really confused."

I must look like I'm going to cry because Will unrolls my paper and looks at it. Then he starts talking like Mr. Win, which is hysterical. "Okay July, Mr. Win says you're a winner, so that will make this problem very easy. Just say it with me. I am a winner."

"I am a winner, "I joke along before turning serious. "Will, I don't understand number six at all. How am I supposed to know the ratio of hearts to all shapes? They never tell you how many circles, or squares, or triangles there are. How am I supposed to know?"

Will keeps reading in his Mr. Win voice: "Six. Matthew drew sixteen hearts and eleven circles. What is the ratio of hearts to all shapes? Well July, how many shapes are listed in the problem?"

"Sixteen hearts and eleven circles," I reply.

"Winner. And how many shapes are there altogether?" he says, still in the goofy Mr. Win voice.

"There are twenty-seven hearts and circles, but I don't know how many other shapes there are because it doesn't tell you," I complain.

"Correct, winner, winner," Will announces.

"What the hell, Will?" I beg. "Just tell me the answer without all the Mr. Win crap, please. "

"July, the only shapes they tell you about are hearts and circles, so the total number of shapes is twenty-seven. The ratio is 16:27," he says easily.

"That's it? I can do this," I say, like there's a light going on in my brain.

"Don't overthink it and you'll do fine," he says convincingly.

The math test turns out to be a breeze. I don't overthink. All the problems are from our homework, even the tricky one about the ratio of hearts to other shapes. I finish the test in about ten minutes and happily bring it to Mr. Win.

"Put your test here, winner," he says. "Now you can read or do this extra credit paper." I do the extra credit paper, which is the same homework paper from last night. You have to be a moron not to get an A in Mr. Win's class. If you even look like you do your homework you get a hundred percent. He never collects it. He just says, "Mr.

Win wants to see who did their homework. Raise your hand if you didn't."

What idiot is going to raise their hand when Mr. Win asks who didn't do the homework? Well, there was one time that Kaitlyn Seaver didn't finish her homework because she was at a student council meeting until late. She raised her hand to explain this to Mr. Winters and, get this, he says, "Kaitlyn, your civic duty is very important, so no worries." He probably even gave her extra credit.

Later I meet Maddie for lunch. It was good to see her. I want to tell her about my mom going missing, but at the same time I don't want to tell her. I get a slice of pizza and a salad from the hot lunch line and find Maddie outside and get this—she's sitting with Nate Green. Yup, hot, shirtless Nate Green.

I'm not sure what to do. Does Maddie want me to intrude on her chance with Nate, or should I just go to another table?

Nate looks up, "Hey July, I was just telling Maddie that some of us are going to play laser tag after school. My brother works there and can get me and my friends in for free. Why don't you come?"

Boy, am I flabbergasted, but Maddie speaks before I can even sit down. "We'll be there."

"What time?" I ask.

"Around 4:00," Nate says. "Nick's going to be there, and I know he would love to see you, July." Nate says this last part casually as he stands up and saunters over to his usual table of hotties.

I look over to where Nick's sitting and catch his eye. He smiles at me, and I get this warm feeling all over.

Maddie's screams bring me back to reality. "Can you believe it, July, Nate Green asked me to play laser tag! Me, oh my God, oh my God!" Maddie's smile was bigger than her face.

Suddenly I realize my real-life dilemma. "Maddie, I can't go. I have no idea where my mom is, and I had to leave Abe with my Aunt Susan. Who knows what's happening over there? She's probably drunk while Abe's wandering around the projects. I can't play laser tag today."

Maddie looks like she's going to cry. "Come on, July, if we don't go, we'll never get another chance to be with Nate and Nick. Can't your aunt keep Abe until six o'clock? And what do you mean you have no idea where your mother is? You know I can't show up alone! That would be weird."

I explain everything to Maddie. It feels good to share this part of my life with someone, but Maddie just looks at me in disbelief. "When you tell me things like this, it makes me feel better that my mom split when I was a baby. At least I can count on my dad to be there for me. Hey, I bet my dad would watch Abe for a little while," she adds hopefully.

"Oh Maddie, you should go play laser tag with Nate. Nate says he's bringing his friends, so you know Jeremy will be there. Talk to April—she'll definitely go with you if Jeremy's going."

"If you're absolutely sure," Maddie says, glancing back at Nate's table. I hate leaving you behind, but it's Nate Green."

"I'm absolutely sure. Talk to April on the way home. I'm positive she'll go with you, so you won't be alone. If she says no, which she won't, ask Julia. I know she's not your favorite person, but she lives next door and she'd be thrilled to do something with the popular kids."

"Oh, July, I'll ask April, but if she can't go, I'll track you down and bring you with me, even if you have to bring Abe. There's no way I would let Nate think that geeky Julia is my friend."

I look at Maddie. Part of me wants to go with her but another part is too worried about Abe. I need to be with him alone after the day I imagine he's having. If Mom is home who knows what condition she'll be in.

"Oh Maddie, I have to stay home with Abe. He's had a crazy couple of days, and I want him to have a quiet night."

"Abe sure is lucky to have you for a sister. You do what you need to, but I'll keep hoping you show up."

I wish I could show up too, I think. Why do I know what's best for Abe, but my mother doesn't? When she gets home if she's not messed up, I'm going to tell her that this is enough. Roger's sure to find out she's using drugs again. She can't hide this forever.

CHAPTER 8

After school I go to the guidance office to get a bus pass to go on Dom's bus. Mrs. Lovell, the secretary, won't give me a pass because I don't have a note. I think she can tell that I'm about to cry because she says, "Call your mother and let me talk to her." She hands me the phone and asks me what number to dial.

"We don't have a phone, Mrs. Lovell," I plead. "My brother's at my aunt's house and it's super important that I pick him up on time because my aunt has to work." I'm surprised by how quickly my lies come. "If I'm not there on time I'll get in a lot of trouble and my aunt might get fired."

"Okay," Mrs. Lovell says. "But next time, get a note."

I grab my pass and run to the bus just in time. Dom isn't there, but loud, obnoxious Corey Rice is. Maybe if I just slink down, he won't notice me. I sit on an inside seat and scooch way down—so far, so good.

When we get to Dom's stop I try to hold back and let Corey get off first. He still doesn't notice me. I'm safe, I think. Then I feel it: a rock grazes my shoulder as I get off the bus.

I run as fast as I could to Aunt Susan's house. Corey's screaming all kinds of nasty things as he chases me down the street. Because he's so fat I have the advantage. I run up the stairs of Aunt Susan's apartment and barge into her living room, slamming the door behind me.

"Whoa, July, you look like hell," Aunt Susan says, kind of laughing. "What happened, are you being chased by a rabid dog?"

"Stupid fat Corey Rice is chasing me because I kind of tripped him," I admit.

"Good for you, July, that kid's an asshole," Aunt Susan says. "Don't worry about him. It's almost dinner time, so he won't bother you for at least twenty minutes." She comes over to me and wraps me in a hug. This is really strange—I don't remember the last time she hugged me. I can smell alcohol on her body, but it isn't as strong as the cigarette smell. I wonder when the last time she had a shower.

Suddenly, I panic like something's wrong. "Is Abe, okay? Where is he?" I can't hide the fear in my voice; I can't see Abe anywhere.

"Relax, the kid's sleeping. Boy, I forgot what it was like taking care of a two-year-old. Your mom owes me."

A new panic fills me. "Aunt Susan, do you have any idea where Mom might be?' I imagine my mother dead somewhere. That thought makes me start to think what that would mean for me. Would I have to go to a foster home? Abe would probably go to live with his dad and grandmother. That would mean I'd never see him again.

I can feel the tears begin to flow. Soon I'm sobbing. I realize that I'm more worried about not seeing Abe again than about not seeing my mom again. In some ways I haven't seen my mom since before Abe was born.

Aunt Susan walks over, and I grab onto her and just cry. "It's okay, my summer girl," she says.

Suddenly I stop crying and look up at her. I haven't heard her say that since I can't remember when. Aunt Susan used to call me her summer girl all the time when I was younger. Memories of a beach house came floating into my mind. I think I must have been like three or four because my grandfather was still alive. He had a little beach house right on the ocean in North Hampton. His house wasn't really a house, it was called a fish house, I think. There are a lot of those little places along the beach. I start to remember going there in the summer with my mom, and Aunt Susan and Dom would come, too. I stop crying and just look at her.

"July, I have to be honest," Aunt Susan says. "When you came over this morning I was pissed. I didn't want to watch Abe. I'm having a hard enough time watching Dom. After you left my first instinct was to grab a beer, and then Abe did something so cute. He crawled up in my lap and said, 'Love you, mama.' That threw me for a loop. I looked down at his sweet face and knew I couldn't drink while he was here. I had to help him and you. But mostly I remembered how your mom helped me after Dom was born. If she hadn't been there for me, I would've lost him. He had so many problems when he was born. Anyway, she needs me now."

Aunt Susan lights a cigarette, then walks over to the fridge and grabs a beer. Her hand's a little shaky. As she takes her first swig, you can see her body relax.

"July, I don't know where your mother is, but I'm sure she's fine. If she isn't home when you get there, come back here. We can figure something out." As Aunt Susan takes another drag of her cigarette and another sip from her beer, I realize I'm not sure if she's the right person to help me. I tiptoe into Aunt Susan's bedroom and see Abe sleeping on her bed. He's curled up in his blankie, thumb in his mouth. I hate to wake him, but I know I have to leave Aunt Susan's. "Come on little guy," I whisper," time to go home."

Abe opens his eyes and looks at me, a huge smile stretching across his face. He gives me a big hug. I pick him up, still wrapped in his blankie. "Thanks, Aunt Susan," I say grabbing the rest of Abe's stuff. "If Mom isn't home, we'll be back," I lie, knowing I won't come back tonight no matter what happens. Once Aunt Susan starts drinking, she's just as bad as Mom, if not worse. Abe and I are better off on our own.

CHAPTER 9

As I leave Aunt Susan's I look around for Corey. Fortunately, he's nowhere to been seen. I hurry off Pleasant Valley Way toward Summer Street. It's difficult to maneuver because I must carry my sleepy brother, his bag, and my backpack.

Walking down Summer Street I notice a mother out in the yard playing catch with her son. She has a Boston Red Sox hat on, and her long ponytail is swinging out the back. I can hear her encouraging her son, "Ready, Tyler, this is going to be a high pop up. You really have to look up and keep your glove right under where you think it'll land. "

Her son is probably five or six. He has a big smile on his face as he catches the ball. I notice that his top two front teeth are missing. "I caught it, Mom, I caught it!" he yells, running to show her the ball.

I wonder if Abe will ever experience anything like that. I imagine our mother just playing with us. It's really hard to picture her playing with us now. I remember when she used to play with me. I remember warm summers building sandcastles with mom at my grandfather's beach house. Mom loved the summer and the beach. She would swing me in the water, twirling me around over the waves. I hope someday Abe will experience that mother, the one I believe is still inside the skinny, drug addict now living with us.

Abe starts squirming, bringing me back to reality. "We're almost home, little guy," I whisper, and try singing a lullaby that Mom would sing to me before she, well....

Too La Loo Ra Li
Too La Loo Ra Loo Ral
Hush now don't you cry.
Too La Loo Ra Loo Ral
Too La Loo Ra Li
Too La Loo Ra Loo Ral
That's an Irish lullaby.

I guess I'm singing louder than I thought because I hear Mrs. White's voice. "Oh, July, my grandmother used to sing that song to me when I was little. I'd forgotten how beautiful it is. You have a lovely voice." Mrs. White then starts singing the lullaby herself. She has a lovely voice, too.

Abe is too heavy, so I put him down. He beelines it for Mrs. White's house, screaming, "Play with toys, play with Annie."

"Abe!" I shout, running after him.

Mrs. White smiles. "Oh July, it's fine if Abe goes into my house. I was just starting dinner. Would you like to join me?"

I'm not sure what to do. Of course, I want to stay. Mrs. White is an amazing cook. I have no idea what I might have to face when I get home, but at the same time I don't want to bring any attention to my problem with Mom. "That would be great, Mrs. White," I say, "but I'll probably have to check with Mom."

"Oh, of course you should. Why don't you invite your mother to come over too?" Mrs. White asks in her grandmotherly voice, all concerned. "I haven't seen her in quite a while. How is she feeling?"

"Oh, Mom still isn't feeling well. I don't know if she would want you to risk catching her bug," I lie easily.

"Oh dear," Mrs. White says. "Of course, you should check in with your mom. Why don't you leave Abe here with me while you run home? I'm making some fried chicken and mashed potatoes. Would you prefer green beans or peas for your vegetable?" The look of concern Mrs. White has on her face gives me a hint of what it might be like to live with someone who really cares about what I eat.

"I like both, Mrs. White. You decide whatever you think is best. I know it'll be delicious. I'll be right back." I walk out the front door and toward the apartment that's somehow my home. I still don't know what to think about Mom. If she's home, what will she be like? If she's not home, where is she?

Slowly, I pull myself up onto the third stair. A small mouse scurries by. I open the door to our apartment and slowly climb the stairs. No music is playing, so I'm not sure what to think. If Mom is home, she usually has that awful music blaring so the whole world can hear it.

I cautiously enter the living room. Lying on the couch unresponsive is my mom. She looks like she was in a bad car accident. Her sunken eyes are swollen shut. Her nose is double its normal size. Her lips are bruised and cut. Her skinny bird arms are shaking, so I knew she's alive. She's breathing, but it's not normal breathing. I hear small gasps as she tries to breathe in air.

I kneel next to her and take her small, shaking hand. "What happened, Mom? What happened?"

I know she can't answer. I'm terrified. She can't die like this. She can't leave us. Should I call for help? Who would I call?

My mom tries to talk. It comes out in a small whisper: "July, where are the bags that were under the couch cushions? You need to tell me." Mom pleads through closed eyes.

Now I'm pissed. "Are you kidding me?" I scream at her. "You're almost dead. I flushed all that stuff away, Mom. I know you'll get more, but I can't handle this. Get your act together. Why are you trying to die? Why do you want me to go into a foster home!?" I can't believe this half-dead person is so worried about her drugs. This is ridiculous.

My mom falls back into unconsciousness. I leave her on the couch and run to Mrs. White's house. I don't have time to think, I just react. As I run into Mrs. White's house, I can feel the panic bubbling inside me. I still don't know what's happened or what I'm supposed to do.

"July." Mrs. White grabs me, "You're white as a sheet, what happened? Sit down, dear, sit down."

"I can't sit," I gasp. "It's my mom…she's, she's…oh, Mrs. White, I think my mom is dying." I start sobbing.

"Oh dear, dear, what do you mean, July? Where is your mom? Deep breaths, deep breaths." Mrs. White tries to calm me down, but she can't.

Abe comes running down the hall. "No cry, Sissy, no cry."

"Oh, shoot, Abe." I start crying again.

Now Mrs. White's getting concerned, "July, should your mother go to the hospital? Why don't we go over to your house? Let me just put this food in the fridge."

I'm numb, but I know I don't want Abe to see Mom. "Mrs. White, my mom's pretty bad. I don't want Abe to see her. I don't want you to see her. I just don't know what to do." I start crying again.

"July, you stay here with Abe. I'm going to your house to check on your mom. You two just stay put." Mrs. White grabs her cell phone, puts her jacket on, and hurriedly walks out the door.

I feel paralyzed. I don't know what to do or what to say. I'm holding Abe, grabbing him to my chest. I can't stop crying.

A few minutes later Mrs. White comes back, "Listen, July, I got some help for your mother. You and Abe are staying with me. Now let's have some dinner. She's all taken care of, and you and Abe are safe with me."

"I can't just leave her alone, Mrs. White. I should be with her. Can Abe stay here with you?" I ask.

"July, dear, you sit right down. Your mom is where she's supposed to be, I promise. When I saw your mother, I said some prayers. Oh my, my. Your mother is safe now. No one needs to know that you're here. You and Abe are safe. You're staying with me. That's it, that's all." Mrs. White sits down and starts serving us dinner.

I'm so relieved not to make any more decisions that I just let Mrs. White take care of me. I listen to her words, "You and Abe are safe." I don't remember the last time I felt safe. I think it must have been when Roger lived with us before Abe was born.

CHAPTER 10

We don't really say much at dinner. Mrs. White keeps the conversation light. She starts telling Abe the story of the Three Little Pigs and then Little Red Riding Hood. As she talks, I keep thinking about Mom. I can't really eat my dinner, which is amazing because the food looks so good.

"It will be so nice to have kids sleeping in Jason's room again," Mrs. White smiles. "Tomorrow I'll go to the store and pick up some things for you kids. What do you need, July? I know I should get some diapers for little Abe. How about you?" Mrs. White just takes over, like she's, our parent. It feels so good not to be in charge and not to worry, but at the same time it doesn't seem right.

"No, no, Mrs. White," I argue. "Abe and I will be fine. We can go home after dinner. It won't be the first time that we've been left alone without our mom." As I say the words, I realize that maybe I've said too much, so I add, "Well, there've been a couple of days that Mom just needed a little break. It doesn't happen all the time. We really are fine. I just need to find out what's happening with Mom."

Mrs. White gets all motherly and concerned. "I saw your mother, July. I think she's been ill for a long time. I wish you had shared some of this with me. I called the ambulance. She's in the hospital. You are NOT to stay alone in that apartment. You can NOT go home. Now, tonight you're just relaxing, and there won't be any more worrying. There are bunk beds in Jason's room, one for you, and one for Abe.

Tomorrow is a new day. You're safe, safe, safe. After we tuck Abe in you can help me make some cookies and then we'll talk about what to do next."

The way Mrs. White says this makes me a little uneasy, "You're safe, safe, safe." She keeps repeating how safe we are. I'm not really sure what she means. At the same time, it does feel good to just make cookies with an adult who wants to make decisions and keep me safe. I'm too tired to worry, too tired to argue. *Sure, let's make cookies, have a bath, and sleep.*

After Abe goes to sleep, Mrs. White and I go into her homey kitchen. She begins pulling out mixing bowls, measuring cups, flour, sugar, eggs, butter, and some cookie cutters. "I can't remember the last time I had some young people sleep over," she says. "This will be so much fun."

I have to admit, it's nice, but at the same time I'm thinking that the reason we're here is because my drug-addict mom is dying in the hospital. It's not like she asked Mrs. White to care for us. "It's nice having you take care of us tonight, Mrs. White, but really, we can go home tomorrow."

Mrs. White comes over to me and gives me a big grandmotherly hug. She's a little taller than me, and a lot chubbier. I can smell lavender as she's hugging me. It's such a great feeling. It's genuine and I accept it. "Thanks," is all I manage to say. No one has made me feel like this for a long time.

"No more talk of going back to that apartment," Mrs. White says firmly. "I'm taking care of you and Abe and that's that. Now let's make some sugar cookies." She smiles and hands me an apron. "I was thinking, Mrs. White is such a formal name, it's fine with me if you call me something else. My first name is Mary, but if you like, you can call me Grammy. I'd really like that, July. Do you think you could?"

Mrs. White is so kind. I always dreamed what it would be like to have a grandmother. My mother's mother died when she was a little kid. I guess she had breast cancer, but Mom never really talked about that. After my grandmother died, my grandfather started drinking pretty heavily. My mom never really talked about it. I guess it's one of those memories you'd like to forget.

It would be easy to call Mrs. White Grammy. I think she needs grandchildren as much as we need a grandmother. "Sure, Grammy it is," I say, smiling. Mrs. White—I mean, Grammy—wipes flour down my nose and laughs.

While we're making cookies, I decide it's okay for me to ask Grammy about Jason. It's a difficult conversation to start, but I think if I'm having this new family I want to know. "Mrs. White—I mean, Grammy?"

When I say the word *Grammy* Mrs. White just smiles. "Yes, dear?"

The look I get from her is something I haven't experienced in a really long time. It's like I'm the most important person in the world. "Umm, I just I hope it's okay to ask you this, um..."

"July, you can ask me anything, don't you worry. I would never do anything to hurt you." Mrs. White pats my hand and again looks at me in that caring way.

I'm a little confused as to why she'd say she would never do anything to hurt me, but I carry on. "Well, I was just wondering, what happened to Jason?"

Mrs. White stops rolling the dough and looks at nothing across the kitchen. Her face becomes sad.

Suddenly, I wish I hadn't asked. "I'm sorry, Grammy, you don't need to tell me," I add regretfully.

Mrs. White turns to me and smiles a sad smile. "Oh honey, it's okay. Jason and his dad were killed in a car accident in 1980. It was the worst day of my life. I relive that day sometimes. It's getting less painful, but it's always there. Jason was just four years old. Bob, my husband, was taking him to see his mother Jason's Grammy. I wasn't feeling that great, so I decided to stay home. There were so many days when I wished I was with them. It's just been so hard."

She stops for a minute and says nothing, then smiles like everything's fine. "But now look, I have you and little Abe. I feel like I can start my life once again. It's been so long since there's been any joy in this house. Having Abe here the other day was so wonderful, and now that you're here, well..." She begins rolling the cookie dough again and humming a happy tune.

I'm a little confused about what's happening—what does she mean now that I'm here? I decide she's just a lonely old woman who needs to feel wanted. I also suddenly realize that I'm a little kid—no, really. Okay, I know I'm twelve, but I haven't been allowed to just be a kid for a while. It feels so great to have someone who wants to take care of me.

After we make the cookies, Mrs. White tells me I can have a long bath in her tub. She has one of those old-fashioned deep clawfoot tubs. She brings me this old lady nightgown and tells me to take a good long soak while she cleans up the kitchen. She shows me how to turn on the tub like I wouldn't know. She also gives me some bubble bath. I recognize the smell: it's the lavender I smelled on her earlier.

I climb into the relaxing, warm, bubble-filled tub. I can feel my body start to relax as the years of worrying about Mom, taking care of Abe, having to keep our family secrets from everyone—all of it seems to melt away. "I have a Grammy now, she'll make everything better," I smile as the bubbles encase my body.

CHAPTER 11

"Grammy, Grammy." I hear Abe giggling as I wake up. It takes me a few minutes to remember that I'm in Mrs. White's house and not our apartment. I realize that I have no idea what time it is and I'm probably late for school. I jump out of bed, race to the kitchen, and look at the clock: 8:45.

"Shit, I'm late for school," I announce to no one in particular.

"Now July, please watch your language, especially around little Abe," Mrs. White says. "After the difficult evening you had I decided you had to sleep. I called the school and explained that I'm your grandmother and you're not going to school today. Last night was very difficult and you need at least a day to unwind. Missing a little school isn't going to be a problem," she assures me. "Today, you, Abe, and I are going on an adventure. Will you watch Abe for just a bit while I buy some things at Target?" Mrs. White tells me more than asks me.

"Sure, Grammy, "I say, remembering she's the grown-up who's now taking care of us. I don't have to worry about this anymore. I get to just be a kid. I try to forget that my mother is dying or dead at the hospital. I'm a little concerned that she told the school she was my grandmother, but not having to worry sounds good. Besides, it's Friday, and I won't have to suffer through Mrs. Masterson's guidance lesson. Maybe having a grandmother is a good thing.

"I made you some waffles—they're in the oven keeping warm. Let me get them for you." Mrs. White brings me a plate of waffles with strawberries and maple syrup.

Taking a bite, I'm sure I must be in heaven. The waffles are light and fluffy. The warm maple syrup tickles my tongue as the flavors dance in my mouth.

"Oh my God, these are the most wonderful waffles I've ever tasted," I exclaim. "How did you do this?" I ask, finally swallowing the first amazing bite.

"They're made with love, dear, made with love." Mrs. White kisses my cheek and hugs Abe. "I won't be gone too, too long. You two relax. When I come back, we're going to my favorite place. I can't wait to share it. I washed your clothes, July, so they're clean and on top of the dryer. Abe is all set for the day."

Abe is playing with Jason's old trucks as I finish my heavenly breakfast. "Can you believe it, Abe? We have a Grammy!"

"Grammy, Grammy, brrroom, brrroom," Abe singsongs as he zooms his trucks around the kitchen.

A small part of me is feeling guilty. What about Mom? Is she still alive? Should I call Aunt Susan and let her know that Mom is in the hospital? Should we go over to our house? All of those decisions are too hard. I decide the best thing to do is clean up my dishes and play with my favorite little guy. I grab one of Abe's cars and start making the "brrroom brrroom" car noise. As I drive one of the little cars all around Abe's body, he laughs and yells, "Again, again." As I'm playing with him, I wonder if this is what it's really like to have a little brother, not worrying about whether he's eaten or whether he'll be safe while you're at school, just playing and laughing together.

That thought makes me wonder more about Mom and about school. Even though my life has been tricky, I've managed to get to school every day. Taking this one Friday shouldn't really matter. Fridays just kind of wrap up the week anyhow. I'm curious about Maddie, though. I wonder how her laser tag date with Nate was. I decide I can find out on Monday. Mom's a different story--I know Mrs. White is right. The ambulance took her to the hospital. What could I do if I went to the hospital? They definitely would've sent me to a foster home and Abe off to Roger's house.

Roger—I totally forgot about Roger. It's Friday, and Roger will be at our house around 5:00. When he finds out about Mom he'll surely take Abe, but I can't think about this now. I grab another waffle and pile it high with strawberries and maple syrup. Opening the fridge, I'm psyched to see a can of whipped cream. I pile this on top and gobble it all down, stuffing the fear down deep so I don't have to think. When the waffles are gone, I reach for a cookie.

Abe starts yelling, "Cookie for me, Sissy!"

This breaks me from my food coma. I bring Abe into Jason's— or I guess, our—room and really look through it. There's the set of bunk beds against the far wall that Abe and I slept in last night. They have Winnie the Pooh quilts and Piglet sheets on them. I'm sure they're the exact same ones that were here when Jason was alive. There's a framed Winnie the Pooh and Piglet poster with a saying, *If there ever is a day that we can't be together, keep me in your heart and I'll stay there forever.* Reading that gives me the chills. Poor Mrs. White. I wonder if she bought that before or after Jason died. It doesn't make sense to me that this kind, loving woman lost her child. It's so obvious that she was a great mom. My mom, on the other hand, well, there was a time when….

I start trying to remember good things about Mom. I know that she loved me once and maybe she still does. I think about those long-ago summers before Abe and Roger when it was just the two of us playing on the beach, painting pictures, singing songs. At one time I had that kind of mother, I guess, even if it was for just a little while. "What happened to you, Mom?" I realize I'm saying out loud.

Abe is looking through a cardboard book called *Trucks*. When he hears me say, "What happened to you, Mom?" he says, "Shhh, Momma sleeping."

This is all Abe knows about our mom. She's always passed out on drugs. If she isn't on one of her highs, she's just useless. She doesn't seem to notice anything around her. Sometimes she complains that she's soo soo cold, or itchy. Then she has her drug again and she's really gone. Part of me is hopeful that the people at the hospital will make her get off the drugs. It'd be amazing to have a kind, loving mother again.

In the meantime, do I just stay with Mrs. White? I could probably get Abe ready to go with Roger and tell him Mom went out for a bit. He'd believe this—it's happened before. Mrs. White seems so excited to have kids. It's a little weird how all of this happened. I mean, before Abe stayed with Mrs. White that day, I took Mom's drugs and flushed them, I didn't really know Mrs. White. We would walk by her house and say hi. Sometimes she'd ask us about our day. She was always so happy to see Abe. Looking at a photograph of Jason, I can see why. Abe and Jason have similar features. The same sandy blonde hair and big brown eyes. Jason's smile is different—it's bigger. Not that Abe doesn't have a nice smile, Jason's smile engulfs his entire face. Abe's nose is more of a button shape. Jason has two distinct freckles on his nose.

As I'm checking out Jason's room, I hear Mrs. White come in. "Hello, July, Abe...."

She sounds a little panicked. "We're in here!" I yell as I come to the kitchen to greet her.

"Oh, thank goodness. I've had so much fun. Wait until you see what I bought." Mrs. White puts two good-sized bags on the table. She goes back to her car and comes back with more bags. She also has a car seat for Abe. I'm astonished as she hands me two big bags. "July, these are for you, now you can be honest if you don't like them, or if they don't fit we can go back to the store," Mrs. White says looking really pleased with herself.

Inside the bags are more clothes than I've ever owned in my entire life. There are jeans, pants, shirts, sweatshirts, sweaters, pj's, socks, even matching underwear. I can't believe Mrs. White bought all this for me. "Mrs.—I mean Grammy, I don't know what to say. I never, I just...." I truly don't know what to say.

"Now, now, dear, I've had just the best time. When I did your laundry yesterday, I looked at your size, so I'm hopeful everything will fit. I also got you these, so please tell me if I'm off," Mrs. White says, handing me another bag.

I look into this bag and there's deodorant, a hairbrush, toothpaste, face wash, shampoo, conditioner, a hair dryer, and some maxi pads. I just smile and say, "Thank you, you're very kind to have done this."

The other bags are filled with things for Abe: clothes, diapers, and a little potty chair. Mrs. White explains, "I think we can potty train Abe, he's a smart little guy. One more thing for each of you," she says, taking out some suitcases. "I thought it would be lovely if we went on a little trip. My family owns a cabin up in Maine. Let's go up there and relax and just get away."

I'd like nothing more than to run away from my crazy life, but I don't think this is the best idea. "I don't know," I say. "I mean, with Mom being sick and all, maybe we should just stay here until she's better."

Mrs. White has this kind of stern tone to her voice that scares me a little. "Now you listen to me, dear, your mom is where she's supposed to be. You and your brother deserve to have some fun. I understand after seeing your mother the other night that you most likely haven't had fun for a long time. You're safe now. You're with me, the end, and we're going. Pack your suitcase!"

I just kind of look at her for a few moments. There's a small voice inside my head that thinks, *Wait a minute, what's going on?*

I guess Mrs. White catches on to my concern because suddenly she's all nice again. She comes over and hugs me and sweetly says, "July, I know your mother is involved with some kind of drug and it's not safe for you to be around here right now. You're a smart girl. You saw your mother's face. Whoever hurt her may be back. In the meantime, no one knows you're with me. We can go away and talk and think. I want you to know I believe God has sent you to me to watch and protect. I've been praying for my life to have meaning for so long and now...you are a gift. NO more talk."

How can I argue with that? I never thought about myself as a gift from God. I didn't think that whoever hurt Mom might be back. I wonder if she was beaten because I flushed all those drugs that were hidden in our couch? I shudder at the thought.

"You go pack up, July. I'll get Abe ready." Mrs. White is in charge now.

I guess it will be good to get away just for the weekend. I could use a break from my crazy life. I open my suitcase and fill it with all my new clothes. I think that I should go back to my house and grab a few things like Abe's teddy bear and my Percy Jackson book. When I finish packing, I notice that Mrs. White has put Annie, her cat, in her little carrying case. I guess she doesn't like to leave her alone.

I'm not sure what to do about the Roger situation. I mean, if we're gone and Roger shows up and no one's there, what will he do? I decide to shove a couple of cookies in my mouth and not worry about it. "Mrs. White, I'm just going to run to our house and get a book I'm reading and Abe's teddy bear, "I tell her, dragging my suitcase into the kitchen.

"No, you are not, July. You are not going to that house! Who knows who might be there? I promise I'll buy you a book on our way. There'll be many books at the cabin once we get there. Abe has his blankie and he can certainly take Jason's teddy bear. There's no need for you to go back. And you must remember to call me GRAMMY!" Mrs. White again uses the stern grandmother tone followed by a hug. This is getting a little confusing.

"Okay, I guess, that'll be fine," I say. What did she mean by who knows who will be at our house? What does she know that she's not telling me? Maybe she's just being a safe, safe, safe grandmother.

I help load our suitcases into the trunk of Mrs. White's Toyota Camry. Abe's new car seat is safely in the back next to Annie's little crate. Getting into the front seat, I look up and down Appleton Street and wonder when I'll be back.

CHAPTER 12

"When I was at the store, I asked a young man what music you might like. I told him you were twelve. He assured me that I would have to get this CD." Mrs. White presses the play button and just like that Justin Bieber is singing "Sorry." For some reason it makes me laugh because Mrs. White's like doing this dance move with her head as Justin sings.

I look in the back seat and Abe is clapping his little hands. I guess they're both Bieber fans. Me, not so much, but I don't have the heart to tell her. She's trying so hard to make everything great for us. I believe now that we're saving her as much as she's saving us.

"Thanks, Grammy, I didn't know you were a Bieber fan," I tell her because she seems to be mouthing the words.

"There are lots of things you don't know about me and more things I don't know about you. I guess we can spend some time getting to know each other on our ride up to the cabin. We have about a five-hour ride ahead of us. So, any time you're tired or need a break, let me know."

I think about this for a minute: five hours. I've never been more than an hour or two from home. I think the furthest I've been to Boston. Mom, Roger, and I went to Boston before my mom was pregnant. It was a great day. We took the train from Maplewood. Once we got there, we went to the Swan Boats. I remember sitting on Mom's lap as we sat in the big swan-faced boat. Roger brought a bag of bread so we could feed the ducks. I'd forgotten about that.

Mrs. White begins the let's-learn-everything-we-can-about-each-other conversation. "July, when is your birthday? I don't even know that. I assume it's sometime in July because of your name."

"Actually, my birthday is in August. August third," I share. People usually think my birthday's in July. Mom told me July is her favorite month. Everything good happens in July. That's why she named me July because I remind her of everything good. At least that's what she told me once upon a time. I know a lot of girls named April and Autumn, and I even have a friend named Summer. I like July. It's kind of different. It makes me feel special.

"Now your turn, Mrs. White. When is your birthday? I'm guessing it's sometime in the spring, right?" I ask, not sure why.

"You're right, July, my birthday is May 23rd. I'll be 66 years old on May 23rd. Can you imagine? Where have the years gone?" Mrs. White says.

"May 23rd, why that's Abe's birthday. He'll be three this year. Isn't that strange that you two have the same birthday?"

"Wow, what a great coincidence. I don't think I know anyone else who has the same birthday as me. I'm thrilled to share it with Abe." Mrs. White has this big smile on her face like she was just given a present that she always wanted but no one ever thought to give her.

"I guess we'll have to have a big party," I say.

Mrs. White is quiet for a minute, humming the Bieber songs like she's lost in thought. Slowly she tells me that today would have been Jason's birthday. "He would be forty-two years old today. Can you imagine? Jason and Bob, my husband, shared the same birthday, April 12th. Bob would have been sixty-eight and Jason forty-two. Oh my...."

I can see little tears forming in Mrs. White's eyes. She brushes them away and continues. "I remember the first summer we brought Jason up to the cabin. My parents began staying there year-round after my brother, Harry, was killed in Vietnam. They couldn't go back to our house. I don't think I saw my mother really smile after Harry passed until the summer of Jason. That's what she called it, the summer of Jason, Jason Harry White. I stayed up at the cabin with my parents for the summer that year in 1976. Bob would join us on the weekends. It was lovely. We would visit every summer until the accident took my Bob and my beautiful boy. I just couldn't go back after that. My parents passed a few years later. My dad seemed to understand why happy memories haunted me. He never pushed me to return, but my mother…well, she wasn't as understanding."

I have so many questions for Mrs. White, but I don't know where to start, like: Did you date anyone after Bob died? Did you have a job? Do you have any other family or friends? Does anyone in the world know that Abe and I are with you? Instead, I just say, "How long has it been since you've been there?"

"Oh my, July, probably twenty-five years. I was going to sell the place, but I just couldn't. One of my brother Harry's friends looks in on it for me, but he stays away in the spring. Moosehead Lake is quite a beautiful lake. Have you ever been there? "

"No, I don't think I've been to many places in Maine," I share. "Well, I have been to York and Kittery. Abe's dad lives in Berwick."

Suddenly, Mrs. White looks pale, like I've told her something horrible. "You know Abe's father?" she asks. "I thought…well, tell me about him. Is he involved with Abe?"

I'm not sure why Mrs. White is concerned about Roger. He's a really nice guy. He truly loves Abe, and I think he'd like to keep him sometimes—he just doesn't know how to do it. The last time Roger was at our house I think he was really concerned about Mom. He and Mom got into a fight. I could hear part of it. Mom was yelling all crazy, "Just say it, Roger, just say it!"

Roger came into our room because I was reading Abe a story. He asked me seriously, "Is everything all right with your mom, July?"

Mom freaked out. I thought she was going to pick Roger up and throw him out the door. Roger again told Mom, "Jenny, I'll help you any way I can, but I will not have my son living in a house with a drug addict." As he said this, he looked at me like he wanted me to tell him about Mom's drugs. I wanted to, but I couldn't live with just Mom knowing I'd never see Abe again.

I try to explain Roger to Mrs. White. "Abe's dad is named Roger LaMarche. He lives with his mother in Berwick. He usually takes Abe for the weekend. Roger works a lot. He gives Mom money for Abe and all that. Abe loves to see him and usually comes back from his house all happy with new clothes and stuff. As a matter of fact, I think he's supposed to pick him up today."

"Oh my, I had no idea. Well, we'll just have to figure that out once we get to the cabin." Mrs. White has this far-off look. I decide it's best to just watch the road and be quiet for a while. I look back and notice that Abe seems to be sleeping. I hear soft purring sounds from Annie. Sleep seems like a good idea. Soon, I'm asleep, too.

I awake with a start a few hours later.

"Oh, hello, sleepyhead." Mrs. White smiles. "You certainly were having some dream. You were talking in your sleep. Tell me about Ms. Paulson. You just kept yelling, 'Don't ask me to do it, Ms. Paulson.'"

I have no memory of a dream. I wonder why I was dreaming of Ms. Paulson and think of the poetry contest. "Ms. Paulson is my Language Arts teacher," I tell Mrs. White. "She's super nice. I can't imagine why I'd be having a bad dream about her."

"Do you like school?" Mrs. White wants to know, like she's a concerned grandmother.

Do I like school? I never really thought about this. "I guess I do. I'm good at it. Well, I'm a good writer. At least that's what Ms. Paulson tells me. I also like to read. I think reading helps when things are tough, you know? Sometimes when my life is crazy a book is really good. I pretend I'm in the story. I try to imagine the people in the book as my friends."

"I know what you mean, July. I like to read too. What are you reading right now? Tell me about it." Grammy asks, genuinely concerned about what I'm interested in.

I let this sink in my grandmother wants to know what I like to read and whether I like school. That's kind of awesome. I mean, I don't know the last time a grown-up asked me about me. I tell Mrs. White—Grammy—all about Percy Jackson. How he's this kid from New York who has all kinds of learning issues. He's a real problem and gets into trouble at school. It's just Percy and his mom until one day he learns that his father is really Poseidon, God of the sea. Percy goes to this special camp where other kids who have gods for parents live.

As I'm babbling on about Percy, I look at Mrs. White. She's really interested. She never interrupts, she just nods her head and says things like "Wow" and "Hmm", so I know she's listening.

When I finish my Percy Jackson recap Mrs. White gets off at the next exit and says, "You've convinced me, July. We're going to buy some Percy Jackson books."

And just like that, we're in the parking lot of a Barnes and Noble somewhere in Maine. I take Abe out of his car seat and grab his diaper bag. "Smells like you need a change," I tell Abe, waking him from a sound slumber. He puts his head on my shoulder and tries to fall back to sleep.

When we walk into Barnes and Noble, I tell Mrs. White that I'm going to change Abe. I also need a bathroom break myself. When we're finished, I see Mrs. White looking at the Rick Riordan section, "July, this author is wonderful. He has so many interesting series."

"I know. I just started reading *Sea of Monsters*. I finished *Lightning Thief* last week."

"Well, I'm going to buy these two series so you can have some reading while we're away. Is there anything else you'd like? What about Abe?" She acts like she has a million dollars.

"Oh, no, no, Grammy, that's too much. I can get these books at school, or at the library. Abe is fine. Please, you don't have to spend any more of your money on us," I insist. I keep wondering how Mrs. White has all this money. Why would she live on the lower end of Appleton Street? I mean, her house is way nicer than mine, but still. It just doesn't make sense.

"Nonsense dear," she says. "I love that you like to read. It's my pleasure. Now, look at your brother." Mrs. White smiles at Abe, who's taking those cardboard truck books with little wheels and zooming them around the carpet. "Bring those to me, July. I want to get those books for Abe, too."

Mrs. White must have spent at least five hundred dollars on us so far. How could that be? I wonder if she has a secret stash of money somewhere.

I pick up Abe's little books. He's pretty upset that I've taken them from him. "It's okay, little guy, Grammy's going to let you keep them."

"My books, my truck," Abe whines.

"It's okay, Abe, Grammy's going to buy these for you. They'll be yours forever, just like Grammy. I'll be your Grammy forever." Mrs. White says, scooping up Abe and giving him a kiss.

CHAPTER 13

After five long hours in the car, we end up at Mrs. White's cabin on Moosehead Lake in Rockwood, Maine. It looks like no one's been to this cabin in a long time. Mrs. White tells Abe and me to stay in the car while she looks for the key. I'm kind of surprised she doesn't have the key already.

While she's looking for it, I am looking at the lake. Because it's early in April there's still ice on it. I can't believe the size of the lake. I've been to a few lakes and ponds around Maplewood, but this one seems to go for miles. There are ice fishing huts and snowmobile trails all over the place. I'm anxious to explore.

"Okay, July, Abe, I found the key. Come on up!" Mrs. White hollers to us. She has this big smile on her face like we're about to enter some magical kingdom. "You'll just love it. I know you will. Come on!"

She's like a little kid, clapping her hands and motioning us to climb up the long, steep stairs to the rustic cabin. It's a typical New England log cabin. There's a big porch that wraps around the outside. I notice a strange-looking knocker on the red wooden front door. As I get closer, I notice it's the face of a raccoon—I think. Anyway, it's kind of strange.

As we reach the door Mrs. White opens it and says, "Ta-da! Don't you just love it?"

As Abe and I walk across the threshold I'm hit by a musty smell, like no one's been inside forever. There's a big open area with a big old leather couch and a cozy old chair complete with an ottoman. An end table with a lamp made of driftwood separates the couch from the chair. A big, braided red rug sits in front of a giant stone fireplace against the far wall. Hanging above the fireplace is the head of a deer.

Walking into the kitchen is like walking back in time. The sink is a big old-fashioned white basin with separate hot water and cold-water faucets. I've never seen a refrigerator that looks like the one against the wall. It's almost an oval shape. It's white and has what looks like a lever instead of a handle. It doesn't look like it has a freezer.

Mrs. White is sitting inside a little closet off the kitchen. "Dear me, dear me, I need to turn all of this on. Now let me see. "

Suddenly, the cabin comes to life. The overhead light in the kitchen comes on, and you can hear a gurgling in the pipes like water's coming to life.

"Turn on a faucet, July, would you please?" Mrs. White asks, still in the closet.

I turn on the cold-water faucet and some really strange noise comes out, followed by a small, rusty stream of water, then a steadier stream. "It seems to be working now," I share.

"Try the hot water," Mrs. White yells. "I just want to make sure the hot water heater is working. I may need to light the pilot."

I turn the hot water side on. "Still cold!" I yell.

"Let me try to remember. Bob showed me how to do this many times, but that was years ago," Mrs. White says, but not really to me. She gets up and walks to the old white cabinets above the sink. "Oh, I know there are matches somewhere."

I look in the cabinet as Mrs. White opens it. There are some old spices, cans of food, coffee, and matches, I wondered how long they've been there. I really want to look at the expiration dates. It was like we'd driven back to 1960 or something.

Mrs. White takes the matches back into the little closet. "July, go check on your brother while I get the furnace and hot water heater working. I have to light the pilots, and if I do something wrong, I don't want you to be in here."

"Abe, where are you?" I call. He isn't in the living room. I see a staircase leading up to a loft. Running up the stairs, I begin calling again. "Abe, where are you?" I'm a little worried now.

As I reach the top of the stairs, I see my baby brother playing with some building blocks. "What have you found, little man?"

I look around the loft and begin to feel like I'm in Jason's bedroom at Mrs. White's house. It's kind of creepy in a way. There are the same bunk beds with the Winnie the Pooh comforters. There's even a Winnie the Pooh poster on the wall. In a small closet are toys and clothes for a small four-year-old boy. I find this odd, like maybe Mrs. White couldn't move past Jason's death or something weird like that. I pull out an old Dr. Seuss book and begin reading to Abe.

"July, Abe, come on down here. Grammy has some things to tell you about the house," Mrs. White calls to us.

I carry Abe down the stairs to the kitchen where I find Mrs. White drinking a cup of tea. "Well, this certainly is fun. I guess I'd forgotten how to get the old place up and running, but everything's fine now," she assures us. "There are a few little quirky things we need to go over, so follow me."

Mrs. White puts her tea down on the big oak table and walks down a small hallway into the bathroom. "Oh my, we'll really have to scrub this tub. I just want to show you both some things about the toilet. Now July, the septic system here is tricky, so we only flush after poop. I know that sounds gross, but you get used to it. Little Abe, Grammy got you this potty chair. I know you're a big boy and can start to go potty on the potty chair. Grammy got you these M&Ms, so every time you use the potty, you get to have a few. Won't that be fun?"

I'm confused about the whole thing. First, yeah, it's gross to only flush after you poop. Second, why are we teaching Abe to use the potty if we're only going to be here for two days?

"Grammy, maybe we should teach Abe to use the potty when we get home. He might be confused learning to use the potty here." I try to sound convincing.

"Oh, but July, we are home. Now help me unload the car and then we'll see what else we need." Mrs. White smiles as she heads out toward the car.

CHAPTER 14

I'm a little freaked out by Mrs. White's comment. What does she mean that we're home? I don't even know where we are. It's beautiful and everything, but I need to know what's happening to Mom. I have to go to school on Monday. I have to find out what happened to Maddie and Nate.

"Grammy, Grammy!" I yell as I chase her down the stairs to her car. "Wait, I need to ask you something."

"Help me with these things, July. Little Abe is playing with his toys. You and I can start bringing everything into the house. We'll put all this away and then we'll go to the grocery store. It's about twenty minutes away. I think I remember how to get there. It's quite an unusual store. They have everything you could ever need and then some. I remember one time…." Mrs. White begins jabbering on and on as she hands me lots of bags from the car.

I try to break into her rant, but I don't think she can or wants to hear me. It's like she hasn't talked to anyone for about thirty years and just wants to let all of those thoughts come out at once. "Hey, Mrs.—I mean Grammy," I finally break in, "What do you mean when you say we're home now? I have to go to school on Monday. I need to find out what happened to Mom."

"Oh, July, listen to me very carefully. You are home. You're with me. You're finally with someone who will take care of you and Abe. You can be a little girl and not worry about grown-up things. You're safe now. This is our new home. Isn't that wonderful? God has put us together, finally answering my prayers for a family." Mrs. White is smiling and hugging me.

I'm freaking out. I've just realized that I've been kidnapped, but not really, because if Mom died, I'd have to go to a foster home and Roger would probably take Abe, so…it's still weird.

"Grammy, it's beautiful here and I certainly appreciate all that you're doing, but shouldn't we tell someone that we're here? I'd really like to know what's going on with Mom and I should go to school on Monday. "I'm hoping this will help her understand that we have other lives and that people are probably wondering where we are.

Mrs. White just looks at me. Slowly and sternly, she says, "You're with me now, July. Your life begins today. I don't want any more talk about going home. You are home. Never bring this up again. Do you understand? Your life is here in Rockwood with Abe and me. There is no past, only the future. July, your mother never cared for you. Think about all she put you through. For heaven's sake, your mother was never a mother. Just think about how she looked the last time you saw her. Can't you see that I'm saving you and giving you a much better life?"

As Mrs. White mutters these words, I start bawling my eyes out. I think I believe what she's saying. The last time I saw Mom she was really wasted and unresponsive on the couch at our house. She was also pretty beaten up. Mrs. White's right: Mom can't care for me. What do I have going for me in Maplewood? I need to leave that behind and just move on.

Mrs. White puts her arms around me and hugs me for a few minutes. "Now, now, July you and I will not talk about this again. We're on a new adventure—you and me. Everything will be perfect, you'll see. We're going to be just fine. Now let's go to the store."

As I go to the house to get Abe ready for our trip to the store, I can't help but think of Roger. I mean, Roger really separated from me when he left, but once Abe was born, he tried hard to be a dad. He moved back in with us for a while. He slept on the couch, but he was encouraging Mom to go to these meetings called Narcotics Anonymous. He told Mom that if she didn't quit using pain medication, he'd take Abe away. That was when Mom got herself together. She really stopped using for a while and was a mom. I mean, she made us meals and seemed to care about what was happening to us. That lasted for about a year. It was another sneak peek into a life I might have been able to have if there were no such thing as painkillers.

When Abe was six months old Mom went back to work at Dunkin's. She found this woman who watched Abe while she worked, and I was at school. I don't really know who she was. I never met her. What I do know is that when Abe was about eighteen months old, mom was home every day. She didn't go to work. That's when things changed for the worse. I guess I should have looked for the signs. There were days when Mom was pretty distant. She'd tell me she was tired and ask me to put Abe to bed. She'd just go into her room and put on loud rock music and not come out. Sometimes I'd check on her, and usually she was passed out with her clothes on. I'd shut off her music, do my homework, and go to bed.

Soon there would be no dinner. I'd get home from school and Abe would be wandering around our apartment while my mom was passed out on the couch. I couldn't wake her. On these days it was cereal for dinner. The odd thing about Mom's passing out or whatever was that she knew the days Roger would show up. During these Friday and Sunday afternoons Mom was able to pull herself together. I think she might have been afraid that Roger would take Abe. Maybe she was more afraid that Roger would take away his child support.

Anyway, during this time I saw my real Mom again. She even made a real dinner, like spaghetti and meatballs, or chicken and potatoes. Sometimes Roger would stay and eat with us. Before he left, he always handed mom a check. She had Roger fooled pretty good. As soon as he and Abe were down the street, Mom would run into her room and slam the door. She never said anything to me. It was understood that she didn't need me seeing what she was doing. She would stay in her room for the rest of the night.

Eventually, I was getting up on my own and getting Abe ready for the day. Usually when I left my mother was sound dead asleep or passed out. Most days I tried to be sure the apartment was safe before leaving. The first few times I left Abe I had a pit in my stomach all day.

72

As I started remembering the life Abe and I had in Maplewood, I began to convince myself that we would have a much better life here in Rockwood, Maine. Mrs. White, or Grammy, seemed to care about us. She was buying us all kinds of things. We never had to worry about food. Abe was happy with her, and she seemed to love him. My life would probably be better here.

We drive twenty or thirty minutes to Greenville. The whole time Grammy tells stories about living in Rockwood. She talks about how the times have changed since she first came here years ago. The place is basically the same, but there are some new spectacular homes. Some businesses have changed, but the feeling is the same.

As we drive past Moosehead Lake Regional School, Grammy grows excited, then nervous. "Oh July, this will be your new school. Isn't that exciting? Well, we'll have to make sure they know you're living with me now because of, well, you know."

But I don't know. "What do you mean, well, you know?" I quip harshly. I guess I'm angry that my life has been upturned even if it is better. I like that someone, a grownup, is taking care of me, but I also want Mrs. White to know I need to be in control.

"July, we must be sure to put on a united front. You and I will explain that your mother passed away from a drug overdose and naturally you're living with me, your grandmother."

As Mrs. White says these words so matter of factly, I can feel the tears dribble down my cheek. I want to be anywhere but in this car with her. "You don't know that my mother passed away. You don't, you don't, stop saying that like it's a fact," I cry. Was my mother really dead? How would I know for sure?

"Please Mrs.—I mean, Grammy, can I just call my cousin Dom and find out? I won't tell him where we are or anything. I need to know."

Mrs. White ignores me and turns up the radio. She begins to sing along with the song. It's some old song. "It's a marvelous night for a Moondance," she sings.

She begins her ranting way of talking, again completely ignoring me. "I just love Van Morrison. Do you know any of his songs? I'll have to teach you some. Oh my, they just bring me back. Abe, do you want to sing with Grammy?" Mrs. White starts up again with her singing. Abe is all smiles and clapping and I feel like I'm in some creepy horror show.

We finally get to the store. It certainly is different than stores in Maplewood. It's a good-sized store. On one side there are groceries and on the other there are all kinds of things: clothes, sporting goods, alcohol, toys, books. If you want something, I bet you'd find it in here.

"Now let's get some food and other things we'll need for our home. Why don't we get some party food? I think we need to celebrate. What do you think? Do you want some cake and ice cream, Abe?"

"Hooray, cake." Abe starts dancing around, clapping his hands. He's kind of adorable, and I can't help but smile. I don't remember ever going grocery shopping with Mom and Abe. Maybe this is going to be okay—I don't know. I do know I don't really have a choice right now. I put my uneasy feelings away and try to enjoy my "new" life.

Grammy asks me to pick out my favorite cereal and things like that. I pick up a box of Cinnamon Toast Crunch and look at the price first. It's just a habit. I'm the one who usually grocery shops for us in Maplewood.

"Oh July, don't worry about the price. We have plenty of money. Get what you like. Is this the cereal you and Abe like? Do you like cereal, or would you prefer that I make you eggs and French toast and that kind of thing?" Grammy asks me this, truly interested in my response. I've never had anyone make me breakfast—well, Roger did, but that was a long time ago.

"Um, well, I can eat cereal," I tell her. "You don't need to make a fancy breakfast for us every day."

Grammy just laughs and hugs me. "Oh July, I love making things for you and Abe. For heaven's sake, you're my grandchildren. I have an idea: we'll get both the cereal and things to make a fancy breakfast. You're just so sweet. Remember July, I'm taking care of you now. You need to just be a kid."

Mrs. White puts the cereal in the cart, and I start to relax a little. Yes, I'm just a kid, but for such a long time I was in charge of so much. Grocery shopping continues like this. As we're leaving the store a woman stops Mrs. White and says, "Oh my, what lovely grandchildren you have."

"Why thank you," Mrs. White says. "They are wonderful, aren't they?"

CHAPTER 15

I decide it's best not to talk about Maplewood—for a while, anyway. I feel uncomfortable, like I'm doing something wrong, but not having to worry about whether my druggie mother is alive, or dead is fine with me. I try to push Mom out of my mind, but when I close my eyes the image of her lying on that couch bruised, bloody, and half dead comes crashing back.

After the groceries are away and Abe is down for his nap, it's time for me to explore. I walk out the front door and hear a panicked voice, "July, where are you going? You can't just leave," Grammy scolds.

"Sorry, I guess I'm just not used to having someone care about where I am. I just wanted to walk down to the lake and see what it's like," I explain.

"Oh, I see," Grammy says "Well, you and I are going to have to explore some guidelines. I would be devastated if anything happened to you. Please just always let me know where you'll be. I guess we both must get used to our new living situation."

"Okay, I guess that's fair. Is it all right if I go across the street to the lake?" As I say the words, they sound foreign. I've never asked if it was all right if I did anything or went anywhere. No one ever cared. Heck, I was the one who worried about others. No one worried about me.

"Of course, you can go look at the lake, but don't go on it. You never know how safe the ice is. Please stay close so I can see you," Grammy says as she kisses the top of my head.

I have no intention of going near the ice. It's about fifty degrees. I can't imagine how cold it would feel if I fell through, but I guess saying the obvious is one of those grandmother caring things to do. Moosehead Lake is huge. You can't really see across it from where I'm standing. There's a big mountain on an island in the middle of it. I'm not sure, but it looks like people are living on that island. I can see boats docking, and some houses. I'd really like to get over there sometime. I wonder if there are moose over there. I wonder if there are moose around here. I understand that there are moose all around us, but Moosehead Lake is called Moosehead Lake because the lake is shaped like a moose, not because of the moose population.

I decide to walk down the street. I mean, if this is going to be my new home I'd better figure out where things are, right? As I'm walking, I can see a bunch of little cottages on the right. I don't think anyone's living around here now. It seems like the kind of place people come to in either the summer or the winter. In spring there's just a lot of mud. What's there to do during mud season?

. On the left side of the street there are big old houses with amazing views of the lake. They have huge porches and docks that jut out into the water. I'm curious about a big, old, gray house. It looks like it would be in one of those horror movies. You know, old and spooky; it certainly doesn't seem like anyone's home. What would it hurt to peek inside the window?

I slowly climb the many wooden steps. There's a huge porch that wraps around the house. I find myself slowly creeping along the side of it until I'm all the way at the back where it's literally sticking out above the water. If I jumped off the porch I'd be in the lake. "Wow," I say aloud, amazed by the sight.

"It's pretty spectacular, isn't it?"

I jump when I hear this. Standing next to me on the porch is a boy, I guess around my age or maybe a little older. He's tall, probably around six feet, but he still has a baby face. He's smiling at me like he knows he walked in on me doing something I wasn't supposed to.

"Hi, I'm Bryce Turner," he says, sticking out his hand like he wants to shake mine.

I shake his hand, feeling my face burning. I mutter, "Hi, I'm July."

"Nice to meet you, Julie," Bryce says confidently.

He called me Julie—it's a common mistake. Most people want to call me Julie because July is so, so—I guess, unique, unusual—but July is who I am. For a brief second, I consider how easy it would be to just go with it.

"Um, yeah, Julie, Julie White," I reply, trying to get used to this new identity. I guess I'm going all in and leaving my July life behind.

"Well Julie White, what brings you to Moosehead? Have you been here before? April isn't the best time to visit the lake."

I'm pretty good at hiding truths about my life, but for some reason this has caught me way off guard. Should I tell this guy? I don't know what to do. I just kind of stared at him for way too long. I'm playing in over my head—what do I say? This old lady kidnapped me and my brother because my mom is a dead drug addict. No, that doesn't seem right.

I just start to cry. Now I feel stupid, and he probably thinks I'm a weird freak. "My mother is…." I can't say it—I just cry and cry.

I don't know how long I stay like that, just sobbing. I start thinking about everything I've been through and finally realize my mother is probably dead. After a while I gather some composure, look up, and realize that Bryce has been standing next to me the whole time, probably not knowing what to do. I feel like a big loser.

"I'm so sorry I freaked out like that. I guess just being here, so far away, it finally hit me that my mother's really dead. My grandmother thought it would be best for all of us if we just, you know, started over. She used to come up to this cabin a long time ago before…well, a long time ago. So here we are."

Bryce just looks at me, like he doesn't know what to do. We both just stare out at the lake.

"I should go," I finally say. "My grandmother gets worried pretty easily." I start running around to the front of the porch.

"Hey Julie, wait!" Bryce calls.

I stop and look back.

"This is a good place to heal. I, um, I know how you feel. My mother died when I was a little kid. Anyway, I live down the road. My dad owns the cabins at the end of the street. Maybe I can take you out on the boat one day and show you around the lake."

"Yeah, maybe you could. Thanks." I smile as a walk up the hill toward my new life.

CHAPTER 16

"Oh, there you are, July," Grammy smiles as I walk up the hill. "Abe and I have started making supper. Are you hungry? Where did you go?"

I don't really know where to start. I'm not even sure I should tell her that I met a guy and have a new identity, but something tells me she would be fine with my new name. "I was across the street looking at the lake. I met this kid who lives down the street. He seemed nice, but...um."

"Now, July, what is it? Don't be afraid to tell me anything. For heaven's sake, I'm your grandmother."

I look up at her and just say it. "He thought my name was Julie, so I told him my name was Julie White and that we live here now because my mother died."

Mrs. White gives me a big hug, "I like it, Julie White. I'm happy to have you as my granddaughter...Julie White. Now why don't you play with Abe while I finish making dinner?"

As she walks away, I think I hear her say, "Do you hear that, Jason, you have a daughter named Julie." That's creepy. When Mrs. White says or does things like that it makes me freak out a little.

I go upstairs into the loft. Abe is building a tall structure with his blocks. "Knock it down, Sissy, boom!" he screams and claps his hands.

I wonder what's going on in his head. Does he know he'll never see Mom or Roger again? Does he know this is our home now? "Come here, little guy I need to squish you." I grab him and start tickling him. He's laughing and laughing. I begin laughing, too. "Oh Abe, as long as you're always with me, we can get through anything."

CHAPTER 17

I wake up to the smell of cinnamon buns hot and fresh from the oven. The sun is peeking through the window just a little bit. Abe's still sleeping. He looks so peaceful with a little smile on his face. I can't help it; I just bend down and kiss his little cheek.

I climb down the stairs and see Mrs. White, my "grandmother," humming as she puts icing on the warm cinnamon buns. "Oh, good morning, JULIE, I just love that you're Julie."

I don't know how to react to this. I mean, what's wrong with July? I think of the explanation my mom gave me about my name. "July is everything good. It's the best month. July is warm and sunshiny. In July you get to play and be free." Julie—Julie is just Julie.

"Why? Why do you love that I'm Julie? Didn't you like July? I really like my name and all its uniqueness."

"Now, now, don't get huffy," Mrs. White says. "That's not what I mean. When you said that you told that boy your name was Julie White...I don't know, I just felt like you truly believe I'm your real grandmother. You're part of me now. You want to be Julie White, and that's just so...amazing to me. July or Julie, I'll call you whatever makes you happy. I'm just thrilled that you're here with me. I love you so, so much. Do you know how happy I am to have you here with me?"

I guess I do. I also know that Mrs. White really did save me from whatever was happening to Mom and my life with her. But how can she love me so much? I don't really know how I feel about her.

"I'm grateful for all you've done, Grammy. It's just, I....." And then the tears start again.

Grammy wraps her grandmotherly arms around me and kisses my forehead. "You're really going to be okay my sweet, sweet girl. Now, how about you and I have one of these delicious cinnamon buns before they get cold. Cinnamon buns must be eaten hot!"

And just like that, the subject is changed and life is good. Abe comes down the stairs and runs right to Mrs. White. "Grammy, Grammy!" he screeches happily as he climbs into her lap.

Mrs. White just looks so happy; her eyes seem to be dancing. She kisses Abe on the head. "My beautiful grandchildren. It's a miracle that you two have been given to me, just a miracle from God in heaven. You are the answer to my prayers. I'll never be lonely again. Do you hear that, Bob?" She's looking up at the ceiling as tears trickle down her cheek.

Are we the answers to Mrs. White's prayers? I don't really feel like we are. I get so confused during moments like this. I mean, she seems a little creepy when she talks about God and her dead husband. I don't know how to act.

Suddenly, Mrs. White turns serious. "Tomorrow is Monday and it's a school day, so I think we should register you for school."

So many thoughts and emotions swim through my brain when she says this. Am I ready to leave Maplewood behind? Will I ever see or talk to Maddie again? Maddie, who knows more about me than I know about myself? Maddie has been my best friend for a long time. I know Mrs. White will understand that yeah, I'm moving to Moosehead Lake to escape, but I need to put it out there. I need to at least talk to Maddie.

"Um, Grammy, if we um, register me for school, won't there be a lot of questions. I mean, don't they have to call my old school and get my records and shots and things like that? I also need to call my best friend Maddie and let her know what happened to me. She'll freak out if she can't find me and I just disappeared. And what about Roger?"

Mrs. White kind of stares at me and says in a calm, slow, stern voice, "July, you've told me that you're Julie now. Believe me when I tell you I've given this much thought. You must, must, *must* follow what I'm telling you. Your mother, my daughter, was very, very ill. Because she was so ill, you couldn't attend school because you didn't want to leave her. I moved in with you. I've been homeschooling you for the last three years. If you don't stick to this story, there's a very good chance you'll end up without me and in heaven knows where. Do you want to be with people who don't love you like I do? Do you want to never see Abe again because his father's taken him away? Now we can start a new life here. You are safe and loved. I deserve this, JULIE WHITE!"

What does Mrs. White mean that she deserves this? When she says things like that in that mean way it freaks me out. I try to calm her down. "Umm, I'm sorry, it's just that everything's happening so fast. I just...." It's too much for me and again I'm sobbing.

Mrs. White once again turns into a kindly grandmother hugging me and repeating the story in a loving way. "July, I saw your mother and your apartment. No child should live like that. Trust me dear, our life here will be wonderful. You'll make new friends. When you go to school you must tell the story that your mother died, you were homeschooled, and now you're living with me."

This story kind of makes sense, but I'm afraid I might screw it up. What if I just tell the truth, that my mom is a bad drug addict, and she was wickedly beaten. Mrs. White—our neighbor, not my grandmother—decided it was best for me to get out of that situation, so she moved my brother and me to this house in Rockwood.

I guess that does sound like Mrs. White kidnapped us, but come on, she's trying to save us, and if she hadn't done that, who would I live with? Aunt Susan? Abe would move in with Roger and I'd never, ever see him again. I couldn't take that. After careful thought, I agree. Julie White will be a sixth-grade student at Moosehead Lake Regional School.

CHAPTER 18

When I tell you that my new school is the antithesis of my old school, I'm not lying. I mean, there are only eight sixth graders in the whole school. EIGHT! There were twenty-eight kids just in my homeroom at Maplewood. There were about one thousand kids in my old school. I'm not sure if I can handle just the eight of us. I mean, I tried my best to blend in and not be seen in my old school. I tried to just be kind of average so no one would ask me any questions.

I was pretty good at not calling attention to myself until I ended up in Ms. Paulson's class and she decided I was a fabulous poet. I do miss her class. I wonder if there'll be any similarities at all between Maplewood Middle School and Moosehead Lake Regional School. I don't really see how there can be. One big difference at Moosehead Lake is that the teachers teach all the middle grades. There are twenty-seven students in the middle school section of the Moosehead Lake Regional School and twenty-four high school students. The middle school is grades six through eight, while the high school is grades nine through twelve.

My first day at MLRS is surreal. I stand in the principal's office while Mrs. White tells this long story about the trauma I endured to the secretary, Mrs. Mitchell. Much of it's true: my mother wasn't able to care for me for the last few years, since she was so ill. Apparently she was suffering from a horrible, rare cancer. Each day that she was alive was a miracle. I, of course, couldn't leave my mother's side, so my grandmother taught me as best she could. When my mother finally passed away, Grammy thought it best that we make a new start.

I had no known father. Grammy explains away my father, who was also Abe's father according to her story. Once dear old dad found out about mom's illness he split. They were never married, and he would come and go. Grammy tears up as she explains that my dad was a bad drug addict who abused her daughter. Once he was gone, she felt this was the best thing. No one knew where this horrible abusive man was, and she'd like to keep it that way. The way she explains this so convincingly even I believe her.

Mrs. Mitchell looks at me with sympathy that makes me feel uncomfortable. "My, that's a tragic story, Julie. I'm so sorry for your loss. However, we do need to have your medical records and birth certificate before we can accept you into our school. Do you think you can get those for me?"

Mrs. White becomes quite teary at this part of the questioning. If she were auditioning for a play, she'd definitely would have the part. "Oh, I don't even know where to begin. I had all the children's important papers in a box. On our move they must have gotten misplaced. You know these things take so much time. Please, could Julie begin at her new school? I promise I'll get those records to you as soon as I figure out how. Because of all the trauma she's endured she just needs to meet some friends her own age before summer."

"Well, this is a special case," Mrs. Mitchell says. "I suppose you can get started, Julie, since I know your grandmother has your best interest at heart. Why don't you come with me? School is over at 2:45. Are you going to pick her up, or should she take the bus home?"

"Julie, why don't I pick you up after school today? That way if you need supplies, we can get them right in town. Have a wonderful day, darling," Mrs. White says, kissing my cheek. "Thank you so much, Mrs. Mitchell. I know this is just what my Julie needs. Please take good care of her. Come on Abe, we have to see if they have some books for you at the library."

And with that, I was in. My new life was really beginning.

CHAPTER 19

I follow Mrs. Mitchell down a colorful hallway with a giant picture painted on the wall. It's definitely Moosehead Lake, but from a long time ago. In the picture there are lots of logs in the water. A steamship with the words Mt. Katahdin is pulling the logs. Moose and black bear stand at the water's edge. The painting is so real it looks more like a photograph than a painting.

At the end of the hallway, we come to a big area with some lockers and four good-sized classrooms. "This is the middle school area, Julie. Hold on and let me just tell Mrs. Clark you're here."

Mrs. Mitchell goes inside the first classroom. What am I doing here? I have a classroom—I'm one of Mr. Winters's winners. I wonder how I did on the math test. I guess I'll never know.

Mrs. Mitchell comes out of the classroom with an older woman I assume is Mrs. Clark. She has a long, gray braid down her back. She's tiny, with lots of lines around her eyes when she smiles. She's definitely the type of person who spends her life outdoors, you know what I mean? She has a natural look about her. She's wearing jeans and a sweater she probably knit herself. "Welcome, Julie. I'm Mrs. Clark, and I'll be teaching you math. Come on in."

Mrs. Clark brings me into the classroom. I start to imagine what Dorothy must have felt when her house landed in Oz. This classroom is so different than the one I left in Maplewood. The size of the room is the same, but there is so much that's different. There are tables instead of desks. Everyone has a computer and there are only eight other kids. I make number nine.

Mrs. Clark brings me into the classroom.

"Everyone, this is Julie, and she just moved here from... whereabouts did you move from? I don't think Mrs. Mitchell said."

Great—I thought Mrs. White and I weren't going to talk about this. "Um, I was living in New Hampshire before my...." A little voice in my head begs me to stop. I look pleadingly at Mrs. Clark, who's able to rescue me.

"Well, welcome! Why don't each of you tell Julie your names and one thing she should know about our school."

I try to focus on what each kid is saying. I'm also trying to picture who I would be in this group. There are three girls (now four with me) and five boys. They seem nice, smiling and telling me things I don't comprehend because I'm trying to focus on the story, I need to make up about myself.

"Why don't you sit at that table over there with Jackson and Sarah?" Mrs. Clark says as she goes over to a little closet. "They can fill you in on what we've been doing."

Sarah starts right in telling me everything really quickly in her thick Maine accent. "Well, we ahhh studying ratios in math. The sixth grade is doin' a project on the environmental problems affectin' the lake afta yeahs of loggin'. Mrs. Clahk is helpin us with the math portion of the project. You're gonna get a Chromebook I assume because all of our work is on Google Classroom. Right, Jackson?"

"I suppose so," Jackson says. "I mean we ain't got no books or nothing. Everyone does everything on their Chromebooks. Did you have a Chromebook at your old school?" I almost start to answer about my old school when I realize I need to stick to the homeschooling story. "Well, I've been homeschooled for the last three years. We had a computer. I used it for research and things like that."

Mrs. Clark calls me up to her desk. Sarah and Jackson go back to work on their Chromebooks. "Julie, this will be your Chromebook while you're at Moosehead Lake Regional. Have you used a Chromebook before?"

At Maplewood Middle School there was one computer lab for all of the fifth and sixth grade. My teachers had computers, but none of the students had one. We didn't have a computer at home. We were lucky to have pen and paper. "No, I never used a Chromebook. Are they difficult to use?"

"I don't think so, Julie. I'm a learning-by-doing kind of person. Tell you what, I'll give you your own private tutor. Haylee, can I see you, please?"

A tall girl with the most beautiful, straight, jet black hair comes up to Mrs. Clark's desk. "Haylee is our computer expert. She seems to understand Chromebooks better than most college students."

Haylee blushes. "I don't know about that."

"Haylee, would you help Julie today? I'm hoping that you'll show her how to navigate Google Classroom. Everyone in our school has a similar username, but your password is unique and only you'll know it. You know how to get set up, right?" Mrs. Clark asks Haylee knowingly.

"Sure, I can help you," Haylee assures me. "It's pretty simple. Come on over to my table and we'll get started. "

I follow Haylee to her table. There are four tables in the classroom for students. I guess there are no desks because there aren't that many kids. The classroom is a decent size. It's probably the same size as Mr. Win's room with only nine kids in it, so there's a lot more space.

There are two other kids at Haylee's table, but they're really into their computers and don't seem to notice us. "Hey, Ben, will you move your stuff? We need a little more space," Haylee tells the short kid who's sitting on his knees.

He's totally engrossed in his computer and doesn't even look up. He just slides his stuff over. I notice on the top of his pile is Rick Riordan's book *Sea of Monsters*. This kid can't be too bad, I guess.

Haylee gets right down to business. "To access Google Classroom, you need an email address. Did Mrs. Mitchell give you one with a temporary password when you registered?"

I'm think back to all the things my "grandmother" and Mrs. Mitchell discussed and I can't remember anything about an email. "No, at least I don't think she did."

"Okay, come on." Haylee gets up and I follow her out of the classroom. She doesn't say anything to Mrs. Clark, she just leaves. At Maplewood you couldn't just leave—you had to ask permission, sign a paper, and take a pass.

"We need to go back to the office to get you your temporary information so I can help you log in. It's really easy once you have all the pieces. So how do you like Moosehead so far?"

"It's really different." I almost say that it's really different from my old school, but I stop myself in time. "I was homeschooled for a while, so it's kind of nice being with other kids."

"Carly was homeschooled too, until last year. She lives on Keneo, so it's hard for her to get here, but her mom thought it was important for her to be with other kids. Her place is pretty cool. I've been out there a couple of times."

Haylee is telling me this and I'm trying to remember who Carly is. I have no idea where Keneo is. "Is Keneo far?" I ask, confused.

Haylee smiles like I've just said the dumbest thing. "It's that island in the middle of the lake with the mountain on it," she explains as we enter the office.

"Hello, girls. How can I help you?" Mrs. Mitchell asks.

"Julie needs her Google information so I can help her log into Google Classroom," Haylee explains.

"Oh dear, let me see. I don't know why I didn't bring it with us when we took you to Mrs. Clark's room. Give me a minute."

As Mrs. Mitchell leaves, I get a little nervous. I'm scared that the lie Grammy told has been found out somehow. Haylee's talking, but I can't really understand what she's saying because I'm terrified that social services or the police will bust into the office.

Soon Mrs. Mitchell comes back to her desk with my folder. "Here you go, Julie," Mrs. Mitchell says, smiling and handing me a paper with a username and password on it. "I'm sorry I didn't give you this before. I know you'll like it here. Just remember that if you need anything you can talk to any of your teachers. Of course, Haylee will probably be the best one to show you the ropes. Have a good day. "

"Thank you," I say.

As I turn to walk out the door Mrs. Mitchell adds, "Don't forget to remind your grandmother that we'll need those papers as soon as she can find them."

I can feel my face turn red. There are no papers. If Mrs. White tried to get them, she'd probably be arrested. Hopefully Mrs. Mitchell will just forget the whole thing. I'm not sure how Grammy will pull off creating magical papers from nowhere.

When we get back to our classroom I sit with Haylee for a few minutes as she explains how to sign into my new Chromebook. She explains my username and then tells me to think of a password that only I will remember. There are so many things swimming through my head; I have a whole life that I'm supposed to forget, maybe I can remember who I really am by my password. Would that be too risky? I don't know, but I decide if I use my real first name, I can explain it away. "Okay, I have one," I say confidently.

"Great," Haylee says. "Just put in your temporary password, then click the change password button. Remember to try and use letters, numbers, and a symbol. You might want to write it down, so you won't forget."

I type in my new password: JulyK603-555-7489. My name and Maddie's phone number. Like magic, my computer comes to life.

I have an overwhelming desire to contact Maddie. I know that she has a Snapchat and an Instagram account. How hard would it be to create one myself?

"Hey, Haylee, can you, like, access your Instagram account on these?" I ask hopefully.

"No, the school blocks that kind of stuff. I have my account on my phone. What's your name on Instagram? Maybe we can be friends."

"I don't have an account," I tell her. "My grandmother is really strict about that kind of thing. I was hoping I could get one through school so I can keep in touch with my friends in New Hampshire."

"Oh, well I can help you set up an account if you want," Haylee says. "I can be pretty sneaky if you need some help. Why don't you come over to my house after school? I don't live that far from here."

I'm surprised that Haylee already wants me to come to her house. I mean, I guess it would be okay, but do I really want to go? I feel kind of odd, like, yeah, I should make some friends, but can I really let someone else into my life? It would be cool to have a way to get in touch with Maddie. I really miss her, but on the other hand, if I start hanging out with Haylee, I'll really have to keep my real life secret.

"Well, do you want to come over?"

"Oh, I'm sorry," I mutter. "I don't know. I was just thinking about how overprotective my grandmother is. She might want me to come right home. Besides, I live about twenty miles from here. How would I get home?"

Haylee smiles. "Wow, Julie! I'm sure you could get a ride home with Bryce Turner. He works at Miller's ice cream after school, and I think he lives near you. He and my brother are good friends. Anyway, I know he lives in Rockwood. He's really cool."

"Bryce can drive?" I ask, surprised. "I know he's older than me, but I didn't think he was that much older. "

Haylee giggles. "Oh, so you've met Bryce. He's pretty cute right?"

I can feel my face flush. I hate that feeling. "Well, we kind of bumped into each other down by the lake. He seems like a nice guy I don't really know him."

"Bryce is in eighth grade. He just turned fourteen. His older brother, Steve, works at the Hannaford. Steve has a truck. They drive to school together. When Bryce is working at Miller's, Steve gives him a ride home. I'm sure they could fit you in the truck."

This is all happening too fast. I can't handle this right now, hanging out with new friends. I have to keep an eye on Abe, I mean, not like I used to, but still. I don't feel ready to be Julie White. I miss Maddie, and believe it or not, I really miss my mom.

"Haylee, I don't know, I just well…." Stupid tears. I feel them, and I can't stop them.

"What is it, Julie? Did I say something to upset you?" Haylee asks, genuinely concerned. She doesn't act like I'm a weird freak or anything like that, she is really nice.

I pull myself together and tell her my not-really-lie, "It's just, this is all so new. I mean, my mother died, and I really miss her. I miss my best friend, Maddie. I could talk to her about anything, and I haven't been able to talk to her since we left. My grandmother is all about leaving everything behind, including my friends."

"Oh my gosh, Julie, I had no idea your mother died. I guess I didn't really understand that you were living just with your grandmother. I can't imagine how you must be feeling. If I had to move away from here and leave my best friend Kennedy and never talk to her again, wow—I don't even want to think about that. Listen, maybe not today, but I'll have my mom get in touch with your grandmother and see if there's a time you can come over and hang out with Kennedy and me. It sounds like you could use a friend or two."

I just smile and think to myself. I don't even know how to answer.

CHAPTER 20

Grammy and Abe pick me up after school as promised. "Grammy"—a name I'm still not used to—jumps from the car and gives me a big hug. It's kind of embarrassing. I don't notice that Haylee is behind me until I hear her talking.

"Oh, you must be Julie's grandmother. I'm Haylee Littlefield. I was hoping that Julie and I could hang out after school sometime."

Grammy suddenly puts on that creepy fake smile I've learned not to trust. "Well, Haylee Littlefield, I'll have to think about this. What do you mean, hang out? I don't want Julie getting into any trouble. She has chores to do, and of course, homework."

I'm so embarrassed listening to Grammy telling Haylee that she doesn't want me to get into trouble. What the heck does that mean? What will Haylee think? I hope she doesn't peg me as some loser.

"Well, I was just thinking that Julie could come to my house, and we could work on homework," Haylee explains politely. "I could catch her up on some classwork she's missed and show her around a bit."

"Julie and I will talk about this, Haylee," Mrs. White says. "It was nice to me you." And just like that Haylee's dismissed.

"See you tomorrow, Julie," Haylee says, waving as she walks away from the car.

When I sit down in the car Mrs. White—or Grammy, or whoever—just stares at me in this creepy death stare kind of way.

I'm not sure what I've done or why she's looking at me like this. I don't have a good feeling. I want to run. I look in the back seat and there's Abe contently sleeping. I'm afraid to look to my left, so I just let myself focus on my peacefully sleeping brother until finally, Mrs. White begins her stern speech.

"For heaven's sake Julie. Do I have to remind you what we're doing here? Your parents are no longer in the picture. If you aren't careful, you'll be taken from, me, your grandmother, and put into a foster home. You can't just go off with people you don't know. What if you accidentally started telling this Haylee or some random person your real story? Really, you must think to stay safe."

I'm so angry thinking about how I won't be able to have a normal life that I say words I knew will hurt. "Listen, Mrs. White, you're not my grandmother. I know you think you are, but you're not. My grandmothers are both dead. I didn't even know you more than to say hello until a few weeks ago. I'm not sure what you're doing, but I think you'll be in trouble if someone finds out."

My cheek stings as I feel Mrs. White's open hand hit it. She doesn't say anything, she just starts the car and drives out of the parking lot.

I'm terrified. What have I done? What have I done? I don't want to give Mrs. White the satisfaction of tears. I look out the window, struggling with all the thoughts going through my head.

Mrs. White turns on the Van Morrison CD and again and just starts singing along. No one's ever slapped me before. My mom in her worst drug-addicted phase never slapped me, even when I threw all her drugs away. Is this what my new life will be like? I don't know which would be worse. I suddenly have a horrible feeling in my stomach. Would Mrs. White hit Abe? Is he in danger with her?

I turn my gaze toward the singing Mrs. White, trying to figure out how to ask a question without putting ideas in her head. "I'm sorry I upset you," I say. "Just…please, please promise me you'll never hurt Abe."

Mrs. White turns off the music. "Julie, my dear, dear granddaughter. How can I prove my love to you and your darling brother? I would never do anything to hurt either of you. You're my whole life, my world. If anything happened to either one of you, I just...well." Tears begin to flow down Mrs. White's cheeks. "We will not speak of this again. I'm in charge, remember. You're the child. I'm the grown-up. I need to keep you safe—the end. No more talk of going off with strangers."

What does this mean? Am I supposed to not talk to anyone for the rest of my life? This is not better than living with Mom. I decide not to discuss this anymore and just think—think about my life and Abe's. I really do wonder about Roger: I mean, if Mrs. White is going to be a weird abusive control freak, maybe it would be best for Abe if Roger knew where he was. I know that I might end up in a foster home in who-knows-what kind of situation, but Abe deserves more, doesn't he?

This is all too much; how can I live without Abe? At the same time, how can I trust that he'll really be safe, safe, safe, like Mrs. White says? If safe, safe, safe, means hitting him when he does something she doesn't like, then he's not really safe at all. I wish there were someone I could really talk to.

As we get out of the car Mrs. White smiles and again acts like everything's wonderful. "July, Abe, and I made some wonderful cookies while you were at school. Why don't you relax and have a cookie and we'll talk about your new friend, just to be sure we're all on the same page. If anything, ever happened to you or Abe, I just...well, I don't know. My life is finally beginning after so many years, July. I truly can't imagine you not in it. I would never, ever do anything to harm you. But you must never leave. Just promise me that one thing, that you'll never, ever think of leaving me."

I don't answer right away, I bite into a delicious chocolate chip cookie. The butter, sugar, and chocolate melt into my mouth. As I take another cookie from the plate, I look at Mrs. White and realize that this relationship is going to be really tricky. But if I can have these cookies every day, it might be worth it.

CHAPTER 21

I decide I'm going to have to talk to Mrs. White—Grammy—about hanging out with Haylee. I couldn't handle living a life of just going to school and coming back here to our quiet shack. I need to find out what's going on in Maplewood, especially with Mom. I also really miss Maddie. I mean she was my rock; you know? I didn't have to say anything to her, and she knew how I felt. If only I could talk to her about what's happened. We have no way of contacting the world. Mrs. White doesn't own a phone, never mind a computer. I decide this is where we'll start.

"You know, Grammy, I understand that we can't have anyone trying to find us, but I think we should have a phone just in case. Like, what if I'm sick at school and they need to call you?" I'm sure that'll get her attention—I mean, she needs to protect me, right?

"Oh July, I bought this little phone at Hannaford. It's called a Go Phone. We only use it to make emergency calls. Do you hear me? It'll be with me at all times. I don't want you to think you can start calling people back in Maplewood. It's just too dangerous." She's pretty firm about this.

I have to make her believe I would never, ever try to get in touch with Maddie or Dom, never mind Roger or Mom. "I truly understand the ramifications of people from Maplewood finding out about me," I say. "I just want to make sure I'm safe, you know? If something happened, I'd want to get in touch with you right away."

"Oh, now July, what could happen? It's perfectly safe here. The school seems lovely and so small that if anything happened to you someone would notice right away. When I drop you off tomorrow, I'll give Mrs. Mitchell my number."

"Oh, yeah," I say, remembering. "Mrs. Mitchell wanted me to remind you that we need my birth certificate and medical records. How are we going to get these? I don't have a birth certificate that says Julie White. How are we going to make that up?" I was really curious about this.

"Now, you listen to me," Mrs. White says in her stern, scary voice. "Stop this worrying. That's my job. I'll take you to a doctor here and just explain that while you were in your mother's care you were neglected. Let's face it—you were neglected. He'll give you all the proper shots for school. I'll work on your birth certificate somehow. In the meantime, I'll just keep stalling and so will you!"

"Well, um...."

"Just say it, July, what's your concern now?"

"Can I give Haylee your phone number? She said she would have her mother call you and set up a time when I could come over. She's really nice, Grammy, and I just, well, I need a friend." Tears begin spilling down my cheeks.

"I'm your friend, July," Mrs. White says. "I'm the only friend you need. I'll buy you whatever you need, I'll make sure you always have a good meal and a warm bed. No more silly talk about a friend. It's not safe—who knows what you might say or do with this girl?"

"I don't understand. I mean, I'm away from you all day at school and you aren't afraid I'll say anything. How would this be any different?"

"Oh, my," Mrs. White says. "I never really thought this through. You're right. Going to school is just too dangerous. I'll teach you myself. I'm quite capable, and I can teach you all you need to know. I don't need that Mrs. Mitchell snooping around trying to find out about you. I think you'll be safer right here with Abe and me. Now we'll start today with some cooking lessons. Won't that be fun?"

All of a sudden, I realize Mrs. White, (no, not Grammy, Mrs. White), wants to isolate me from the world. Abe and I aren't some kids she's trying to rescue from a drug addict. She believes God put us with her so she could have a new family and never be alone. I picture us locked in an attic with her as a crazy lady from a Stephen King novel. I sure have to be careful. I'm not sure how to react—I mean what if I disagreed? Would she hit me again, or do something worse?

"I don't know, Grammy. Won't the school check on me if I just don't show up? You gave them our address, and, well, maybe they would think it was weird. I promise I won't say or do anything that would make anyone suspicious. I certainly don't want to end up in a foster home."

"Well, Julie White, you've given me some things to think about. I'm worried about that Mrs. Mitchell and her demanding birth certificates. Maybe we just aren't safe here in Rockwood. Oh my, but I do love it so. I have such great memories and just wanted to create some more. Let me just think."

What a mess. I mean, I don't want to spend the rest of my life going from one town to another. I go upstairs to hang with Abe. He's zooming trucks around in his two-year-old voice trying to sound like a man saying, "Back truck up Roger...beep, beep." He then looks at me and says, "Daddy truck, Sissy?"

"Yup, that looks like Daddy's truck," I tell him, realizing he may never see his daddy again.

This thought makes me want to vomit. What have I done? I mean, if I'd just let Roger know about Mom, maybe he could have helped her, and we wouldn't be in this mess. I wonder if it's too late.

ROGER

Rate of pregnant women addicted to opioids skyrocketed in 15 years, CDC says

BY ASHLEY WELCH
AUGUST 10, 2018 / 10:13 AM / CBS NEWS

CHAPTER 22

Walking into the Dunkin Donuts on Main Street in Maplewood to grab some iced coffee that warm July afternoon changed my life. Sure, the coffee was great, medium iced, Extra Extra, but the server was gorgeous. She wasn't gorgeous in a traditional way. It was her spunk, her spirit. She was small—I guess you could call her petite. It was the twinkle in her bright, brown eyes that made me shiver when she said, "May I help you?" A slow, impish smile would spread across her face, causing her button nose to crinkle.

For the next three weeks I found myself going into that Dunkin Donuts even when I wasn't working anywhere near Maplewood. It was almost like an obsession. If it looked like another person was going to wait on me, I'd do stupid things like go to the refrigerator where the water was and stare into the glass door like a lost puppy until I could figure out how to get her as my server and hear her say, "Medium iced, Extra, Extra?"

After three weeks I got my courage up and asked her out for coffee. What a dope! Can you believe I actually said, "So hey, I was wondering if you'd like to, umm, well…." Man was I nervous! The whole time I was talking to her with those crazy brown eyes staring at me, I was melting. Finally, I got it out: "Would you want to go get a coffee with me sometime?"

She had this cute giggle. "Get a coffee? Wow, that would be a different experience," she said somewhat sarcastically. "What's your name, anyway? In my head you're Medium Iced, Extra, Extra."

"I'm Roger, Roger LaMarche, and I guess you're Jenny because you have that Jenny nametag," I said, trying to be suave.

"Nothing gets past you. You know, coffee sounds good as long as it's Starbucks. I'm not really a Dunkin fan." Jenny said, smiling a smile, that I'd come to love and hate.

And just like that I found myself in a world I never imagined.

CHAPTER 23

Our first date was at Starbucks in Portsmouth. I found myself sharing things with Jenny that I'd never told another person. She thought it was cute that I loved NSYNC and the Backstreet Boys. She'd say, "I didn't know guys like you were into that kind of music. Do you like to shop at Claire's, too?" Then she'd smile that impish smile and grab my bicep.

I work out pretty hard, and I work construction, so I was in good shape for a thirty-year old. I knew I looked pretty good: six-one and one hundred eighty pounds of muscle, though I'm not sure if my looks really impressed her, I mean, she never told me she thought I was a stud or whatever, but she always said that I made her feel safe. She'd say, "Hold me, Roger, keep me safe. I never thought I could be this happy with a guy like you." I guess I wasn't her usual type of guy.

The first summer we were together was magical. I couldn't get enough of her. Early on she told me her story. When she was eighteen, she was involved with this guy. She described him as a typical motorcycle-riding bad boy. You know the type—lots of tats, a real rebel. Anyway, she had a kid from the relationship. The guy ended up in prison and she cut all ties.

Her kid is real sweet, a little girl named July. It makes sense that Jenny would have a kid named July—not your typical Katie or Meghan for her, nope, July. Jenny is unique and so is her kid.

Jenny was excited for me to meet her daughter. She said July was all the best parts of her. She certainly had those same brown eyes. Her hair was darker and much curlier, and I guessed it must have come from her dad. Soon it was the three of us: Jenny, July, and me, a nice little family.

In September I moved in with them. I'd been living with my mom at the time in Berwick, Maine because my dad had recently died, and I didn't want my mother to be alone. Also, my dad's construction company was run out of a little office on my mom's property. Once Dad died, I took over, and at the time it had made sense to be close to work and close to Mom.

Once Jenny and I were serious, I thought moving in with her made sense. Mom was financially set, and I would still see her every day because of my business. This did not sit well with Mom. She believed Jenny was just trying to trap me. "Roger, you don't want to be responsible for some other man's child," Mom warned. "That woman sees you as someone who can take care of her, she'll never really love you, trust me." I was so angry with Mom because I have a sister who makes Jenny look like a saint. "Not everyone is like Michelle, Mom. Once you get to know Jenny and July, I know you're going to love them." I said leaving.

I thought moving in with Jenny would be the best decision of my life. I was sure she was the one. For a while she was, and then the whole thing blew up in my face.

CHAPTER 24

I came home one day in the middle of December and Jenny and July had this surprise for me. I had no idea what was going on. July was a typical ten-year-old. She was always smiling and giggling. Everything I told her was hysterical. I think it was nice for her to have a father figure. Anyway, I started walking up the stairs and July stopped me.

"Wait, you can't come up yet!" she yelled, blocking my entrance. "Mom has a big surprise. You have to close your eyes, Close them tight!"

July grabbed my hand and held on. "Keep your eyes closed. I'll lead you to the surprise," she ordered me all giggly.

"Wow, what are you up to? Is it my birthday and I just forgot?" I asked, playing along.

"No silly, we're almost there. Open your eyes!" she told me, clapping her hands.

I opened my eyes and in front of me was a beautiful painting. It was a painting of me holding a little baby. I knew Jenny had painted it because it was her style and she's an amazing artist. I just looked at the picture and then at Jenny who was nodding her head. "Yes."

"I'm going to be a father? You're having a baby?" I asked as the emotions overwhelm me. I lifted Jenny up and swung her around. July started hugging the two of us. "Family hug, we're having a baby!"

I said to my two favorite girls. "I never thought things could get more perfect."

"You know what the best part is?" July asked. "Mom says the baby will probably be born in early July." Her smile told me the baby would have the most wonderful big sister ever.

CHAPTER 25

The first few months of Jenny's pregnancy went great. She felt a little nauseous in the mornings, but she t me it was better than when she was pregnant with July. In January we found out that the baby would be a boy. I couldn't believe we would have a son. I imagined myself teaching him to do all kinds of things: ride a bike, play ball, build houses. It became so real that I got a little panicked.

"I don't know if I'm ready for this," I confessed to Jenny. "There are so many things to learn about babies, and so much responsibility. Can we afford this? Do you think we should talk more seriously about moving in with my mom? Hell, my business is doing okay now, but you never know with construction."

Jenny smiled and grabbed me around the waist. "You're already an amazing dad. I just love the way you are with July. You'll be a natural with this little guy. Deep breaths there, baby, deep breaths. I don't really want to pull July out of school. She's had enough issues in her little life without having to move away from Maplewood. Besides, I don't know if your mom's really warmed up to you having an instant family. I still think it's weird that she has July call her Mrs. LaMarche. I mean, I know she isn't her grandmother, but it puts up an added boundary. Do you think she'll have our new baby call her Mrs. LaMarche too?" she said playfully.

"Look, Mom's old-fashioned. She still goes to church almost every day and to confession once a month. I know she's having a hard time with us not being married and you having a kid, but trust me, once she meets her grandson all this will change. I'm sure she'd be okay with July calling her Memere now. Maybe we should get married. I mean, I can't imagine being with anyone else," I said, suddenly serious. "We've never talked about getting married, but why not? What's holding us back?"

Jenny kissed me softly, looked into my eyes, and said, "Not on your life, buster. I love you too much to force you into a marriage just because I'm having your kid."

This threw me. "I want to be with you forever, Jenny. This isn't just a let's-get-married-because-we're-having-a-kid kind of thing. I love you. I want to be with you," I said, trying to convince her—and maybe myself—that we should tie the knot.

"After the baby's born, I'll see if I want to keep you around," she said as she kissed me deeply.

For now, at least, I understood that the conversation was closed.

CHAPTER 26

Sometime in February things started to change. Jenny had an early shift at Dunkin's She had to be there by five. It was super early and hard for her to get out of bed. She was starting to get bad back pain from the baby, and maybe from being on her feet for so long.

July and I developed an easy morning routine: I'd wake her up and we'd have breakfast together. It was kind of a special time for the two of us. I was really falling for this kid. She had so much of her mother's spunk and creativity. She made up these stories that she'd share with me, so I bought her a little journal and she just wrote and wrote. After breakfast I would wait at the bus stop with her. I knew I didn't have to, but I wanted to, you know? I was all about being a dad.

As things got better for July and me, things with Jenny were getting complicated. At first, I blamed it all on the pregnancy, but then things just got...I don't know. She grew distant. I would get home from work, and she'd be in bed. She was always tired. I begged her to talk to the doctor, but she didn't even want to talk about it with me. She would pull the blankets up and say, "Just leave me alone, Roger." She was still getting up every morning and leaving early for the donut shop. July started noticing things, too. Jenny would be home in the afternoon before July got home from school. Jenny had the five a.m. to one p.m. shift now just so she could be there when

July got home from school. Because I own the company, I changed my hours to eight to four, so we didn't have to worry about paying a babysitter for July. There were a few days when she would get home and Jenny wouldn't be there. I don't know how many of these days there were. When I found out about it, I was disappointed. I mean, was this the kind of thing Jenny would do with our kid? One day I got home, and July was all alone. She was only ten and yeah, I guess she's mature for her age and can take care of herself, but she had no idea where her mother was and neither did I. Jenny waltzed into the house around six-thirty. She didn't say anything and just went into the bathroom, took a shower, and got into bed.

Man was I angry. This wasn't the Jenny I fell in love with, distant and mysterious. That Jenny was a great mom. July always came first, but now something was changing. I walked into our room. "Look at me," I told Jenny quietly.

She pulled the covers over her head. I pulled them back off her and grabbed her face so I could look at her. I had a suspicion and hoped I was wrong.

She looked up at me, her eyes half closed and pretty bloodshot. The look on her face told me a lot: it was uncaring, and she couldn't focus. I'd seen this same look on my sister's face so many times when she was using. *Please God*, I prayed, *don't let this happen to Jenny, not now.*

The next morning, I decided I'd get up with Jenny and really try to talk to her. It was getting more and more useless to talk to her at night. I was so anxious about getting up with her that I actually got up fifteen minutes before her. I decided I'd make her a healthy breakfast before she left for Dunkin's. I knew that she usually ate when she got to work, but I thought a nice breakfast would give us a chance to talk.

Jenny came into the kitchen in her brown uniform that I noticed was starting to get a little tight around her tummy. Fortunately, she was awake and seemed to be in a pleasant mood, just like the person I'd fallen in love with.

"Wow, Rog, what's the occasion? I don't remember the last time you were up this early. Look at this breakfast." Jenny walked over and wrapped her arms around me. She smelled so good, like morning and sunshine. I just wanted to stay like this.

I bent down and kissed her slowly. "I made this for you," I said, pulling away a little, "because I want to talk. I'm worried about you, Jen. You haven't been yourself."

"I'm fine," she said, trying to get back to kissing but figuring that wasn't going to happen just now. "Why are you worried? Yeah, I'm tired at the end of the day, but Jesus, who wouldn't be. I get up every friggin' day at four a.m., then waddle to work where I'm on my feet nonstop until I leave. Look at me—I'm six and half months pregnant and as big as a house. Once the baby gets here things will be better." She sat down and dug into her spinach and feta omelet. "You're the omelet master," she said with a smile.

I couldn't help it—I had to know where she'd been the previous afternoon. I still didn't trust her, and I couldn't put my finger on it. "I know you're tired, babe. If you didn't need the health insurance, I'd tell you to just quit. We'll figure this out. I was worried about you last night—you looked pretty wrecked. Is there anything else I should know?" As I said the words, I knew it was a mistake.

"What's that supposed to mean? 'Is there anything else I should know?' Just say it, Roger. Are you worried I'm becoming a drunk like my sister, or a druggie like yours? Jesus." She threw down her fork, ran from the kitchen, and slammed the door to the bathroom.

Well, that went well, idiot, I thought. I wasn't sure what to do. I didn't want to fight. I was worried she was doing something that could hurt both the baby and her. I'd been around a few pregnant women—I knew they got tired, but this was different. Pregnant women get mood swings, but do they get bloodshot eyes and blurred vision? Do they forget they have a ten-year-old and a partner back at home? It just wasn't right.

As Jenny came out of the bathroom, I could see she'd been crying. "Jenny, I love you," I pleaded. "I'm just concerned. Quit your goddamn job and we'll figure it out."

She didn't even look at me. She just walked out the door.

CHAPTER 27

I was really distracted when I got to work, so I stopped by my mom's for a cup of coffee. My mom's really an old-fashioned French-Canadian Catholic—and so was my dad. She wasn't happy that I was living in sin with a girl who already had a child out of wedlock. She hadn't accepted July and I doubted she ever would. Two of my sisters had kids already, and she was practically raising my sister Michelle's kids because they had different fathers, so she didn't exactly jump for joy when I told her Jenny was pregnant. "Are you sure the baby's yours, Roger?" she asked when I told her Jenny was pregnant. "You can't really trust those kinds of women. I told you she would try to trap you."

As I sat at the table with my coffee, I could see her looking at me with that kind of I-told-you-so look. She knew something was wrong and assumed it was about Jenny, not work. "So, Roger, you seem far away today. Is everything okay at home? Are you having issues with that woman you live with?"

"Her name is Jenny, Mom. We've been together for about eight months. You know she's more than 'that woman I live with.' When are you going to accept that this is my family: Jenny, July, and your new grandson? Why do you always have to be so judgmental with Jenny? It's not like your own daughter hasn't found herself in the same situation four different times." I didn't give her time to respond, I just got up and walked out to my shop.

I tried to throw myself into my work. Sometimes banging nails is just the thing I need. Dave and Fred, my closest friends who work for me, were working on a house in Maplewood. My mind wasn't in a place for tracking bills, so I decided to drive over and see if I could help them out. Physical labor was just what I needed.

I drove down Main Street and decided to stop at Dunkin' and pick up some coffee and donuts for the guys. I knew I'd see Jenny there. I guess I wanted to see her. I wasn't really ready for what I found when I got there.

Jenny was there, but she didn't notice me because the line was really long. I couldn't keep my eyes off of her. She was waiting on some tall, skinny guy with lots of tats. She was smiling and joking with him, just like she did with me when I first met her. As she handed him his coffee, I saw her take something from him and slip it into her pocket. As the guy was leaving, he said, "See you tomorrow, sunshine."

She responded, "I hope so."

I'm not the jealous type, but for some reason I wanted to grab this goon and beat the shit out of him. That was when Jenny saw me shooting daggers at the guy. "What the hell was that about?" I demanded. "'See you tomorrow, sunshine,' and what did you take from him?" I knew I must sound like an ass to the other people in line, but I really didn't care.

"For God's sake, Roger don't do this here," she said as she walked into the back.

I was so pissed I left without picking up anything for the guys. When I got to the job site, I took out my anger and frustration on the demolition. I had the kitchen ripped apart in no time.

"Wow, "Dave said. "We should have pissed-off Roger here all the time."

I know he was kidding, but I just walked out the door. By that time, it was four o'clock so I decided to call it a day and go home.

CHAPTER 28

I could feel the tension as I opened the front door. July was sitting on the couch with her journal. She looked so sad, not carefree like a ten-year-old should. As I sat down next to her, I noticed she was drawing a picture of a girl with tears flowing down her cheeks like big raindrops. I knew how she felt and just gave her a hug.

"Is everything okay with Mom?" July asked.

"What do you mean?" I asked back. What are you worried about?"

"I'm worried about Mom. She doesn't really talk to me anymore. When I get home, she's sometimes cranky, and sometimes it's like she's not even there, but usually she just tells me to do my homework and then goes to bed. I think she needs to go to the doctor or something." July looked up at me, pleading that I'd know the answer that would make everything better. I didn't.

"You know what?" I said, trying to sound reassuring. "That's a great idea. I noticed your mom hasn't been herself either. Maybe you and I can talk to her together and tell her we think she needs to see the doctor."

I thought it was a great idea—now I just had to convince Jenny it was a great idea too. I know she'd been going to the OB once a month, so I hoped they could give her something to help with the fatigue. I had this nagging feeling in the back of my head, though, like something more was happening. Maybe if July and I formed a united front we could come up with something.

"July let's go out for dinner. How about you go and see if you can get your mom up? You pick the place, and we'll go."

July gave me a big hug and ran to wake up Jenny. "Mom, Mom!" she yelled in an excited voice. "Roger's taking us out for dinner. Wake up, let's go!"

It broke my heart to hear Jenny's response. "Leave me alone, July," she said. "I don't want to go out to dinner. I just want to sleep."

"But Mom, you need to eat something, and we haven't done anything as a family for such a long time. Roger said it was my choice, but you can choose the place." July was really pleading I could hear the worry in her voice.

"Get the hell out of here and shut the goddamn door!" Jenny yelled.

"She doesn't want to go," July told me, her lip quivering.

"Well, then it's you and me," I said. "Where do you want to go?" I tried to be happy, but inside I wanted to cry, too.

"I don't care, I'm not really that hungry. We can just stay here." July sounded scared and deflated.

I was so angry with Jenny and vowed that I'd get to the bottom of her moodiness when we got back. "I'm ready. Let's hop in the truck. I really feel like a burger. What do you say you and I go to Wild Willy's over in York? We can even stop at the beach and chase some seagulls."

"Should I tell Mom?" July asked.

Her question only fueled my anger. Couldn't Jenny see what she was doing to her daughter, never mind what she might have been doing to my son?

"Nope, Mom will be fine. Let's go and have some fun. I think we deserve that." Leaving Jenny behind and laughing with a ten-year-old was just what I needed.

July looked towards her mom's bedroom, and I could see the concern on her face. "Burgers and seagulls are waiting," I told her. "Let's go. This boy is really hungry. Grab your coat and a hat. I bet it's cold on the beach," I said as happily as I could.

July grabbed her green and white sweatshirt and hopped into the truck. I turned the ignition just as the start of Carly Rae Jepsen's "Call Me Maybe" came blaring over the radio. I know all the words because you know—I like that kind of music. Anyway, I just started singing. Without missing a beat July joined in. It was just what the two of us needed.

We continued singing crazy pop songs all the way to Wild Willy's. Both of us just laugh and sang. For a while, I think we both forgot about Jenny. It was truly what I needed and watching July smile and dance in the seat next to me, I knew she needed it, too. *Tonight, it'll be just the two of us*, I promised myself.

CHAPTER 29

Things with Jenny went from worse to horrible. She often refused to talk to me. I felt like I was walking on eggshells in my own place. She continued to get up early and walk to her job at Dunkin'. A few times I got up with her, but it was useless trying to talk to her about anything, never mind confronting her about the problem.

Toward the middle of May I learned the ugly truth. I was working near our place, so one day I thought I'd just go home for lunch. I'd made a killer chili the day before and a nice bowl was just what I needed. It was around noon, so I knew I'd have the place to myself. Was I ever wrong.

As I walked up the stairs I could hear loud music, some godawful heavy metal coming from our house. I don't know if I was prepared for what I saw next.

Jenny and this tall skinny tattooed guy were sitting on the couch snorting some kind of powder. Man, did I lose it. I ran over to the two of them, grabbed the stuff, grabbed the guy, and with all the anger I'd built up over the past month, punched him right in the nose. Then I literally picked him off the floor and threw his skinny ass out of the house.

I was beyond angry with Jenny. "What the hell are you doing?!" I screamed, . She didn't fight, didn't yell, didn't respond.

I sat down next to her and just cried, sobbing like a baby. I was terrified for her, but also for the baby that I knew would one day be my son. I never thought I'd have to be worried about this, not with Jenny. How could she do this?

"You need to get help," I pleaded. "You can hurt yourself if you want, but please, please don't hurt our baby."

I left her slumped on the couch; I didn't know what else to do. When I got back to the truck, I banged on the steering wheel a few times. I had to get Jenny some help, but I had no idea where to start.

I drove back to the job site, again happy to be doing demolition. I needed to take my anger out on something. I didn't talk to Fred or Dave, I grabbed a crowbar and started ripping apart a wall.

Dave came up to me and put his hand on my back. "Easy Roge, you're going to take down the whole place."

This broke me out of my anger fog. I looked at what I'd done. We were opening up a wall from the kitchen into the dining room, and I'd been about to whack the support beam." Sorry, man," I said sheepishly. "I've got a lot on my mind."

"I get it," Dave said. "You're the boss, so why don't you take the rest of the day off?"

I realized Dave was right. "I really need to figure some shit out. Do you mind?" I told him more than asked.

"Fred and I are all over this," Dave said. "Take as much time as you need. Your mind really hasn't been on the job lately."

I got into my truck and just started driving. The next thing I knew I was in front of Jenny's sister Susan's house. I didn't really know too much about Susan. She and Jenny were close at one time. Jenny told me she had a drinking problem. She'd been in and out of sobriety for a while. I didn't know if she knew anything about Jenny putting shit up her nose, but she might have known how to help.

I was hopeful as I walked up the stairs to her tiny apartment in the projects. As I knocked on the door my heart started beating really hard. Man was I nervous, or angry, or anxious—or all of the above. I was in over my head and didn't know what to do.

Susan answered the door, a cigarette dangling from her mouth. She looked surprised to see me and tried to straighten out her messy long hair. She closed the door behind her and sat on the front steps. "What brings you here, Roger?" she asked, exhaling smoke in my face.

I wasn't sure how to respond. I breathed out a few times and finally just spilled my guts to this woman I didn't really know, but who I hoped loved Jenny as much as I did.

"I'm so worried about Jenny. She's been acting so crazy. Today I came home early and she and some dude were snorting things up their noses." As I said this out loud, I felt like I was going to lose it again. I really had to fight back tears. "I don't know what to do. She's pregnant for God's sake. I'm afraid for her and the baby."

Susan took a long drag off her cigarette. Then she just looked at me and didn't say anything. I didn't know if she was just thinking, or if she didn't care. I started wondering whether I'd made the right choice coming to see her. Finally, "You want a beer?"

This threw me a little. "Yeah, I think that's just what I want."

Susan got up and walked into the house. *What am I doing here? How is this drunk going to help me? I asked myself.* A few minutes later Susan was back on the porch with two Lite beers. Not my favorite, but beggars can't be choosers, right? I took a long swig and so did Susan.

"That's better," Susan said, putting her beer down and lighting another cigarette. "Look, Jenny's a good kid. She had a problem a few years ago when she was with Bobby. He had her hooked really good. Once she found out she was pregnant with July she got herself clean. She can do it again. I didn't know she was using. I know you're thinking this is really bad because of the baby and all, but I've seen her in worse shape."

I was shocked by this. I had no idea that Jenny had ever had a drug problem. She'd never talked to me about it. I'd known that she didn't drink, but I just assumed that was because her dad was a bad drunk. She'd shared some of her past with me, and it wasn't pretty: I knew July's father, Bobby, was in jail for dealing, but she never told me she'd been using him.

"I don't get it. Why would Jenny go back to drugs? I mean, she had to know what would happen if she started using again, right? Why would she do this to us?" I felt so angry and confused.

Susan took a long swig of her beer. As she brought it down again a sad smile appeared on her face. "Look Roge, it's not really a choice—trust me. You can't turn your addiction on and off. I've been trying most of my life to give up booze. There've been times when I went a whole year without a drop. After Dom was born I had to quit. He had so many issues. His dad couldn't cope with his problems, so he took off. I went back to drinking after that. I tried to kid myself: If I just had one beer, if I just had one glass of wine...."

Tears started trickling down her cheeks. "And there's the problem. I can't have just one. I have to drink until I'm numb. There's no going back once you get started. The guilt kills me sometimes, knowing that I caused my kid to have so many problems, but not having a drink kills me too. I'm guessing it's the same for Jenny. Addiction runs in the family. I guess we just chose different drugs."

Susan gulped the rest of her beer, burped, lit a cigarette, and said, "I'm having another. Do you want one?"

I didn't even know how to respond. I still had half a beer left. Susan had just told me that she drinks until she's numb—obviously, I wasn't going to get the help I needed from her. Shaking my head, I stood up and said, "No, I've got to get going. Thanks for the beer."

"Wait a minute—before you go, don't give up on Jenny," Susan said. "She needs you. She can't do this alone. She's a good mom. I'll try to talk to her."

"Thanks, I guess," I said as she stumbled into the house.

CHAPTER 30

As I drove home, I started feeling guilty about July. Yeah, I was having a hard time with Jenny, but what kind of guy was I letting a ten-year-old stay alone with a drug addict? Who knew what could have happened? Who was this guy Jenny was hanging with? Was he just a dealer? Would he hurt July?

All of this was too much for me. I mean, I didn't think of July as my true responsibility, but I guess she was. I could hear my mother's accusations: *Roger, do you really want to take care of somebody else's child? Do you know how difficult this will be? What are you thinking? Don't think I'm going to help you I already raised my kids and my grandkids; I'm not going to take care of some strangers kid.*

What a mess! It was well past seven when I got home. I really didn't want to go inside. I was still angry with Jenny. I wondered if she even remembered that I'd been home.

July was sitting on the couch watching some kid show. She looked up when I came in but didn't say anything. It was almost like she understood that now she was taking care of herself.

"How are you? Did you have dinner?" I asked, feeling a little guilty. "I'm going to fix myself a sandwich. Do you want one?"

"I had some cereal. Mom's asleep. She's been asleep all day, I think. Anyway, I got home around three and she was already asleep. I don't even think she heard me come in." July's tone was matter of fact.

Inside I was still angry. I wanted to run into Jenny's room and shake the living crap out of her, but I couldn't do that. I had to protect July somehow. I decided to use her matter-of-fact tone, too. "How was school? Have you done any more writing?"

July responded without looking up from the TV. "It was fine."

I left her and went into the kitchen. I was thinking about some cold cuts, but it took me a while to even find them because my mind was so consumed with Jenny and the baby.

As I ate, I gazed at July watching mindless television. Jenny, her mother, the mother of my unborn kid, was asleep in her room. I started asking myself questions: *What are you doing here? Do you love the woman who's having your baby? What about July? What do you really owe this kid? I mean, it sucks for her that her mother's a druggie, but is she, my responsibility?*

I finished my sandwich and went into bedroom; I knew I couldn't stay there—it was all too much. I started throwing some stuff into a duffle bag. Jenny looks up. She's in a foggy haze. "I can't do this anymore. You don't care about me, or July. So help me if anything is wrong with the baby, so help me I'll take him from you and be sure you can never see him again"

Jenny doesn't even reply, It's like she's not even there. I looked up and notice July was standing in the doorway. "I'm sorry July," I said, "I never signed up for this," I walked past July and out the door."

I jumped into my truck and turned on the radio in the middle of Katy Perry's "Circle the Drain." I couldn't help but relate to the lyrics. Man, what was I doing? How could I leave this baby, but at the same time how could I stay? It was just too much. As I found myself driving to my office, I realized I'd probably have to do some explaining to my mother. I wasn't ready for her to tell me I told you so. Hopefully, I could sneak into the office without her noticing.

CHAPTER 31

I woke to the sun shining through my office window. I knew it was morning, but I didn't care. I felt awful, and my neck ached from sleeping on the uncomfortable loveseat in my office. I needed coffee and a shower. I knew I had to go into my mother's house for both, and I knew she was going to give me some looks and ask lots of questions, but the need for coffee was unbearable.

As I opened the back door, I realized Mom was still asleep. *Maybe I can make some coffee and shower before she wakes up.* In the middle of filling the water in the Mister Coffee, I heard the upstairs bathroom door close. I tried to focus on the coffee and not the questions I knew would be coming.

No sooner had I poured the coffee into the mug then I heard my mother's voice. "Is that you, Roger? I saw your truck pull up to the office last night. Did you have a construction emergency?" she called out sarcastically.

"I just needed a little space, Ma. Don't overthink this," was my reply.

She appeared at the bottom of the stairs. "I don't know why you didn't just go up to your room. For goodness' sake, I know you'll be back here once you figure out what kind of woman that Jenny is. I mean, just look at her: a single mother, tricking you into getting her pregnant—and I'm sure she tricked you into it. I still don't know why you think that baby is yours. You know those kinds of women, always sleeping around. Save yourself some trouble and move back home."

I was so angry with everything that I grabbed my coffee and walked out without so much as a goodbye. I knew if I went back to the house Jenny would hopefully be at work and July would be in school. I really didn't want to see either of them. I just wanted to take a shower and do some hard work. Fred and Dave were ripping apart a bathroom today, and I knew the physical labor would keep my mind off things.

As I walked up the stairs to Jenny's I could hear that horrible, loud music. My stomach started to do a little flip. I wanted to run away, but something compelled me to open the door.

Jenny and the tall, skinny dude were all over each other on the couch. Some kind of white powder, little baggies and straws were all over the coffee table—they had no idea I was even in the room. It was clear that before the make-out session—they'd gotten wasted.

The scene sealed the deal for me. I couldn't stay in that place—I couldn't do this. I watched them for a while longer, then I slammed the door.

On the way back to my mom's house, I knew this is going to be really hard. I could hear my mother's *I told you so* and see her judgmental looks. I resigned myself to dealing with her, so I didn't have to deal with Jenny anymore. The women I fell in love with was gone. I needed to face that. I couldn't fix her; I couldn't turn her back into the girl I'd fallen in love with over iced coffee. I couldn't take care of her kid. Hell, I probably couldn't even take care of my own kid.

I walked back into my mom's kitchen. Before she could even open her mouth, I told her, "I'm moving back in, please don't say anything right now. I need you to understand. I loved that woman, she's having my baby, but I can't be with her. It's really complicated, and I don't want to talk about it, so please just let me be."

Instead of talking, my mom grabbed me and hugged me tight. She just said, "Welcome home."

CHAPTER 32

Things between Jenny and me got pretty weird. I hadn't even been gone for twenty-four hours when I got a call from Jenny's sister demanding I come to the hospital, that I had a son.

When I heard the words, I was terrified. I mean, Jenny was taking drugs, and now my son, my baby, had been born two months premature.

I jumped in my truck and headed to the hospital, not sure what to expect. As I approached the nursery, I was overcome with so many feelings. *Will I feel a bond with this guy? Am I going to be able to care for him as my son? Should I leave him with his mother and pretend I never knew her? Should I just run out now before I see him?*

"Roger!" a familiar voice called before I could turn and run. "You have to meet Abe, he's so tiny, but he looks just like you." It was July coming out of the nursery as I was going in. "Come on, he's so cute—don't be scared of all the tubes. The doctor and the nurses told me he would be just fine."

July dragged me to meet my son. I wish there were words to describe my emotions. Looking at him lying there so helplessly hooked up to all these machines made me realize I had to be there for that little guy—and that I was going to take him away from his mother so fast. Jenny had no right to do this, not to my son.

His little body was shaking, and he had this painful, tiny cry, like he couldn't catch his breath. "I'm here, little guy," I told him, "and nothing will ever happen again to hurt you, I swear to God. I promise that I'll always take care of you."

I could feel a trickle of a tear fall down my cheek as July brought me back to reality.

"He's wicked cute, right Roger? I mean he's teeny tiny. I think we better get some doll clothes for him."

"I think you're right—he is pretty tiny. Where's your mom?" I don't know why I asked. I really didn't ever want to see her again. I was afraid I was going to kill her.

Then Jenny's sister appeared from nowhere. "She's asleep. I don't know if you should really see her right now. Maybe leave her be."

I couldn't believe it, her telling me not to see the woman who'd caused my son to have so many problems. "Listen Susan, this is my son. He's a part of me and I have every intention of making sure your druggie sister knows that. I get that she's just suffered some trauma but look at that tiny baby in there with tubes coming out of every part of his body. You don't think he's suffered some trauma too? His body's shaking, and he can't stop crying."

I was furious. I turned and walked out of that hospital as fast as I could. I didn't know what to do. I just sat in my truck, banged on the dash, and cried.

CHAPTER 33

I got back to my mom's house around seven-thirty in the morning. My mom was up and poured me a strong cup of coffee. She knew something was wrong but didn't ask, which was a blessing. I slowly sipped my coffee, trying to decide what to say and knowing that whatever I came up with would be judged.

"So, I'm a father.," I finally said. "Jenny had the baby, a boy named Abe."

I knew what she was going to say before the words were out of her mouth, but I didn't want her to say them.

"Are you sure he's your baby? I mean, don't you think she just trapped you because she believed you had money? Does this baby even look like you? You owe this woman nothing, Roger."

How could a mother be so cold? "I don't even know what to say," I told her. "I knew that's what you'd say. Yes, that little, tiny baby with tubes coming out of his mouth and wires attached to his little chest, yup, he's mine. He's your grandson. Don't worry—he'll never be a burden to you like Michelle's kids are. I'll never leave him with you. You won't ever, ever have to lay eyes on him!"

I was so angry I couldn't see straight. "I really need you to just be a mother now. Come on, can't you say anything, like *Congratulations*, or have some compassion and say, *Roger, what can I do? You must be worried sick about your new little son.* No, you just can't believe that your good little Catholic boy could knock someone up. Well, you know what? I did. I've slept with plenty of women, but I only ever loved one, and now she's had my baby." I couldn't help it, I just start sobbing.

"Now Roger, you're a grown man," she said dismissively. "What would your father say if he saw you crying like this? I'm really glad he's not here to see this mess. Go pull yourself together. No more talk of this."

I just looked at her. I couldn't say anything. The one person who should be there for me wasn't. Boy, did I feel alone. The only place I wanted to be was back at the hospital. I felt drawn to my son—I needed to be with him. Having this blowout with my mother made me even more determined to be there for Abe. I mean, he was already starting life in such a difficult place.

I somehow pulled myself together and drove to a local toy shop. I needed to get him something—something soothing that he could cuddle with. I must have looked lost because a woman approached asking if I could use some help. I explained that I was a new dad and needed a cuddle toy for my son. She showed me all the stuffed animals and I saw the soft white Gund teddy bear right away. I remembered having one when I was a little kid.

"That's it, that's the one," I told the woman.

When I left the store with that cuddly bear, I felt ready to try again. Whatever was going on with Jenny, this baby was still mine. I had to get to a place where I could talk to her and get her the help she needed. I had to get her back to the woman I knew she could be. I saw the mom she was before she started taking drugs. I was pretty sure she could get there again.

I walked into Jenny's room where she was pumping breast milk. She looked up and just started crying. "I'm so, so sorry, Roger. I know you must hate me. I swear to God I'll do whatever it takes to be sure our little boy is okay. I named him Abe, after your dad. I just don't want you to hate me." Her crying turned into sobs.

I wrapped my arms around her and let her cry. I didn't know how to feel. Yes, a part of me hated her because of what she'd done to Abe, to me, to July—but as I held her, I couldn't forget that I also loved her.

"He's so tiny, Jenny. I'm so afraid for him. I'm sure together we can get through this. Just promise me, swear that you'll never take whatever that shit was that got you into this condition ever, ever again. And so, help me God, if I ever see that goon you were with, I'll kill him. If you're still with him, you have to let me know because my little boy is not having anything to do with that creep."

I could feel the anger in my voice. I didn't want it to come out like that. I got up and said, "I'm going to just hang out with Abe so I can think."

I walked down the hall to see my tiny son. He was smaller than the teddy bear I'd bought him. July was sitting in the chair next to him, singing songs and holding his little finger. She was really sweet. Somehow, I got a feeling that she would always be there for her brother, no matter what.

CHAPTER 34

Abe was released from the hospital six weeks after he was born. Because he was born with oxycodone (the drug Jenny was taking while she was pregnant) in his system, he had to be given small amounts of morphine to control his tremors, or I guess, seizures. We weren't sure if he'd make it, and we still don't know if there'll be permanent damage. His heart, lungs, and other vital organs were fine, but the doctors thought he might have some cognitive damage.

Jenny acquiesced to having a social worker assigned to her case and admitted that she'd been addicted to oxy and was getting it from a guy off the street. She also suffered bad withdrawals. She agreed to start Narcotics Anonymous right away, maybe because the state threatened to take Abe and July from her. Whatever the case, I was glad she was getting back to her old self. I agreed to support her and keep a close eye on the kids.

I wasn't sure what to do. Jenny and I were talking, but it was so much harder for me to forgive her than I thought it would be. I knew our relationship was over, but I wasn't going to abandon my son. I was worried about having him live with Jenny, even though she'd promised she was clean. She'd given up the goon, and she truly had a bond with Abe. I also watched July taking care of him, and it was clear that his big sister was not going to let anything happen.

The first night Abe was home, I asked Jenny if I could sleep on the couch. I guess I just needed to see for myself that he would be okay. Jenny left the hospital before Abe, but she didn't really leave. She'd stay there for most of the day and into the evening. She had to be home so July could go to school.

I stayed with Abe at night, which I found really comforting. Soon I could hold him and rock him. I loved this guy so much already. I had a future planned for us. It was going to be tricky, but it would be okay.

Surprisingly, staying that first night with Jenny and July wasn't too bad. July was such a great helper, getting diapers and even changing Abe. She had these cute songs she made up about him. Jenny had no problem breastfeeding. She had a little portable crib set it up next to her bed. It seemed like they had things under control—I just couldn't be separated from him.

It was hard to sleep on the couch. I heard Abe cry and got right up to go to him. The first time I peeked in Jenny was feeding him. She looked so beautiful. She was kissing his toes and smelling his little head. This is what I thought our life would be like before she got herself involved with that tattooed guy and those drugs.

She looked up and smiled at me. "He's so beautiful. Come on in. It's really okay. I want to be able to parent together. I know I screwed up, but this beautiful boy deserves two parents."

"You're right, he certainly does." I put my head down on her pillow, realizing what could have been, and what could still be. "He'll always have me—I'll never, ever abandon him. I'll be here whenever you need me. We have to figure this out, but I can't move back in, not now. I hope you understand. I love my son, and I won't have him be another kid raised without a dad. I know you're trying to stay clean and I'm proud of you for that, but I need to be sure Abe will always have a mom who's sober."

Jenny began to cry. "You're a really good guy, Roger LaMarche. I'm going to prove that I'm quite capable of raising this boy. I know you don't trust me, but I swear I won't do anything to hurt him. You'll never have to worry that I'll put either of my kids in danger again."

And I believed her…for a while.

CHAPTER 35

For the first year of Abe's life things seemed good. Jenny was in love with this amazing little guy. She worked really hard getting him all the help he needed. Because of the way he came into the world, he had lots of visits from social services, which was fine by me. Jenny spent hours reading to him, singing, doing anything she was advised to do. I'd come over after work and hang out with July and Abe so she could go to her meetings.

After a while I got caught up in a big project at work and it was hard for me to visit as regularly as I wanted to. Abe was getting bigger, and I felt like it might be time for him to start hanging out with me on the weekends. Jenny and I were drifting apart. I mean, she was involved with her NA friends, and I didn't seem to have much in common with her besides Abe. July was eleven. She actually seemed more like an adult. What a responsible kid she was. A few nights when I couldn't make it over, July would watch Abe for an hour or two while Jenny went to her meetings.

I agreed to give Jenny two hundred fifty dollars a week for child support. She was working again and had found a nice woman to watch Abe. I also gave her money for the babysitter. The situation was working out okay. Not ideal, but I thought it could work. I knew Jenny was really depending a lot on July, and I wanted her to know how much I appreciated her help. I usually gave her twenty bucks just for herself as I left with Abe.

Once Abe started hanging out with me at my mom's house, my mom fell in love. She took hundreds of pictures of him to show her friends. She spent days on end at the outlet mall buying him outfits. It was hard to walk in the house because there were so many toys for him. "I can't believe how much he looks like you," she would gush. I guess she started believing that he really was my son.

Things started changing around August. Jenny's landlord sold the house they were living in, so Jenny had to find a new place to live. She moved into an apartment that certainly wasn't my choice. We actually got into a fight about it. We'd been getting along well, but this was—wow. I mean, she moved to a really bad part of town. The apartment was in an old three-story house that was really rundown. It was obvious the landlord's priority wasn't taking care of the place. There were signs of rodents and cockroaches. The front steps were broken. I couldn't believe she thought this was a good place to raise kids.

"Listen Roger, you don't have to live here, and I can save a ton of money. This place is three hundred dollars cheaper than the other place," she said dismissively as her NA friends helped unload the truck and move my son into a house, I wouldn't want a dog to live in.

"If it's the money, I can give you more. I just don't want my son growing up in a slum."

"Oh, for God's sake, it's not that bad. The apartment is clean. It's still in Maplewood. It's not like I'm moving the kids to a drug-infested project in the South Bronx. It'll be fine for now."

I walked up the stairs, carrying a box of things that belonged to Abe. July and Abe were in their room. July was setting up a shelf with all of Abe's things, and Abe was in a playpen. I overheard her talking to him: "Abe, this will be okay, I mean it's not as nice as our other place, but we're closer to the park. I can take you there after school, and we'll walk around downtown. I bet Maddie will come with us."

There was something about July. She has an old soul, I guess. Whenever I saw her with Abe, I felt better. I knew she was just a kid, but she had common sense and was so smart. If she was around, I knew Abe would be fine.

CHAPTER 36

After Christmas I noticed a change in Jenny. It was subtle at first. I would go to pick up Abe on Fridays and she would seem tired. Another time she seemed disoriented or confused. It was a Friday, and I knocked on the front door and walked inside. That awful loud music Jenny would always listen to was coming from the apartment. As I walked up the stairs, I got this sinking feeling.

Jenny was lying on the couch obviously asleep. "Jenny, hey Jenny!" I yelled.

July appeared with Abe. He was all packed and ready to go. "Daddy," Abe called, running to my arms. I picked him up and looked at July. She seemed nervous.

Jenny started to stir. She looked up at me and said in a slurred voice, "Roger, why are you here?"

I almost cried. *Please no, don't do this again.*

July spoke first. "Mom, remember, it's Friday. You got Abe's bag all packed. You asked me to watch him until Roger got here because you had a headache, and you were going to take a nap."

This seemed to pull Jenny out of her fog. "Oh, how long have I been sleeping?"

"About two hours, I guess," July said.

"Oh, wow. Come give Mommy a kiss, Abe," Jenny said.

Abe ran over to Jenny and gave her the sweetest kiss. "Bye-bye Mommy. Bye-bye Sissy."

"Are you sure you're okay, Jenny?" I asked, not really sure if she would tell me the truth.

"To be honest, I hurt my back at work," she said nonchalantly. "I'm taking some time off, so hopefully it'll heal soon."

She must have sensed the panic in my face because she added, "You don't have to worry. I'm not going back to that stuff. I've been clean for nineteen months and twenty days."

I couldn't help but think that she'd been clean for ten years when she was pregnant with Abe. Her back was hurting from standing on her feet and she went back to drugs so easily. This time, though, she wasn't pregnant. She'd have a much easier time convincing herself she was just taking what she was taking so she could feel better. These thoughts terrified me.

"I really hope not," I told her. "I don't want anything to happen to Abe. If you do anything stupid, I won't hesitate to…."

"To what, Roger?" she challenged, getting off the couch and walking toward me with anger in her eyes. "I can't really picture you keeping Abe full-time," she said accusingly. "And your mother certainly won't watch him while you're at work."

Even though Jenny was angry, she had a point. How could I watch Abe if I was working? I guess I could find daycare if I really needed it. Mom truly loved Abe but I didn't think I could handle the guilt she'd throw at me if she had to watch him. I had to do what was right for Abe. Having a sober mother would be best for everyone, but how could I be sure she was staying sober? *Once an addict always an addict*, I kept thinking.

"Let's not fight about this. I'm sorry if I said anything to offend you. I'm just looking out for Abe's best interest. Do you want me to take him more often? Maybe you should go to extra Narcotics Anonymous meetings while you're in pain?" The Narcotics Anonymous meetings were what got her clean, so I hoped she was still going.

I looked up and saw July staring at me. She looked scared, and I could understand why. She's not stupid—she knows the kind of meetings her mother goes to, and she remembers what happened before Abe was born.

"I can watch him," July said. "I usually take him to the park after school. Most nights I read him a story before he falls asleep. Mom knows he's okay with me."

"That's right," Jenny said as she planted another kiss on Abe's cheek. "Abe is just fine with the two of us. You have nothing to worry about."

I grabbed Abe and walked down the stairs. I couldn't stop thinking about the look on July's face. I also didn't trust Jenny. I had a nagging feeling all weekend that I shouldn't leave Abe alone with her. Would she fall back on using painkillers? Would he be safe with her?

When I came back on Sunday Jenny seemed great. She made a nice dinner, and I stayed a while just to make sure everything was okay. In my head I always had this struggle about Jenny—I guess I didn't have faith that she'd stay clean.

After that weekend, whenever I picked Abe up, Jenny seemed okay. The two of us didn't talk too much. Usually, I'd pick up Abe and hand her a check. He always seemed happy to come with me. Of course, he's still only two, but he'd often say, "Shhh Mommy sleeping." What the hell was that supposed to mean?

I also noticed that Jenny was getting awfully thin. I wasn't sure why, and I tried not to be suspicious. On Sundays when I dropped Abe off, she'd have a nice dinner waiting and she always invited me to stay. Most of the time I did. During those meals it seemed like things were fine, until one Sunday in April.

Something was going on—July wasn't her usual self. She seemed distant, sad somehow. I asked her how things were going, but she gave the typical "Okay" response and it was obvious I wasn't getting any more. Something was happening and she was afraid to tell me. I wondered if I should push the issue but realized she didn't trust me. I'd left her before, so of course she was afraid I'd leave her again. Would I? I mean if I realized Jenny was unfit to mother Abe, what would happen to July?

Was this my job? I wondered. *Who else does July have?*

Abe was always more excited to see July than Jenny. I know they're close, but don't kids usually want to see their moms before their siblings? Abe ran over to her yelling, "Sissy, Sissy, read book."

My mom had bought him a few books and some more clothes that weekend. July picked him up and hugged him tightly—she never seemed jealous or dismissive of Abe. "I missed you so much," she said as she took him back to their room. "Let's go sit and read your new truck book."

There wasn't any dinner ready like there usually was, but I didn't know how to bring up my concerns without starting a fight. I had to be careful, so I decided to try a different route. "What's going on with July?" I asked.

Jenny just dismissed this, saying, "I don't know. She's reaching that teenage mood and doesn't really talk to me. When she gets home, she stays in her room."

"I thought she was spending a lot of time with Abe. He tells me she takes him to the park and to get ice cream. She reads books to him. Abe's always talking about Sissy." For some reason, what I couldn't say was, *Abe never talks about you. He never misses his mother. The only thing he ever says about you is, "Shhh Mommy sleeping."*

"Look, why are you so concerned about July all of a sudden? You're the one who took yourself out of her life. What's this really about?" Jenny asked.

"I don't know, you tell me. You don't seem right. I'm worried. Are you sure you're okay?"

This was the wrong thing to say. I couldn't tell if Jenny was angry because of the accusation or guilty because she was using again. "Just say it, Roger. Just say it! Get it off your chest!" Jenny yelled as she picked up a wet sponge and threw it at me with all her strength.

"Calm down—what the hell is this about? I don't need this. I'm trying to be a good dad and a supportive co-parent. Tell me honestly, are you using again?"

"Get the hell out of my house. Just leave!" By this point Jenny was yelling and crying.

I wasn't sure what to do. I walked down the rotting stairs and sat in my truck. I was afraid to leave but wasn't sure staying would do any good. When I finally drove away, I told myself everything would be fine until I came back the following Friday.

CHAPTER 37

It was a tough week. I threw myself head-on into my work. Thankfully, I'd won a bid to rebuild an old factory—it was pretty cool, but more importantly, a lot of work. I had to hire a couple of extra guys since it was too much work for just Fred, Dave, and me. As I opened up a wall I realized the place was loaded with asbestos. I should have been expecting it because of the age of the building, but I hadn't budgeted for it. "Beautiful, friggin' beautiful! What else can go wrong!" I screamed, whipping a big piece of plaster toward the trash pile and missing Dave by inches.

"Roge, for God's sake, take it easy! I only have one head," Dave said, trying to shake me out of it.

I stopped then and looked at Dave, my best friend since middle school. We'd been through so much together; high school track and football, early girlfriends who broke our hearts. I was the best man at his wedding. He came to work for me after my dad died. He had his own small carpentry business, but I convinced him we'd all do better if he teamed up with Fred and me. He was my rock, the one person I could count on to have my back. I can't imagine what would've happened if I'd hit him.

"Sorry, Dave. I just—ah! I've had a rotten few days and now this. It just feels like too much."

"Anything I can do?" Dave asked as he easily put the piece of plaster I'd hurled at him onto the pile.

I told him my suspicions. "I think Jenny might be using again and I don't know what to do about Abe. The last few weeks when I've dropped him off, she's just been distant, kind of like she was the last time. She's also lost a lot of weight—not that she had much to lose."

"That's a tough one," Dave said, thinking. "Are you sure she's using? I mean do you have actual proof? Has July seen anything?"

"I don't know. I mean, July's been acting differently too. She seemed almost scared the last time I was there. It's strange how connected Abe is to her. He acts more like July's his mother than Jenny is. When he's with me he talks about Sissy. The only thing he says about Jenny is, 'Shh Mommy sleeping.' That bothers me a lot. I think I seriously have to talk with Jenny about taking Abe, but I can't take him away from July. And if Jenny's using, how can I leave July with her too? I can't take both kids. It's just a mess." I had no idea how Dave could help me, but it felt good to just tell someone everything.

"Why don't you come over after work and talk to Robin? She's good with this kind of stuff. She's seen all kinds of things during her teaching. I know she'll have some advice," Dave said.

"Yeah, thanks. I just might do that. I'm picking up Abe on Friday, so I'll see how he is then and more importantly, see how Jenny is. If I need Robin's help, I'll let you know."

That Friday I decided I'd pick up Abe a little early. I thought if I got to Jenny's apartment before July got home, I could really see how Jenny. I put Fred in charge of the afternoon and headed over to Jenny's. I replayed what I'd say over and over again, even though I wasn't sure how to start. Jenny, I think you've been using again, and I'm taking Abe until you get help. No, that wouldn't work—I didn't want her to get defensive. Hey, I got out of work early and thought I'd take Abe away from his drug-addicted mother. No, not by a long shot. In the end, I decided to just show up and see what happened when I got there.

I pulled up in front of the rundown slum that was my son's home five days out of the week. This was another problem—their apartment just screamed druggies. It was such a gross place. Even if Jenny wasn't using drugs, I needed to get Abe out of there. As I jumped over the broken step and up to the front door, at least I didn't hear the usual loud, horrid music, which seemed like a good sign.

I couldn't have been more wrong.

CHAPTER 38

As I got closer to their apartment I smelled a horrific stench like a rotting potato. It smelled so bad I felt like I was going to gag. Now I really didn't want Abe around that apartment. I climbed more quickly, calling Abe's name, and dreading what I might find.

The closer I got to the top of the stairs the worse the smell became. When I still didn't hear anything, I started to freak out. "Abe, Jenny!" I yelled, ripping open the door and running toward the putrid smell in the living room.

The smell was coming from Jenny, who was lying on the floor dead. Her eyes bulged and her body was bloated. Her face looked like it had been beaten pretty badly. It was too much. I ran to the bathroom and lost everything in my stomach.

After that I ran down the stairs and called 911. "9-1-1, what is your emergency?"

I heard the words, but for some reason I couldn't talk, I just started sobbing.

"9-1-1, what is your emergency?" I heard again. "Hello? Take a deep breath."

I'm not exactly sure what happened, but I remember I started screaming. "Jenny's dead! Abe's missing! Oh God, help!"

"Sir, can you please tell me your location?"

"I don't know, I don't know, um Appleton Street, lower Appleton Street, hurry! Jenny's dead, oh my God! My son's missing!" I was sweating and sobbing into the phone.

Soon I heard the sirens. It seemed like hours but was probably just a few minutes.

The police officers got out of the car. "Did you call to report an emergency?"

"My son's mother is dead," I told the officers, "and my son is missing. Please help."

One of the police officers, a younger woman with short, brown hair, tried to get me to calm down. "What is your name, sir?"

"Roger, Roger LaMarche, please, you have to find Abe!" I pled, not knowing what to think. *Is Abe dead, too? Did whoever do this kidnap him?*

Just thinking that Abe might be in danger made me throw up again. I heard the other officer, an older guy who looked a lot like my dad, start speaking. "I'm Officer Moore, and this is Officer Cruz. Why don't you show us where the body is and then we can help you find your son?"

"I can't go back up there. I just...." I said and started puking again.

"Sir, please stay here with Officer Cruz," Officer Moore said as he walked up the stairs. "I'm going up to see what I can find."

"Roger I'm going to ask you a few questions," Officer Cruz said as she pulled out a pad of paper. "What is your full name?"

"Roger Abraham LaMarche. Really, I need to find my son. I have a two-year-old son, Abe. Please, we have to find him. What if the person who did this to Jenny took him? Can we put out a news story? Can we get information out? Should we search the neighborhood? Maybe July knows what happened."

I knew I was talking fast, but I was scared. As I explained what I could, more police officers showed up. Officer Moore came down the stairs and walked up to a guy in a blue suit. "Good seeing you detective, looks like we have a homicide. I called the state coroner. They're on the way."

When I heard that I had to sit down.

"Got it. Who's Cruz talking to?" the detective asked.

That's when I jumped up. This guy seemed like he was in charge. Maybe he could start looking for Abe. I ran over to him.

"I'm Roger LaMarche. My two-year-old son was in that apartment, and he's gone missing. My ex is dead. I don't know what happened to my son. His half-sister July should be in school. She might be able to help figure out what happened. I think Jenny, my ex, was using again. I bet the guy who killed her took Abe as ransom or something. July would know who he is. I can go over to her school and get her."

"Slow down, Mr. LaMarche. I'm Detective Harrison. Tell me what you know. What do you think happened?"

I tried to calm myself down as I explained everything to the officer. "I don't know what happened. I came over to pick up my son Abe. When I got here, I saw Jenny was dead and Abe was missing. I called the police."

"Jenny—was that the victim's name? Can you tell me everything you know about her?" Detective Harrison said as he started writing.

Soon more official-looking people arrived. The apartment was roped off. People entered with gloves and booties over their shoes.

"Jenny is my son's mother. My son should be here, too. Maybe he's hiding in the apartment." I started walking toward the apartment and Detective Harrison stopped me.

"Mr. LaMarche, you can't go near the crime scene. We'll do everything we can to find your son, but you need to help us figure out what happened. I'm going to ask you some questions, and you tell me what you know." Detective Harrington was speaking more forcefully now. "What is the victim's full name?"

"Jennifer Crowley, "I answered and started weeping again. *Jenny is a victim. Jenny is dead. Jenny, we could have been so happy if you'd just....*

Detective Harrington's question pulled me out of my thoughts. "What time did you enter the apartment?"

"I'm not sure of the exact time—about ten minutes ago, I guess. I came over early to pick up my son. I walked in and didn't hear anything. I found Jenny on the floor. There was no sign of Abe." I started panicking again. "How could Abe be missing? If he's been kidnapped, I hope July's with him. Oh God if July and Abe are both in danger...."

Before then it hadn't occurred to me that July could be in trouble too. I'd assumed she was at school. But maybe Jenny's murder had happened some time ago.

Detective Harrison continued his questioning. "You said your son's missing. What did you mean when you said you hope July's with him?"

"July's his older half-sister. She lives here, too. I assume she's at school. She goes to Maplewood Middle School." Part of me hoped July was at school where she'd be safe. Maybe she knew something useful she could tell the detective.

"I'll send some officers over there to check things out. In the meantime, why don't you go to the station with Officer Cruz and tell her everything you can think of so we can start searching for your son," Detective Harrison said. "I don't think you can be any more help here. If we have any questions, we'll give you a call."

Officer Cruz told me she'd follow me to the station. I don't remember getting into my truck or driving, but soon Officer Cruz was pounding on the window, "Follow me, Mr. LaMarche," she said, waiting for me to get out of the truck. "Is there anyone you'd like to call? Maybe come down for some moral support?"

I started thinking. *Who do I want to be here?* If I called my mom she'd be devastated and start blaming me for picking Jenny as Abe's mother. Fred and Dave are busy. I also knew Jenny's sister should know what had happened I didn't want her support, but I thought she should know.

"Jenny has a sister named Susan," I told Officer Cruz. "I should let her know what's happening."

As I walked into the police station, I saw a poster of missing kids on the wall. Abe's picture could have been on one of those posters. *Where are you, Abe? God, please keep him safe.*

I sat down next to Officer Cruz's desk. She got a call while I was waiting and told me the most bizarre thing.

"The police officers that went to the school to check on July said her grandmother called this morning saying she wouldn't be in today because of a family emergency. Does July have a grandmother, Mr. LaMarche?"

JULY

Nation's opioid crisis overwhelms foster-care system

Author: Perry Stein, Lindsey Bever, The Washington Post
Published July 1, 2017

CHAPTER 39

Abe and I are playing and soon Mrs. White comes up the stairs. She doesn't say anything, she just watches Abe playing with Jason's trucks. I notice a little tear trickle down her cheek. Finally, she sighs, picks up Abe, and starts kissing him.

"No, Grammy, no kiss, play with trucks," Abe demands, squirming down from her lap.

Mrs. White smiles and looks at me intently. "July, I've decided on some rules to keep us safe. First, you're now going to be Julie White all the time. You must listen to me, dear. I understand you like your July name, but this is too dangerous. No one can know your true identity. I'll call you Julie from now on. Little Abe calls you Sissy. He'll learn to call you Julie too as he grows up. Second, staying in Rockwood for the time being makes sense for us. For heaven's sake, who could possibly know we're here? I don't think roaming the country and being afraid to stay put is good for anyone. Third, while I don't think you'd risk being put in a foster home with strangers when you could be with a grandmother who loves you, I'm worried about you making friends and accidentally sharing something that'll give us away. That's why the third rule is no talking about your past life with anyone, especially those people at the school. Now you must agree to these rules. I've made a contract and I want you to sign it. I hope you know everything I'm doing is because I love you so, so, much. We're going to have a wonderful life together. Now come give Grammy a hug."

She hugs me and kisses the top of my head. "I'll go get that contract for you to sign."

I don't know what to say so I don't say anything. I need to think. Signing a contract sounds crazy, but so does Grammy. This seems like something I'll need to do to appease her. If I gain her trust, maybe I can eventually catch her off guard.

Grammy comes walking back up the stairs with the contract. I wonder what would happen if I didn't sign it. I'm a little afraid to find out.

"Here you are, Julie, now you see everything we discussed is on here. You're welcome to read it over, but it's quite straightforward."

I look down at the contract. It reads:

I promise to always be called Julie White. July Krativitz no longer exists. I will not tell anyone about my former life. I will be evasive if anyone asks. I will always tell Grammy everything I tell my friends. If these rules are not followed there will be very serious consequences for all of us.

As I read this "contract" I really start thinking about what I can do. I really don't have a choice. I mean, if I don't sign the contract, what will happen? I don't want to find out. I have to make sure Grammy believes I'm all in. I need her to believe she's the only person in my life who matters. If I don't convince her she might chain me to a bed—or worse.

I take her pen and sign my name in big loopy letters: *Julie White*. Then I hand the contract back to my new grandmother and smile. "It's so amazing to finally have someone in my life who loves and cares for me. I'm happy to leave July behind and start my new life with you, Grammy," I said as convincingly as I can. I even try to cry a little.

"Oh Julie, you've made me so happy!" Mrs. White cries. "I just don't know how to explain how much this means. I now know God has given me a second chance. You and little Abe are my whole world.

I never imagined that day I promised to watch Abe for you would be the start of my living again."

Mrs. White looks up at the ceiling and says, "Do you believe this, Bob and Jason? I finally have a reason to live." She looks back at me and says, "Now stop dillydallying, Julie, and let's get you ready for school."

CHAPTER 40

The next morning, I wake up to the smell of blueberry muffins baking in the oven. I forget for a minute where I am. Looking around, I remember that I'm Julie White living in Rockwood, Maine with my beautiful baby brother and my crazy grandmother. I hop in the shower, then grab my new Maine outfit: a wool sweater, jeans, and new LL Bean boots.

I comb my hair and walk into the kitchen where Grammy's putting all kinds of treats into my lunchbox. I wonder if I'll be able to eat all of it. She's packed me cookies, a sandwich on homemade bread, an apple, chips, and a hot muffin wrapped carefully in foil. I really could get used to this. It's not so bad having a grandmother who loves to cook.

"Oh, there you are, Julie. I made your favorite blueberry waffles this morning. It's important that you have a hearty breakfast before you're off to your studies. Abe and I were just sitting down to eat." As Mrs. White says this, she cuts Abe's waffle into small bites.

"Sissy eat, yum, Grammy yum," Abe says, happily stuffing waffle pieces into his mouth.

"You're some handsome little guy, "Mrs. White says, rubbing Abe's head. "Now Julie, I was thinking last night about our safety. I'm thinking it may be best for us to start calling your brother Jason instead of Abe. I know you said something about Abe having a father who might wonder where we are. This isn't safe for us. I think we need to be sure this father of his isn't looking for our little Abe. Can you imagine what life would be like without our sweet boy, Julie? Oh, I can't, I can't," Grammy whines as she pats Abe's head.

Okay, it's one thing for me to be Julie, but how can I suddenly call Abe Jason? Plus, it would be creepy to call Abe Jason since Jason is Mrs. White's dead son. I chew on a piece of waffle as I think this over. Thank God for food—it really does help me think.

"Hmmm, I see your point, Grammy, but Jason might be hard for Abe to get used to. Maybe something like Al would be better," I say, putting another piece of glorious waffle into my mouth.

The look on Mrs. White's face goes from normal to downright frightening. "His name is Jason. J-A-S-O-N. Do you hear me? He IS Jason! Maybe you don't see it, but I do. His little smile, the way he plays with trucks, his sweet voice. He is my Jason. God has given Jason back to me. I demand this, Julie. I will not have you tell me his name is Al or Abe. He doesn't belong to that father. He's my little boy. Don't confuse him by calling him Abe. His name is Jason! When you're with him you call him Jason, Jason Robert White. END OF DISCUSSION!" Mrs. White screams this last part and Abe starts to cry.

How can I leave Abe with her today? What the heck is happening? I feel like I've gone from a bad dream to a nightmare. I can't upset her—she really is crazy. Why didn't I see it before? I have to calm Abe down and get Mrs. White to trust me before I go to school. It's going to feel like leaving him with Mom all over again.

I pick Abe out of his booster seat and say loudly and convincingly, "It's okay, JASON, Grammy and Sissy are here. We'd never do anything to hurt or upset you, right, Grammy?"

"Oh Julie." Mrs. White hugs me and takes Abe from my hands. "Oh Jason, you're my whole world. I would never, ever do anything to harm you. I'll never lose you again" Mrs. White says as she kisses the top of his head.

CHAPTER 41

As Mrs. White—or Grammy—drops me off at school she hugs me and says, "Jason and I will have a fabulous day, Julie. You remember that you signed the contract. Don't let anyone know the truth about your past. You don't want to be taken away and placed in a nasty foster home. I would just die, and I can't imagine Jason without his sister. Have a wonderful day. We'll pick you up at two forty-five. NO going off with any strangers after school—not yet."

I say goodbye, then walk to Mrs. Clark's room and sit next to Haylee. Mrs. Clark's busy at her computer. She soon looks up and says, "Good morning, Julie. I hope you're adjusting well to Moosehead. Do you have any questions? Anything I can help you with?"

Well, I think, *the woman pretending to be my grandmother has kidnapped me and my brother, who she now thinks is her dead son. She's starting to scare me. Is it okay with you if I call my friend Maddie and let her know? I'd also like to see if my mother is alive, and I really hope she' is recovering at Maplewood Hospita*l. Instead, I smile and say, "So far, everything's good."

"Okay," Mrs. Clark says, coming over to my computer. "In that case, since you weren't in a traditional school and we don't have your records, we'd like you to take an assessment test. It shouldn't be too hard. You're going to take the test in Ms. Ellis's office. She should be here soon. I don't think you met her yesterday—she's the guidance counselor for the middle school."

"Sure," I say. "Will it take a long time?"

"Hmm, I don't know," Mrs. Clark says. "I'm sure you can take breaks if you need them. Ms. Ellis will be better able to answer your questions—and here she is."

A woman I'm guessing is Ms. Ellis just walked in the door. She's pretty tall, like maybe six feet. I'm guessing she's twenty-three or so. Her hair is the color of wheat, and she wears it in a ponytail that hangs down her back. She's also wearing jeans and a wool sweater. I guess that's the Moosehead style.

"Hello," Mrs. Clark says. "This is Julie White. She just moved here from New Hampshire."

"Oh hello, Julie, it's so nice to meet you," Ms. Ellis tells me. "I'm sorry I wasn't here to meet you yesterday. I was at a conference. We're going to walk down to my office for the academic assessment. I also want you to know that I was sorry to hear about your mother. If there's anything I can help you with, let me know. That's what I'm here for." The smile on her face and the way she says this makes me believe she's sincere, not like Mrs. Masterson at Maplewood.

"Well, there's one thing, I guess. Um, I'd like to email one of my friends in New Hampshire, but I don't have a computer at home. Is that something I can do from…here?"

After I say this, I get really nervous. *What have I done? If Mrs. White finds out…*

"That shouldn't be a problem," Ms. Ellis says. "You got a Chromebook yesterday, right?"

"I did, but I thought it was just for school things. Haylee told me Instagram and Snapchat and those types of things are blocked in school."

"Well, yes, you can't access social media, but everyone has an email account attached to their Google Classroom. I'm sure your grandmother had to sign off on that when you registered. I'll check with Mrs. Mitchell," Ms. Ellis says as she opens the door to her office.

I'm nervous about Mrs. Mitchell for some reason. Maybe it's because Grammy is sure she'll send me to a foster home because I don't have a birth certificate. "No, that's okay," I say. "I can check with Mrs. Clark. I did a lot of things on the computer yesterday. Haylee helped me set up my email."

I'm starting to wish I'd never brought up the subject. I really want to get in touch with Maddie, but I need to think this through.

When I walk into Ms. Ellis's office, I notice her giant bookcase. How could she have possibly read so many books? Some of the books seem like guidance-counselor type books, but I even see *The Tenth Good Thing About Barney*. That was the book Mrs. Masterson read to us when Natasha Spinoza's brother died. I hope Ms. Ellis doesn't think she should read that to me.

"Julie, I know you've been through a lot these past few weeks. I really do want to help you. When you're through with the test, I'll help you contact your friend and see about getting you involved with some organizations at Moosehead Regional. How does that sound?" Ms. Ellis asks, smiling.

It sounds terrifying. I'm not sure what to tell her. If Mrs. White even thinks someone is meddling in my life, she'll homeschool me and probably lock me in a closet or worse. Still, I can't help but notice that Ms. Ellis has the whole Percy Jackson series, so she can't be too bad. I also notice there's a *Magnus Chase* book by Rick Riordan on the little round table. I pick it up and read the back cover.

"It's pretty good," Ms. Ellis says. "Magnus is an interesting character. If you like Rick Riordan books you should give it a try." She smiles as I put the book down.

"Thanks. Right now, I'm reading *Sea of Monsters*. When I finish that series, I'll let you know."

"Well, I suppose you should get started on the test," Ms. Ellis says. "It's all on the computer. I logged you in, so you can just answer the questions. Once you're done with the reading section, let me know and you can move ahead to the math. Take your time and answer as many questions as you can. I'll be in and out of my office, so if I'm not here and you have a question, just let Mrs. Mitchell know and she'll page me. Do you have any questions?"

Looking at the test, I almost say, "Oh I've taken these STAR tests for like the last four years." Instead, I just say "I don't think so."

"Okay, then just let Mrs. Mitchell know if you need me," Ms. Ellis says as she walks out the door.

As I start clicking through the test, I realize I'm not really focused. I can't believe I just told Ms. Ellis that I wanted to contact my friend. *Just focus, July, just focus.*

The reading test is pretty easy, and I finish in less than a half hour. I'm not sure what to do now. I mean, I know I should tell Mrs. Mitchell so I can move on to the math section, but I don't. For some reason I open a new tab and log into my Google account. There's an email attached to my account. I'm not really sure if I should use it to email Maddie since someone might be checking it, If someone in Maplewood finds out where we are I'm not sure what would happen to me or Mrs. White. I do know how to access Maddie's account and decide this will be safer.

I quickly log into mflynn15awesome@gmail.com. I hope her password is still the same—and just like that, I'm in.

I quickly send her a message, but I'm a little afraid to tell her too much. *Hey Maddie,* I write, *it's July. I'm alive and miss you soooo much. You wouldn't believe what's happened to me....*

As I'm typing, Ms. Ellis comes back, so I quickly press send and switch back to the test.

ROGER

New Hampshire is at the Heart of the Nation's Growing Crisis of Opioid and Heroin Addiction

CHAPTER 42

By this point I was really starting to worry. Abe was missing and now July was too. Some older women had called saying she was July's grandmother. Could this have been true? Had an old lady kidnapped July and Abe? Or had some drug dealers kidnapped them and called the school pretending to be an old lady?

"This is just too much," I screamed at Officer Cruz. "It's obvious someone's kidnapped Abe and July. Why are we just sitting here? I understand Jenny's dead, but my kids are missing!" I hoped somehow that they were still together. "If anyone's harmed them in any way...."

But I couldn't even finish. I just started crying again.

"Mr. LaMarche, I know this is difficult..." Officer Cruz began.

"Difficult? I said between clenched teeth. I could feel my jaw tighten as I put my hands firmly on the desk. I leaned in toward Officer Cruz and continued. "Do you even have kids? Difficult isn't the word I'd use. Terrifying, scared out of my mind, unimaginable— those are words I'd use. Difficult is what you say when you're pulling into a tight parking spot. This is way beyond difficult. I need to find July and Abe!"

"Please, Roger," Officer Cruz said soothingly as she placed her hand on mine. "We'll do whatever we can to help you, but you have to calm down. There must be someone I can call to be here with you. You need support from family and friends. I don't have any kids, but

I do have two nieces who mean the world to me. I don't know what you're going through, but if it was me, I know I'd need someone to be with."

I tried to calm myself down. Who would make the most sense to call? I decided Fred and Dave would be willing to come down without judging me. I also realized Officer Cruz was right. I needed people who had my back. Dave, Fred, and I have been through a lot together, not just in our business. Dave and I are the same age and go way back, but my dad hired Fred when I was about ten. He's more like an uncle than a coworker. I can't imagine how much harder Dad's death would've been without Fred.

"I have two guys who'd be here in a heartbeat to help me. I can call them myself. I also think Jenny's sister might have some insight into what happened. I don't have her phone number, but her name's Susan Crowley and I know where she lives. I don't think she should find out about Jenny over the phone, though."

"Okay," Officer Cruz said. "We'll send an officer to her house. Why don't you call your friends? Can I get you something to drink—soda, coffee, water?" She looked at me with a calm expression. "Please trust us. We really want to help you."

"I'll have a coffee with cream and four sugars, thanks." I got up from my chair. "I'm just going to step outside for a minute so I can call my guys and think."

When I walked outside, I noticed it was a bright, sunny day, but the wind was biting cold, which for some reason really pissed me off. I hopped into my truck to get out of the wind and call Dave. As I dialed his number, I noticed Abe's car seat in my rearview mirror. "Where are you, little guy?" I asked no one.

Dave picked up right away. "Hey Roge, what's the good word?"

"Dave, I need you, buddy," I said, trying to keep my voice steady. "Abe's missing and Jenny's dead."

"Holy shit, Roger. Where are you?"

"I'm at the Maplewood police station. I really need you to just be here for a while. I'm losing it. I don't know where my boy is and it looks like July's missing, too. Jesus, Dave, this is just too much." It was all I could do to keep myself together.

"Give me a few minutes to take care of things here and let Fred know what's happening. I'll be right down."

"Don't worry about the job. Close up for now and bring Fred with you. I need both of you so I can be sure of what's going on. I also need to find my kids."

"We'll be there in fifteen. Is there anything you need?"

"Not yet—just people to keep me calm. See you soon," I said, hanging up the phone.

I hopped out of the truck, reluctant to go back into the station. I couldn't get the image of Jenny bloated and lying on the floor out of my head. I started thinking about the creep she was with, the guy who was giving her drugs while she was pregnant. Did he do this to her? Had he taken the kids? I wished I known the guy's name, or anything more about him.

I decided I needed to tell Officer Cruz about the tattooed guy. I hated the guy and wanted to kill him. If he did this, I prayed he'd rot in hell.

As I got closer to the station I saw Jenny's sister Susan getting out of a police cruiser. She looked awful. Her stringy gray hair was hanging in her face, and she was obviously crying. I wondered if she'd been drinking. She noticed me and started coming my way, though I had no idea what to say to her.

"Oh Roger," she sobbed, pulling me into a tight hug. "I can't believe this. Tell me it's not true. Jenny can't be dead—she just can't be." The stale smell of cigarettes and beer wafted from her body.

"I know, I can't believe it either. I also can't believe Abe and July are missing. We have to find them. Do you have any idea what happened?" At that point I started sobbing too, and we held each other for what seemed like a few minutes.

"I didn't know the kids were missing," Susan said, still crying and starting to shake. "Jesus, this is like a horrific dream. Oh my God, where are they? Who could hurt two innocent kids?"

At that point Officer Cruz came outside to ask if we could come back in to answer a few questions. I needed a few more minutes—I was a mess, my body was shaking, and I felt nauseous. I just kept reliving the moment I saw Jenny dead, bruises all over her tiny body, that horrid smell. Her once beautiful impish smile gone and replaced by a bloated, swollen lip. This isn't how I wanted to remember her. I couldn't help but blame myself for her death. If I had just trusted my gut and got her the help she needed … .

"I'm just going to wait out here for my friends. I'll meet you as soon as they get here," I said.

Officer Cruz told me that wasn't a problem and introduced herself to Susan. "I assume you're the victim's sister?" she asked.

"I'm Jenny's sister. Please don't call her that. She has a name." At this Susan started crying again, harder this time. She put her head on my shoulder.

"Sorry, I should have introduced you," I said. "This is Susan Crowley."

"Ms. Crowley, do you mind if I ask you some questions about Jenny? Anything you could share with us could help," Officer Cruz told Susan as she led her into the building. "Mr. LaMarche, you can come inside whenever your friends get here."

"I need to find Abe and July," I assured her. "I'll do whatever I can until the two of them are safe."

After Susan and Officer Cruz went inside, I started thinking again about that creep with the tattoos. He had to have been the one who'd done this to her. Maybe someone at Dunkin' would know where to find him. It wasn't far from the police station. *Maybe when Dave and Fred get here the three of us can head down there to get some answers.*

I heard Dave's truck before I saw it. Fred leaped out of the passenger door. He put his calloused hand on my shoulder, his brown eyes full of concern, just like they were when Dad died. In so many ways Fred reminded me of my dad; both about five feet eight and balding, but so strong both in stature and character. "How are you doing, Roger? You know I'd do anything for you. I promised your dad I'd always look out for you, buddy." "Oh Fred,' I can't," and I just started crying, so thankful that if my dad couldn't be with me, Fred could. His strong arms wrapped me in a hug. I buried my face in his shoulder and just let myself sob. "I'm here, Roger. Dave's parking the truck, you're not going through this alone. We would walk through hell for you."

I took a deep breath and tried to get myself together as I saw Dave running toward me. With his long strides, he reached me in seconds. I looked up into those blue eyes that knew more about me than anyone else.

"Jesus, Roge, What the hell is going on?" Dave asked. "Is Jenny really dead? What do you need, man? Just say it."

"Thanks, for coming guys," I said. "I feel like I'm living in a nightmare. I went to pick up Abe this afternoon like I told you I would, but when I got to their place Jenny was dead. It looked like someone beat the hell out of her. I yelled for Abe, but he was nowhere. July's gone too."

"Holy shit, Roge. I can't even wrap my head around any of this," Dave said as he took off his stocking hat and wrapped it into a ball. "What happened? What happened? Why would anyone do this to Jenny?"

"Remember that creep Jenny was seeing while she was pregnant? I feel like he has something to do with this. I need to find this punk and get some answers." I said feeling the anger rise in my body. I found a big rock on the ground and hurled it with all my might at the side of the police station as I let out a loud yell. It felt good to get out some tension.

"Listen Roge," Dave said, pulling me in for a hug and just holding me for a bit. I could feel him taking deep breaths. I knew he was trying to process how to help me. We stood like this for a while, then he pulled back, holding me at arm's length without letting go, and spoke calmly as he looked into my eyes. "I've known you for more than half your life. I haven't seen you like this since—well, ever. Maybe you should tell the police about this guy. It makes more sense that they find him. You don't need to get yourself in any trouble."

Fred nodded. "We'll do anything to help, but we should do this the right way. Don't become a vigilante."

"Jenny's dead. Abe and July are missing," I reiterated. "No one knows how long they've been missing. I don't know how long Jenny's been dead. I can't just hang out here and do nothing. I'm losing it. I need to find the kids. Why isn't anyone looking for them? Or finding that creep and forcing answers out of him?" I kicked the tree Fred was leaning against hard. The frustration I felt was getting the better of me.

"Calm down, Roger," Fred said quietly.

"Calm down! How the hell do I do that! I keep seeing that creep's face. I know he had something to do with this. If I had that guy in front of me right now...."

"Roger, look at me," Fred said sternly just like my dad would have to get my attention. "No one should be going through what you're going through right now. You need answers, but finding some punk when you're in this condition is not the answer."

"Fred's right," Dave said. "You wouldn't be helping find the kids if you found this guy and took your frustrations out on him."

I got where Fred and Dave were coming from—and I knew they were right. I just couldn't get that creep's face out of my head. I knew he had something to do with this—he was the one who'd gotten Jenny addicted. But when I saw the concern on Fred and Dave's faces, I knew they were thinking more clearly than I was.

"Okay, let's do this your way. Thanks for having my back," I said. "Officer Cruz and the others want to do this right. I think you have a point. Let's go in and I'll tell them about the tattooed guy."

"Good idea," Fred said with a smile.

Fred, Dave, and I walked into the police station and headed toward Officer Cruz's desk. She was in a deep conversation with Susan. I heard her saying, "My sister was an amazing person who got involved with drugs. I know she got them somewhere."

That's when I interrupted. "She got the drugs from the tattooed freak she was seeing right before we split up," I said.

"Please Mr. LaMarche, have a seat," Officer Cruz said. "Ms. Crowley was telling me about her sister's addiction. Do you think you know where she was getting the drugs from?"

"I'm sure she was getting them from that creep she was seeing before our son was born. I never learned his name, but he was tall and skinny. He had tattoos all over his body, even his face," I said.

"Do you have any idea who this person might be?" Officer Cruz asked.

"Listen, I loved my sister and there were times we shared everything," Susan said, "but she never told me where she was getting her drugs. How much longer do you need me here, officer? I should get back to my kid."

"If there's anything at all you can think of, Ms. Crowley, please call me. Here's my card—the number rings right to my desk," Officer Crowley said.

"Um, can I get a ride back to my place? Another officer brought me here and it's a long walk," Susan said.

"I'll give you a ride," Dave volunteered. "Fred, you stay here with Roge."

"I really appreciate that," Susan said.

I looked at Dave, knowing he was giving Susan a ride to help me out. He knew I didn't have good feelings toward her. "Thanks," I said, smiling and knowing I wasn't alone.

"No problem, I'll be back before you know it. Come on," Dave said to Susan. "It's been a rough day."

"Rough is one way to put it," Susan said bitterly. "Did you ever have your sister murdered and her children go missing?"

"Uh, no," Dave said quietly, his face turning red as he placed his worn-out stocking cap over his blonde curls. "I'm so sorry that you're going through this. I keep seeing little Abe's face laughing as he kicked a soccer ball. We all need to find him. I love that kid, too."

I stood up and look Susan in the face. Jenny was the only family she had besides Dom. She was in as much pain as I was. I gave her a hug. "Be safe, and stay in touch," I said.

"You too, Roger. You too," she said. "And Roger, be in touch. I know you loved Jenny as much as I did. I can't imagine life without her. We have to find Abe and July—we just have to."

I let out a deep sigh and just nodded.

CHAPTER 43

We stayed at the police station for just over an hour. I told Officer Cruz everything I could about the tattooed guy. She showed me a bunch of pictures and surprise, surprise, I found one of the scumbags. I also sent a recent picture of Abe to Officer Cruz. I didn't have a recent picture of July, though, and this really bothered me. I tried to think of where I could find a picture of her and remembered that July has a friend named Maddie who might have one, since they're pretty close.

"Thanks," Officer Cruz said. "We'll want to get pictures of the kids out to the public as soon as possible. Why don't you go home and try to rest? We'll be in contact to let you know how the investigation's going. If you think of anything or have questions, don't hesitate to call."

I had so many thoughts going through my head. *Where are Abe and July? Who killed Jenny? Are the police going to help me or not? Should I be looking for the tattooed killer? How can I go home and sleep knowing my baby's out there somewhere?*

"Yeah, and you call me too. I'm going to be right by my phone twenty-four-seven until my son's safely back with me," I said, maybe more for my benefit than hers.

"Come on, man, Dave's outside," Fred said. "Why don't you leave your truck here and get a ride home with him? One of us can pick you up in the morning. I don't think you're in any condition to drive."

"I really appreciate the offer," I told him, "but I can get myself home. It's only fifteen minutes. Look, I'm beat—I promise to drive safely and listen to the radio turned way up so I don't nod off," I said, knowing all I wanted was to just get back to my bed and my mother. *What am I even going to say to her?*

"Your call," Fred said. "Look, Dave and I can handle the business while you work this out. Just take care of yourself, OK? Promise you'll call one of us if you think you're going to do something crazy, like taking on creepy tattoo guy." When he said this, Fred reached out and gave me a hug.

"Thanks," I told him. "I appreciate your help more than you'll ever know."

When I got to the truck, I turned on the radio. "Call Me Maybe" was playing. That song reminds me so much of July. The two of us would sing it together once upon a time.

"July," I said aloud, "I promise that once you're found I'll never let you go. I'm so, so sorry I left you in such a horrible world for so long."

JULY

The Opioid Crisis Has Affected More Than 2 Million Children
*New research examines how children's lives have been
disrupted by the nation's deadly drug epidemic.*

By <u>Gaby Galvin</u>, Staff Writer   **Nov. 13, 2019, at 9:58 a.m.**
US NEWS AND WORLD REPORT

CHAPTER 44

"How did you do with the reading section, Julie?" Ms. Ellis asks. She doesn't seem to notice that I emailed Maddie.

"Pretty good I think," I say.

"Okay," she says. "In that case, it's easy to access the math section. Just go back to the login page and click the Math Assessment button. I'm going to do some work at my desk, so if you need anything, let me know."

I start the math test, but I'm a little distracted by the email I sent to Maddie. I hope I can get back on at some point to share more. I finish the test in about thirty minutes. It was harder than the reading test, since math never was my thing.

"I finished," I say as I stand up from the computer.

"Oh, great!" Ms. Ellis says. "Let me just finish up this email and I'll be right with you."

"Sorry about that, Julie, let's see—it's 9:45, so I believe your class is in science. Would you like me to walk with you?"

"No, I think I can find my way. Thanks anyway," I say, getting up from my seat.

"Okay. I can come by your classroom later to help you email your friend. You must be anxious to be in touch with her. What's her name?"

Without thinking or being evasive I say, "Maddie."

"I can help you contact Maddie, then. Where does she live?"

Now I'm a little concerned—here's where I should be evasive. I can't let Ms. Ellis know what town Maddie lives in, but if I don't say anything, Ms. Ellis might get curious. "Um, she lives in New Hampshire," I say hoping she'll let it go.

No such luck. "Whereabouts in New Hampshire, Julie? I went to college at the University of New Hampshire in Durham," Ms. Ellis says.

Great, lots of college students work at Maplewood Middle School since it's the next town. What if Ms. Ellis was one? I can't let her know that's where Maddie goes to school. She will ask too many questions. I need to change the subject. Maybe if I ask a lot of questions about her college, she'll forget that she asked.

"Wow, my mom went to UNH," I will myself to say.

"Oh Julie, I'm sorry. Losing your mother is really horrible. I meet with a few other students at Moosehead Regional who have lost their parents. We're meeting today at lunch in my office. Why don't you join us? Sometimes it's important to know you're not alone. It's a small group, but you'll make it five," Ms. Ellis says.

I'm concerned that I may say something I'll regret in this group. A smaller number of kids might trip me up. "I don't know if I want to talk about my mom with people I don't know," I say.

Ms. Ellis smiles. "Tell you what, why don't you come today and if you don't like it, you don't come back—no questions asked."

"Okay, I'll give it a try," I say.

"I'll pick you up from your classroom. Do you need to get lunch from the cafeteria?"

"No, my grandmother packed me plenty of food. Do I have to say anything?"

"Of course not," Ms. Ellis says. "Just do what you feel comfortable doing. The other students in the group have been together since January. They're great kids, and I think you'll like them. There are two boys from eighth grade, one girl from seventh grade, and one girl from sixth grade. They're very welcoming. I'm sure you'll feel safe with them." If I don't agree to go, Ms. Ellis might think something's wrong and start asking more questions that could get me in trouble with Mrs. White. If I go and just sit there, nothing really bad could happen, right? "Okay," I say. "I'll see you at lunch."

CHAPTER 45

Ms. Ellis meets me and another girl from my class named Sarah. Sarah is very quiet, and small. She looks like she should be in fourth grade, not sixth. Walking towards Ms. Ellis's room I begin to get nervous. What am I doing? I don't even know if my mother is dead.

The first person I see when I walk into Ms. Ellis's office is Bryce Turner. I forgot that his mother died. He smiles at me, and I can feel my face turn red. I wish I could control this. It's so frustrating.

"Hi, Julie," Bryce says. "It's great to see you again. I was hoping Ms. Ellis would ask you to join our group." As he talks, he takes out his lunch from the cooler. He isn't a big person, but he has two sandwiches, chips, a giant cookie, and an apple. I wonder how he can eat all that in twenty minutes.

"You two know each other?" Ms. Ellis asks.

"Let's just say we bumped into each other the day Julie moved in," Bryce says, smiling.

"I was looking at the lake and Bryce came up from behind and surprised me," I share.

"We appear to be neighbors," Bryce adds.

"Why don't the rest of you introduce yourselves and share anything you think may help Julie," Ms. Ellis says.

"Sure," Bryce says. "I'm Bryce Turner, so I guess you all know that now."

A chunky kid with big brown eyes goes next. "My name is Tim St. Germain. I'm also in eighth grade. My dad was killed in a logging accident when I was ten."

"Hi, I'm Bethany Taylor" a tall seventh-grade girl with shiny auburn hair shares. Her brown eyes look sad as she continues her story. "My mom died of breast cancer last year. It's still hard to talk about. Sometimes I forget that she's really dead. I like coming to this group because everyone is patient and understanding," Bethany tells us. I notice she's playing with a ring on her right ring finger. It's a really beautiful diamond ring. I wonder if it was her mom's.

Sarah shares last. Her voice matches her size. I'm not sure she wants to be there. The other kids sense this, too. "My name is Sarah Dionne. My dad died and my mom couldn't take care of me, so I live with my grandmother."

"I live with my grandmother, too," I share naturally. I promised myself I wouldn't say anything, but there's something about Sarah that makes me want to protect her. I want to know how her dad died. All the other kids have no problem sharing. I wonder if he was involved with drugs like my mom.

There's something shameful about having a parent involved in drugs. Parents aren't supposed to do that kind of thing. When you have a parent who's addicted to drugs it makes you grow up fast. I know for me I ended up being the parent. I had to make sure we had food and keep our place clean. I also had to watch Abe. I don't know if I want to share my shame with these kids. I try to remember what Mrs. White told Mrs. Mitchell. Did she say my mom was beaten to death by her dealer? Did she share that she died of a drug overdose, or did she say she had cancer?

Having a parent with cancer is easier than having a drug addict parent. You don't have to be embarrassed by a parent with cancer because they didn't choose to have that disease. Drug addicts make a choice. That's what I believe anyway. Sure, people say drug addiction and alcoholism are diseases. I guess I can understand that, but not really. When you have cancer and you have kids, you're devastated and will try to do anything to stay alive for your kids. You always see the parents in those Hallmark movies with cancer trying to figure out who their kids should live with if they die.

I don't know if that ever occurred to my mom. I mean, she cared more about her drugs than about me or Abe. There were times when she didn't seem to notice we were even there. She was able to put down the drugs after Abe was born, but then she started again, and nothing could get her to stop. Her drugs were always more important than us.

I soon realize Ms. Ellis is talking to me. "Julie, do you have any questions?"

"Oh, um no. I'm sorry, I was just thinking about my mom." As soon as I say this, I can feel the stupid tears. I try to hold them back, but it's no use.

"No worries about tears here, Julie. I still cry a lot too," Bethany says.

"Listen," Bryce tells me. "All of a sudden something will change, and you'll be able to talk about your mother and smile instead of cry. My mom died when I was six. I remember her, but sometimes she starts to fade, and some days I realize I haven't thought about her at all. That scares me, like I'm not being loyal to her."

"Bryce is right," Tim says. "My dad died four years ago. Last week my brother was telling a funny story about a time he and my dad went fishing up near the Ripogenus My dad thought he'd hooked a big salmon, but in reality, he'd hooked his own leg. The water was so cold my dad couldn't feel it until he pulled hard and knocked himself down. They had to take him to Greenville Hospital to get the hook out." Tim started laughing as he told the story and Bryce joined in.

"I think that's a good place to wrap things up," Ms. Ellis says. "I hope you'll join us next week, Julie."

"I do, too," Bryce says.

"It was great meeting you," Bethany says.

Sarah doesn't say anything. She gets up from the table quietly and walks back to our social studies classroom. I want to catch up with her, but Bryce stops me on the way out.

"Julie," he says, "you know my brother Steve gives me a ride to school. There's plenty of room in his truck if you'd like to come with us. It's not out of our way. I know Steve wouldn't mind. He's a junior and a great driver."

"Well, umm, thanks for the offer," I say, "but my grandmother is pretty overprotective, especially since my mom died. I don't think she'd be comfortable letting me go with you guys."

"Well, maybe Steve and I should come by and pay a visit. I think my dad must know your grandmother if she's been coming up here for a long time. I'll talk to him, and maybe you can all come for dinner."

"NO!" I scream, and then feel really embarrassed. If Bryce and his family show up at our place or invite us for dinner, I can't imagine what Mrs. White would do. I think about the contract I signed and the consequences this would have, which could be truly terrifying.

Bryce kind of looks at me, "Um, well…" he stammers.

I feel my face turning red again. *What am I supposed to say to get out of this?*

"I'm sorry I reacted like that," I say, hoping Bryce will stop the questioning, "but my grandmother's having a really hard time right now. It's just not a good time not yet."

"I get it, Julie. I mean, after my mom died everyone was a mess for a while. Somehow the people who are living need to live and move forward. Your grandmother will come around. In the meantime, why don't you meet us down by the lake for a boat ride? The ice is pretty much gone. You need to live, too."

Being evasive and not sharing is going to be harder than I thought. I need to keep us safe from Mrs. White until I can figure out what to do.

"Maybe," I say as I head back to class.

CHAPTER 46

Mrs. White is waiting outside the school for me at 2:45. I hurry to her car before anyone can stop me. I don't want to get another slap across the face. I know that I can't share much of what happened at school, and I especially can't share that I joined this private group. I know she'd freak if she knew.

I decide to begin the conversation positively by explaining how delicious my lunch was, then focus on her day with Abe. "Thanks for the amazing lunch, Grammy. I can't even tell you how wonderful everything tasted. It really helped me get through the day knowing I'd get to have some more of your amazing cooking when I got home."

"Oh Julie," Mrs. White says, gushing. "I've made some wonderful cookies with Jason today. Made with love for you dear. That's the secret ingredient. Right Jason?"

"I Jason, no Abe, Jason," Abe tells me from the backseat.

This really freaks me out. Did Mrs. White do some kind of shock therapy on him? It was weird that he'd say this. He didn't even say Sissy, Sissy like usual.

"Oh, my Julie, how cute is little Jason?" Mrs. White says. "You are my Jason. That's right, Jason, no Abe, Jason."

"Hi, Jason," I say, wanting to cry. What happened to my sweet Abe while I was at school? I check his body for bruises and don't see any, so that's good—I hope.

"You no Sissy, you Julie," Abe continues, very sure of himself.

I look at Mrs. White. I'm really angry, but now I have to come off sounding sweet. "Wow, Grammy, how did you teach Abe all of these changes so quickly?" I ask.

"What do you mean, Julie? What changes? I was just very firm with Jason, telling him he was Jason, not Abe. When he said, 'I Jason,' I gave him a treat. If he didn't say, 'I Jason' he got no treat. He caught on quickly. He's very smart." Mrs. White's beaming as she says this.

"What about calling me Julie instead of Sissy? How did you do that? I mean, he's been calling me Sissy for as long as he could talk. I think Mom even called me Sissy around him," I say.

"Well, he must learn that you are Julie White. There can be no confusion. Do you understand? I mean, we don't want some stranger meeting us and Jason telling these crazy stories. We have to erase Maplewood from his memory. For goodness' sake, what if we're at school one day and he says something to that snoopy Mrs. Mitchell? We just can't take that risk."

I was fuming inside, it felt like Mrs. White was deleting everything about us. I didn't want Abe to stop calling me Sissy. I like it when he looks up at me with his big brown eyes and says, "Sissy." Julie is fake. Would he even remember that I am July? Would he remember his dad, or Mom? This is too much. I'm not sure what to do. Mrs. White pulls me out of my thoughts. Maybe she knows I am angry.

"So, tell me, Julie, how was school?" Mrs. White continues. "What did you learn? Is there anything I can help you with?"

"Well, I had to take an assessment test to see how my reading and math compared to the other students. That took most of the day," I say, not wanting to share anything else.

"Oh, I see. I'm sure you did just fine. You're such a smart girl. Was it difficult?"

"Not really," I say trying to remember the tests. "The reading test seemed easier than the math."

"Well, you do like to read. You seem to be zooming through the Percy Jackson books we bought."

Without thinking I say words I immediately regret. "Oh, I took the test in Ms. Ellis's office. She's the guidance counselor, and she has all the Rick Riordan books. She said I could read them if I wanted."

"Why on earth would you be seeing a guidance counselor?" Mrs. White screams at me. "There is absolutely nothing wrong with you. You stay away from that Ms. Ellis. Guidance counselors are always stirring up trouble. She'll ask lots of questions about your life, Julie. You must promise me you'll stay away from her. Oh my, I must add it into the contract that you will say nothing at all about your life to this woman. DO YOU HEAR ME?!"

"Julie no talk, promise me, "Abe repeats.

This is creepy. I mean, things were going well and suddenly I'm back at crazy town and my baby brother has joined in.

"I didn't tell her anything you didn't tell her when you signed me up. She gave me the math and reading tests. She also wants me to know she can help me or talk to me about my mother's…" I can't bring myself to say "death."

"That's just what I mean!" Mrs. White continues in her loud screaming voice. "She'll want to talk to you about how your mother died and the next thing you know I'll be in jail and who knows what will happen to you. I don't even want to think about it. Do you really want that to happen?!" Mrs. White asks me this like she's totally out of her mind.

"I didn't tell her anything about Mom, or you, or Abe—I mean Jason," I try to say convincingly. "We talked about the assessment and Rick Riordan, that's all."

"I hope so, Julie, for all of our sakes. I don't want to lose you, not after I've been alone for so long," Mrs. White says, pulling into our driveway. "Now you play with Jason for a bit while I get things ready for dinner."

As I walk into the house I notice a big container of jellybeans. Abe runs to it and starts yelling, "I Jason, I Jason." Mrs. White smiles, takes out some jellybeans, and says, "That's right, you are Jason." She then points to me and says, "Who is this, Jason?"

Abe runs over to me and says," Sissy, Sissy!" I pick him up and give him a big kiss.

Mrs. White says very firmly, "Put him down right this minute. Jason, this is Julie, not Sissy. Julie. Say this, Jason. Julie."

Abe looks like he's going to cry. Mrs. White's voice is very firm. "Say Julie, this is Julie. Jason, you must say that this is Julie. Do you hear me? Julie, not Sissy. Now say it or no more jellybeans and you'll go back to your room."

I can't handle this. ,"Stop this, Grammy! Look at his little face. You're scaring him. He's just a little kid who's been through so, so much. You say you love him, so stop this now!"

"Listen, Julie, I'm doing what's right to protect this family. Jason needs to learn who we are. He is Jason, I am Grammy, and you are Julie! He can do this. I am the adult. I know what has to be done to keep us all safe!" Mrs. White screams.

Abe begins to cry and through his tears he says," No Sissy, Julie." I grab him and run out of the house.

"Julie, where are you going?" Mrs. White yells. "Get back here. There's nowhere to run to. I love you, come back now!"

I keep running, carrying Abe, and running away from this crazy lady. Where am I going? I hear her yelling for me, but all I can think about is keeping Abe safe. This wackadoodle sure isn't going to do it. I keep running, I don't really hear Mrs. White's voice anymore.

"Hey Julie, are you okay?'

Looking up I notice I've run right into Bryce Turner's yard.

ROGER

*America's opioid crisis means many grandparents
are now raising their grandchildren.*

April 22, 2019

By Amy Morona, Washington Week digital content and social
media producer

CHAPTER 47

I parked in front of my mom's house and noticed it was 7:30. How could this be? How was I going to face my mother? Abe was such an important part of her life. What was I going to tell her?

I took a deep breath, opened the door to the house, and saw my mom sitting at the kitchen table with a red kid's fire truck. She looked up, puzzled. I must have looked like hell because she said, "Roger, is everything okay?"

I just looked at her and the tears started flowing down my cheeks. "No," I sobbed. "Abe is missing, and Jenny's dead."

She jumped up from the table and ran to me. She grabbed me in a tight hug, and I just lost it.

"I don't know what to do, Mom. I don't know what to do," I repeated over and over.

"Sit down and let me get you something to eat," Mom said, leading me to a kitchen chair. "I want you to tell me everything you know. This is horrible."

She warmed up some beef stew in the microwave. A picture of Abe and me playing in the snow was on the wall next to the table. I took it off the wall and started crying again, "Where is he, Mom?"

Mom started crying, too. She didn't say anything, she hugs me hard both of us were sobbing. Finally, the ding from the microwave stopped us from carrying on and Mom took the warm stew from the microwave.

As she dried her eyes Mom said, "I know you aren't a drinker, but I think you and I both need a glass of wine to settle our nerves."

She went down to the basement and came upstairs with a bottle of red wine from my dad's collection. She was right. As I sipped the wine and took a bite of the beef stew, I realized how hungry I was. I didn't think I was ever going to eat again, but everything tasted wonderful.

Mom let me eat in peace while she waited for me to start the conversation. I was surprised, but I imagined she must have been gathering her thoughts too. Maybe she'd realized the last thing I needed was judgment. I also knew how much she loves Abe. I finished eating and put my plate in the dishwasher.

"Would you like a little more wine?" Mom asked, pouring some for herself.

"No thanks, I might need to go back to the police station and want to have wits about me. Let's go in the living room and I'll tell you everything."

I told her how I'd found Jenny in her apartment. I left out some of the details about how she'd looked. I also explained that Abe and his sister were missing, and that the police had a lot of people on the case. They were doing an autopsy on Jenny, so hopefully they'd have some answers. I also told her I might have known who killed Jenny.

"Oh my, Roger this is so horrible. You think Abe is with some drug dealers? Why would they take a little boy? He must be so scared. We have to find him, we just have to," she said, and began to cry.

"We'll find him, Mom," I said. I feel it deep inside. I'm not giving up on Abe. I'm sure wherever he is July's with him and she's keeping him safe. She's a tough kid and loves her brother. I can't imagine how terrified they must be. I don't want to think about it."

Mom stopped crying and poured herself another glass of wine. She looked truly distraught. "Roger, have the police contacted the newspapers and TV news reports? We need to get Abe's picture out to the public. Maybe someone's seen him. I'm going to call Father Dube and have him come over. We need prayers. He may also have some ideas on how to handle this horrid situation."

Mom went into the kitchen, and I heard her talking to Father Dube. He's been the parish priest at St. Vincent's in Berwick for I don't know how long. I wasn't sure what he can do to help us, but I was willing to take all the help I could get.

I then heard Mom talking to someone else. "Hi Stephanie, something horrible has happened…."

That caught my attention. I needed Stephanie to be here. She's my oldest sister. The one person in my family who never judged me. She's great; she has three kids, and her husband Joe is a nice guy. Steph's always had my back. She was helpful when I first started bringing Abe to Mom's. She's got three kids: Joey's ten, Aiden's seven, and Audrey's four, and they're truly Abe's cousins. They all love him, and I know that. Having Stephanie here may not be a bad thing. She knows how to handle Mom.

My sister Michelle is a different story. She has four kids. All of them have different fathers. Michelle's oldest daughter, Olivia, was born right after Michelle graduated from high school. Her dad, Mike, is a good guy, but they were just too young and never got married. Three years later Michelle was waitressing at a diner in town and got pregnant again. She swears she doesn't know who the father of her son Ben is, but he sure looks like the owner of the diner, a dirtbag who's easily twenty years older than her. Amber was born four years later. Her dad, Gil, was around for a while, but then he moved back to Canada. I don't know if he ever sees Amber. Now Michelle's with a great guy named Dan, and it seems like she finally has her act together. They have a little guy named Tyler who's around Abe's age.

When I was with Jenny, I felt like my mom was hypocritical. I mean, here's my sister with all these kids by different guys. Michelle would often leave her kids with my parents, so they always had at least one of them, and sometimes all of them. My mother never said anything about watching Michelle's kids to her face, but she was always complaining to Stephanie and me about it.

Now that Michelle's with Dan, we don't really see her or the kids anymore. I really hope Mom doesn't call her. She has a way of turning any tragedy into her own personal tragedy.

My other sister, Beckie, has some issues. She's a drug addict just like Jenny. She's managed to keep herself clean for a while. Her sobriety is fragile. Whenever there's just a little stress in her life, she uses it as an excuse to start using again. I don't want her involved in this. I'm afraid if she knows about Abe, she'll use it as an excuse to start using again.

Beckie's addiction was hard on my dad. She was a sweet kid when she was little. She loved playing with dolls and dressing up. She was tall and thin, so she had the perfect ballet body. She took lessons for a long time and had a part in *The Nutcracker* in Portland for a few years. I think she started using in high school. She started hanging out with a bad crowd and was dating this guy JD. He was your typical bad boy: tattoos, long hair, and a motorcycle. My parents tried to forbid her from seeing him, but that just made it worse. She'd sneak out at night and sometimes not come home. That period of time really aged my father and made my mother super Catholic. She started going to Mass every day and saying a whole rosary before she went to bed.

I think Mom thought that if she just spent enough time at church that Jesus would save Beckie. She tried forcing Beckie to go with her, but the only times Beckie went were when she was stoned. Like Jenny, she was able to clean herself up for a while. My parents spent a lot of money sending her to a rehab place in Portland.

After my dad died, she started using again. She was really angry that my mother didn't give her any of Dad's inheritance. When Beckie realized that I'd inherited Dad's business, she went into the office and trashed the place. I don't know if she was looking for money or was just angry because I got something, and she didn't.

I called the police and reported her. Mom was upset about that because she thought people would start talking about us. That's a big piece I don't get about my mother. She's always so concerned about what people will think. Anyway, Beckie didn't get jail time, but she had to do some community service.

I haven't talked to her since. I'm not sure whether Mom or Stephanie have talked to her. I don't even know where she is.

Mom got off the phone and told me both Stephanie and Father Dube would be here soon, "We need support, Roger. Father Dube is wonderful and caring. He's a man of God, and his prayers will certainly help. Your sister's devastated. Joe's home with the kids, so she's planning on staying over. She told me to make sure you know how much you and Abe are loved."

Take deep breaths, I told myself. *If anything happens to Abe or July, I don't know what I'll do.* This was just too much. Why didn't I take them away from Jenny before this? If I'd just listened to that little voice in my head instead of pretending everything was okay, those two kids would be safe. Also, why did I ignore July? *That kid doesn't have a chance without some stability in her life. I even thought of her as my daughter for a while. When they're found—and I do mean when—I'll fix this, July, I promise, I'll fix it. Keep my boy safe,* I beg, *just keep him safe.*

My sister Stephanie showed up about fifteen minutes later. It usually takes at least 25 minutes to get from Stephanie's to Mom's. She ran into the house crying and grabbed me in a bear hug. "Oh Roger, I'm so, so sorry." When she finally pulled away, she looked me in the eye and asked, "How are you doing?"

I wasn't sure how to respond. I just looked at her and tried to find words to explain the emotions I was carrying. Finally, I said, "I found Jenny's dead, beaten body. My son's missing and so is July. I'm blaming myself for this. I mean, in the back of my head I knew that Jenny had started using again. Why didn't I take those kids away from her?" I felt the tears spilling down my face again.

That's when my mother stepped in. "None of this is your fault. Yes, you chose a bad person to be the mother of your son, but you didn't cause her death or neglect Abe. You can't take responsibility for that girl. She's not a part of you. It's tragic that she's missing and her mother's dead, but you need to focus on our little Abe."

I could feel the rage building in my body. My fists clenched as I backed away from my mother toward the door. "You still don't get it, Ma," I yelled. "You still don't see that I stepped in and was a father to July, not 'that girl.' Her name is July. She's an amazing sister and Abe adores her. I refuse to split them up. Please stop saying Jenny is or was a bad person. She was wonderful and caring. She was an addict, Mom. You should understand that. Look at how you bent over backwards trying to help Beckie. I need some air." I stormed out into the yard, slamming the door behind me.

Soon Stephanie came out with two glasses of wine. "Hey, have a glass of wine with me. I need one and I thought you would too."

I looked at my sister, knowing she was trying to smooth things over. I took the glass, drank a little, and said, "When I find Abe and July, I'm keeping both of them. I can't imagine where they are, but wherever Abe is, I know July's with him. If you could see them together," I started, getting choked up. "She's an amazing kid and she doesn't have anyone. She has a dead mother and a drunk aunt. As soon as I find them—and I will find them, I swear to God I will—July's coming home with Abe and me. If Mom can't handle that, I'll get my own place."

I knew then that I was taking July, no questions asked. I just had to find her first.

CHAPTER 48

The next morning, I got a call from Detective Harrison.

"Mr. LaMarche, we picked up Larry Sanderson, the guy you identified. He admitted to having a relationship with Ms. Crowley. Is it possible for you to come down to the station? I have a few questions I'd rather ask you in person."

"I'll be right down," I said. I poured my coffee into a travel mug and ran out to my truck. I was sweating, which was weird because it was April and still cool outside. My stomach was doing flips, and I started taking deep breaths and talking to myself. *You've been through a lot. Focus, deep breaths, deep breaths. Abe and July are safe, Abe and July are safe.* I pictured them huddled on a cozy bed, July reading books to Abe curled up on her lap. *I'll find you; I promise.*

I got to the station not really remembering how I got there. I found Detective Harrison, who welcomed me in to sit down in his office.

"Thanks for coming in, Mr. LaMarche," he began. "We picked up Mr. Sanderson last night." ." "That's great news, " I said jumping out to the chair and leaning onto the desk. "Did he tell you where to find Abe, and July? Did he confess to Jenny's murder?" "He told us he hasn't had a relationship with Ms. Crowley for a while. He'd heard she was using again, but he's been clean and has a good alibi for where he was during the approximate time of her murder. He told us he might have some leads, so we're going to follow up."

I pictured the day I saw Jenny and this guy on the couch, both stoned, knowing he was the one who got her started on drugs. I still wanted to hurt this guy. I didn't believe he was all innocent.

"Are you sure about his innocence , Detective? The guy's a good liar. He must know something," As I said this, I realized I was squeezing the heck out of my coffee mug causing it to fall on the ground. Coffee spilled everywhere.

Detective Harrison grabbed some napkins from a drawer in his desk and handed them to me. I was angry and felt foolish as I mopped up the coffee Detective Harrison assured me his alibi was rock sold. "In the meantime, the media's been all over this "Detective Harrison said. "I don't know if you watched the news today, but the story was picked up by the Boston media. I'd like to put out a statement. I need recent pictures of Abe and July so we can get them out to the public. Maybe we'll get lucky, and someone will recognize them."

I pulled out my phone and showed the detective all of the pictures I had of Abe. "I just want to find them. I'll do whatever I can. I don't have any recent pictures of July, but I'm sure one of her friends must, or maybe her Aunt Susan does."

"I have a call out to the principal of Maplewood Middle School. I think once this story gets out it'll be hard for some of the kids in July's class to hear. Mrs. Stevens may also have an idea of where we can find pictures of July."

I felt myself taking deep breaths. I was getting that overwhelmed feeling again.

"Mr. LaMarche, this is an unbelievable situation," Detective Harrison said. "No one's ever prepared to have a child missing. We'll do everything we can to find Abe and July. Please believe me. We're going to get them on the national registry of missing persons as soon as we have their pictures. I'm going to have you work with Officer Cruz on this."

Right then I felt horrible that I didn't have any recent pictures of July. "Thank you, Detective. I know the school will have a recent picture for July. Jenny had a picture of her that was taken at school this fall framed in her apartment. "

I left Detective Harrison's desk and sat down in the lobby. I started scrolling through my phone and found a picture of July holding teeny, tiny Abe. It was probably from when he first came home from the hospital two years before. She really is a cute kid, and her smile told how important Abe is to her. This gave me hope. I wiped away a tear as I heard a familiar voice.

"Hi Roger, I hope you were able to get some sleep last night," Officer Cruz said, pulling me out of my thoughts.

"A little, but not much. I'm not sure I'll be able to really sleep until I find my son and his sister."

"Why don't you come down the hall with me?" Officer Cruz said, leading me to her desk. "We can get started finding pictures and anything else you can tell us about Abe or July."

I tried to visualize Abe and July. What were some special things about them? They're both beautiful kids. It's obvious that they love each other. Their bond is stronger than most siblings, maybe because they've been through so much. I looked at the picture of July staring so intently at Abe that was still on the screen. I knew it wasn't the best picture of July, but I felt like I had to at least show it to someone. "She's such a cute girl," Officer Cruz said when she saw the picture. "Do you have any more?"

I scrolled through my phone hoping to find something. There was one picture I'd forgotten about, from maybe two months before. It was a really sweet picture of July reading to Abe. He was looking at July laughing, and July had a huge smile on her face. I remember it was one Sunday when I dropped Abe off at Jenny's and she invited me to stay for dinner, one of those days when I had a glimpse into the life I wanted.

"This picture is from February," I told Officer Cruz.

"I like this picture because their faces are really clear and they're together," she said very professionally and handed me my phone. "I'm sure this one picture will be enough for the news media. We will need individual pictures to put on the missing children report." Officer Cruz must sense that she has been insensitive because her tone changes.

As I stared at the picture of July and Abe on my phone, she comes behind me and puts her hand on my shoulder, "They are very sweet. We are doing everything we can to find them."

My cell phone starts ringing and I see that the call's from Dave.

"Hey Roger, I'm free for the day," he said. "Robin is adamant that I be with you even if you don't want me. Where are you, buddy?"

"I'm back at Maplewood Police Station putting together a missing report about the kids," I told him. "This is really hard. I actually could use you—I feel like I'm floating in a fog. I need another set of ears down here."

"I'll be there in a half hour. Do you need anything?"

"I need to know where Abe and July are," I said. "That's all I need."

CHAPTER 49

The police meeting with the press went well. WMUR, NECN, WBZ, and WCVB were there. There were also reporters from the *Union Leader* and *The Boston Globe*. Detective Harrison was very thorough in discussing what happened. There weren't many questions from the press.

The picture I gave to Officer Cruz of Abe and July was shown on the TV stations and put in the newspapers. There was also a picture of Abe from Christmas and July's school picture. July's teachers, David Winters, and Allison Paulson came down to the station with JoAnne Stevens, the principal. They talked to the police about starting a search party to look for July and Abe.

My mom and sisters came to help—and even Beckie was there and sober. She came up to me and gave me a genuine hug. "I'm so sorry Roger." She said. I felt her tears on my shirt "This is the worst thing I have ever heard. I will do anything to help you. I promise."

"Thanks, Beckie, "was all I could manage to say. I am overwhelmed by the people who were there for me. Father Dube and some of the parishioners from St. Vincent showed up. Dave, Robin, Fred, and his wife Jess were there, as were a lot of kids from July's school with their parents.

The police were incredibly organized about putting groups together. My mom and some of her friends were given posters with

Abe and July's faces on them. They covered the town, putting posters in every store and on every corner.

Jenny's sister was there with her son Dom. I didn't really spend time talking to them. I noticed Dom talking to a young girl I realized was July's friend, Maddie. I felt compelled to talk to her, and when I walked over, I could sense Maddie's relief. I don't think she wanted to be alone with Dom.

Dom started the conversation. "Hi Woger, dis sucks so much. I can't bewieve Aunt Jenny is dead. We wiw find Joowhy and Abe. I know it."

"I hope so Dom, "I said. "How are you doing, Maddie?"

"I don't know," Maddie said, holding back tears. I don't know what I'll do if anything happens to July."

"I have a good feeling," I said. "I think July and Abe are fine."

"I wiww also tell you Roger. Don't wowwy," Dom said.

"Thanks, to both of you, and thanks for coming out and helping with this," I said.

Officer Cruz got the crowd's attention. There were police dogs, officers, kids, parents, and ordinary citizens—I guessed there were about one hundred people there to help. Some of what Officer Cruz said freaked me out a little and I tried not to think about it. Like, if you see a body that's not moving, don't touch anything and quickly get in touch with a police officer. She assigned officers and groups of searchers to different sections of town.

She had me stay with her and interview people in the Appleton Street neighborhood. We started across the street from Jenny's house. I think when some people saw Officer Cruz in her uniform, they were afraid to open the door. If there was no answer, we left a flier with pictures of Abe and July and instructions on who to call.

It was getting frustrating with so many people refusing to answer the door, though we know they were home. Finally, we got a break—or what I thought was a break. An older man, Rodney Smith, answered the door to number 22.

Officer Cruz explained what had happened and showed Mr. Smith the pictures of Abe and July. "We believe their mother's murder took place on Thursday sometime between six and eight in the evening. Did you notice anything unusual during that time?"

"Well, now, them's the little kids that's been hanging around with Mary White across the street," he said. "I believe I seen her driving with them in her car on Friday morning. Let me see those pictures again." He took a pair of glasses out of his wrinkled sweater, grabbed the picture with his gnarled fingers, and looked at the pictures more closely. "Why yes, I do believe those are the kids who were with Mary when she drove away."

JULY

'Become My Mom Again': What It's Like to
Grow Up Amid the Opioid Crisis

Call them Generation O, the children growing up in families trapped
in a relentless grip of addiction, rehab and prison.

By Dan Levin
May 31, 2019

CHAPTER 50

I was so afraid of what Mrs. White might do to Abe I wasn't paying attention to anything. I just ran. I had no idea I'd run into the Turner's yard. I look up at Bryce realizing I'm carrying a crying two-year-old. Before I can say anything, Mrs. White pulls up in her Toyota.

"Julie, where are you going? I don't understand why you ran from the house. You must listen to me. It's very important to listen to me. I'm keeping both of you safe. I love you and just want what's best for all of us. Now, please get in the car," Mrs. White says. She doesn't seem upset or angry. She's calm and acting like she's just stating facts.

Bryce's cute golden retriever starts barking. This is an awkward moment and I'm not sure how to handle it. *I'm running away from this crazy woman*; I want to say to Bryce. *This is not my grandmother; this is my kidnapper. She's abusing my brother. Help!*

But I don't. I'm afraid of what this woman will do.

Abe stops crying and starts squealing in delight. "Doggie, doggie." I put him down.

"This is Ivy," Bryce says. "She's really friendly. You can pat her if you want."

Ivy begins licking Abe's face. Abe's giggling and Mrs. White gets out of the car and comes up to us. "Jason don't let that dog lick your face. She could have lots of germs. You never know what she may have eaten. Now it's time for us to go back home and get some dinner. No more of this silly business," she says firmly.

I look at Bryce and lamely say, "Ivy seems like a great dog." I'm not in a hurry to get into that car.

"She really is. Come over sometime with your brother when you have a chance," Bryce says.

"Julie and Jason, let's go," Mrs. White says. "You must have homework, Julie. I know you have chores. No more talking to this boy. Let's go."

"Um, Grammy, this is Bryce Turner. He goes to school with me. Bryce, this is Mrs. White." I purposefully don't say the word "grandmother" hoping that Bryce will pick up on something wrong.

"Oh, for heaven's sake, I'm Julie and Jason's grandmother," Mrs. White says, laughing. "It's nice to meet you, Bryce, but Julie has too much to do to be running around with her brother. Now I'm sure you get upset when your parents ask you to do things you don't want to do, but you don't run away." She's back to her charming self, the person I first met who was warm, caring, and made cookies.

"Well, actually, Mrs. White, there are sometimes I want to run away, especially when I have to clean the bathroom," Bryce says, smiling.

"Well, it was nice meeting you," Mrs. White says with another laugh. "Now let's go. Perhaps you two can get together another time."

"I'll see you tomorrow, Julie," Bryce says. "Also, Mrs. White, I told Julie that my brother drives me to school. I know he could give Julie a ride, so she doesn't have to take that long bus ride."

"Well, that's nice of you to offer but I enjoy driving Julie to school in the morning. It gets us up and out of the house. Little Jason and I drop Julie off and then go to the library or run errands," Mrs. White says.

"Okay, but if there's ever a time you don't feel like driving, I know Steve wouldn't mind," Bryce says.

"Thanks, Bryce," I say getting into the car, "I would like driving to school with you.".

As I shut the door Mrs. White screams, "Well, that's not going to happen. You are not to see that boy again!! "Enough of this!"

Feeling defeated, I say nothing more. . I'm not sure what to do. I'm ready for the crazy woman who claims to be my grandmother to do something crazy, hit me, or yell at Abe some more. I decide to go on the offensive—what do I have to lose?

"I don't want you to torture Abe anymore," I say quietly. "If you do. I have no problem getting in touch with his dad even if that means getting sent to a foster home. I don't want you to make him call me Julie. I don't want you to make him be Jason." I can hear the tremor in my voice as I try to keep myself together.

Mrs. White says nothing. She doesn't look at me but drives the short distance to our house. She leaves Abe and me in the car and walks into the house.

"Well, that went well, Abe, don't you think?" I say to him.

"I Jason, no Abe," he says. "Jason."

CHAPTER 51

I know I can't stay in the car forever. Abe is starting to get whiney and wants to play with his toys, or get more jellybeans. "You Julie, you Julie," he yells kicking his feet. "Out, out, out, you Julie!"

The sound of his screaming, you Julie sends a shiver up my spine. I don't know how much longer I can handle this. Maybe it's time for me to share what's happening to us with someone, no matter the consequences. I take Abe out of the car and slowly climb the stairs to the house not ready to face Mrs. White.

Opening the door, I see Mrs. White sitting at the kitchen table with a cup of tea. She hasn't started making dinner yet, which makes me nervous. I'm worried about what will happen next. "Julie, put Jason up in his room to play while you and I have a serious talk," Mrs. White says in a tone that tells me I'd better do this.

I took Abe upstairs and set up his trucks. I'm nervous about talking to Mrs. White. What is she going to tell me? I'm not sure I'm ready to listen to this crazy lady.

When I get back downstairs Mrs. White's waiting in the kitchen. She looks at me intently. "First, you need to believe I love you, Julie. You must believe that everything I'm about to share with you I did because I love you, so, so much. Tell me you believe this."

I'm not sure what to say. Do I believe she loves me? I don't know. I'm not even sure what that means, but at this point I know that if I want to get answers, I have to tell her yes. But here's the bigger question: Do I want to know what she's about to tell me?

"Of course, I believe you love me. Look at all you've done for me. You've given me beautiful clothes, my favorite books, and even a Bieber CD. You make amazing food. No one has taken care of me the way you have." As I say this, I realize it's true. I think the last time I felt safe, loved and cared for is when Roger lived with us, but that was only for a short time.

"Oh Julie, when you first asked me to watch Jason, I was surprised. I mean, I had no idea where your mother was. Yes, you told me she was sick, but even when I had a horrible stomach bug, I took care of my Jason. Mothers don't just send their children off to school, especially when one of them is only two. I knew something wasn't right. I knew in my bones that I was outside on that day because you needed me, and I needed you. When you ran to my house and told me something was wrong with your mother, I had no idea how much you needed me until I saw her."

"When you saw her and called the ambulance, right?" I ask.

"Now Julie," Mrs. White says, "this is the part that I need you to really understand. Your mother—well, no, I didn't call the ambulance. That's why I couldn't let you back in that apartment."

I start to panic. "What do you mean? You said you called the ambulance. Did you lie to me? Why didn't you call the ambulance? I should have called 9-1-1 myself. What if no one checked on Mom? She could be, she probably is…." I couldn't even think it, and start to cry.

"Julie, listen, to, me," Mrs. White says slowly and calmly. "The woman I saw on the floor of your apartment was no mother. She was a skinny bird drug addict. She had no right to beautiful children like you and Jason. You were in great danger with her. God wanted you to stay with me. That is the truth. You must accept this."

"My name is JULY, not Julie," I say not at all calmly. "Call me July. Maybe there's a chance my mother is okay. Maybe someone else found her and took her to the hospital. She was alive and breathing when I ran to your house. Maybe she's looking for us right now!"

"Oh, my dear, dear Julie," Mrs. White says, wrapping me in a tight hug. "Believe me when I tell you your mother is not looking for you. You're with me now and you're safe. You'll never have to take care of Jason alone. You'll never have to worry about drug dealers or come home to heaven knows what."

"How do you know Mom isn't looking for us? She did love me. I know she loved us when she wasn't using drugs. She was a great mom. She and Roger are probably together trying to find Abe and me."

"Julie," Mrs. White begins.

I start screaming. "My name is July! My name will always be July!"

"Your mother isn't looking for you because she's dead, JULY! She isn't looking for you because she was already very dead before I came back to my house. That's how I know she isn't looking for you. I told you I called the ambulance because I didn't want you to worry. I'm hoping you can see that now," Mrs. White says matter-of-factly.

"When we first got here you told me Mom was probably dead," I say hoping Mrs. White is wrong. "How do you know she's really dead? Did you check her pulse? She was breathing and talking when I ran to your house. You weren't gone very long."

"Listen carefully to everything I'm telling you," Mrs. White says. "When I got to your apartment, your mother was moaning, 'Help me, help me,' and she was having a very difficult time breathing. She was so bruised. I said a prayer and helped your mother, July. I helped put her out of her misery. I told her not to worry, that you would be safe and well loved. Once she stopped breathing and moving, I came home," Mrs. White says.

"Mrs. White, did you kill my mother?" I ask in disbelief.

"Julie, she was such a mess and, in such pain," Mrs. White says like it's the most natural thing in the world. "God helped me to see that if I could just put her out of her misery, it would be best for everyone. I helped her, Julie, you must believe this. By helping her I'm able to help you and Jason. You were put in my life for a reason. Don't you see that?"

CHAPTER 52

How could Mrs. White think that God wanted her to kill Mom? I don't get this part. I mean, I guess I understand why she thinks she needs to rescue us, but she didn't need to kill Mom.

If she'd called the ambulance Mom would still be alive, I'm sure of it. She'd probably get better and this time she might get sober. She would be the mother I know she could be, the one I remember playing with on the beach. The mom who read stories and painted beautiful pictures.

I don't say anything to Mrs. White, I just grab my sweater and run down to the lake. The idea that Mom is dead is too overwhelming. I guess part of me knew that she'd died, but there was always that glimmer of hope. I guess I thought Mom would get better and she and Roger would come find us. We would live together like one happy family. Now that I know that Mom is really dead and Mrs. White killed her, I'm not sure what I'm supposed to do. How do I live with the woman who killed my mother, even if my mother was a bad drug addict?

This really makes me understand that Mrs. White is crazy. Why would she think God told her she was supposed to do this? Then again, did God really tell her to do this? I don't know much about God. Mom and I never went to church or anything like that. She never had us say prayers. I talked to her about religion once, but she told me she thought it just caused problems. I don't know what I believe. I mean, I guess there's a heaven. People always talk about how when you die you go to heaven.

Mom told me that heaven is better than any place you could ever imagine. Whatever you want to do you can do in heaven. I hope Mom is in heaven, but I also hope there aren't any drugs in heaven. I know all Mom wanted to do was take her drugs and pass out. That's not really living. I hope for Mom that heaven is the beach and she's painting. I remember her painting. I remember the look she would get on her face when she was really into one of her creations. I think you would call that look serenity. She was so calm and peaceful when she was painting.

When Mom painted the picture of Roger holding the baby, I helped her pick out the paint colors. She let me watch what she was doing. She even bought me my own sketchbook and watercolors. I started painting my own pictures, but Mom, wow—she sketched out a picture of Roger that looked just like him. His eyes were astonishing, like he was the happiest guy in the world. I still don't know how Mom was able to capture that look on Roger's face like that.

Roger—I wonder if Roger knows Mom is dead. I wonder if Roger found Mom dead. I wonder if Roger knows that Abe and I are alive and safe—well, I guess we're safe. I don't think Mrs. White would kill us. But then again, if I did anything to cross her or upset her, would she think that God was telling her to kill me?

That's when I realize, holy cow, Mrs. White says she loves me, but she really loves Abe more. I know this because she truly believes Abe is Jason. That creepy time that she told me Abe was her Jason, I think that's when I knew she was crazy. Knowing this makes me want to get away from her, but where would I go?

If I go back to Maplewood, who would I live with? Aunt Susan's my only relative and she can't even take care of herself. I don't want to go back to that. I can't go to a foster home. I know some foster care people take in kids just for the money and treat them like slaves. Girls like me could be abused by a drunk guy every night. I can't imagine how horrible that would be.

"Mom what do I do?" I say aloud. "What do I do? Help me, Mom. Show me how to get out of this. Why did you pick drugs over me? Why wasn't I enough?" As I say this, I feel a dam break inside me and just start crying and crying.

I'm not sure how long I'm at the lake. I never hear any answers from Mom about what I'm supposed to do. God definitely doesn't show up and guide me to kill Mrs. White.

When I get up from where I'm sitting, I turn and standing behind me is Mrs. White. She scares me half to death.

"How long have you been standing there?" I ask.

"Oh, Julie, I see how difficult all of this is for you," she says happily as she hugs me. "I never meant for you to be sad about your mother's death. I thought you'd be relieved that you wouldn't have to deal with her anymore. She certainly wasn't a mother. Now you have me, and I'll never abandon you. You'll be safe with me and Jason forever. You'll see, your new life is going to be wonderful and it's starting right now."

How can my life be wonderful if I have to live with the person who killed my mother and pretend it was a great thing? How can it be wonderful if I'm living a lie and keeping Abe from his father?

ROGER

The Breaking Point: Young Parents Battling Heroin
Addiction to Get Clean for Their Kids

Families ruined by heroin addiction share their stories.

By KETURAH GRAY, NICK CAPOTE, GLENN RUPPEL,
LAUREN EFFRON and LAUREN PEARLE ABC News

March 11, 2016, 5:41 PM

CHAPTER 53

After talking to Rodney Smith, Officer Cruz and I went back to the station. "You know how someone claiming to be July's grandmother called saying she wouldn't be in school?" I asked her. "Do you think that could have been this Mary White? Could she have taken Abe and July?" Part of me was hoping July and Abe were with a nice old lady—that seemed safer than being with a bunch of drug dealers. At the same time, why has she taken them? And more importantly, where were they?

"We certainly will check all possible leads. " Officer Cruz assures me. "This does sound promising, but you have to let us do our job without jumping to conclusions. I know it's hard not to get your hope up, but we must be methodical and get this right."

Mom, Michelle, and Beckie came into the police station followed by Dave, Fred, and their wives. They'd had no luck finding the kids. Posters were up all over the city with pictures of July and Abe. I looked at the people I was closest to in the world and knew I wasn't in this alone. I felt overwhelmed by their support.

"We may have found something while we were talking to Jenny's neighbors," I shared. "It sounds like there's an older woman who lived down the road who may have the kids."

"What do you mean?" Mom asked. "Why would an older woman have Abe and his sister? Is she connected with the drug dealers? Do you know where she's taken them?"

My mother can be too much sometimes, but I knew she sincerely wanted to find Abe "No one's sure if this is true, but the officers are going to work on it," I said, looking hopefully at Officer Cruz.

"We're doing all we can, Mrs. LaMarche," Officer Cruz told my mother. "At this point we have a lot to work on. Why don't you go home? I'll be in touch as soon as soon as we know anything."

"Officer, why don't you put a trace on the car?" my mother asked demandingly. "Can't we call the news people back and let them know about this woman? If the news stations can get the information out, someone must have seen them. What's the name of this woman? When did she take them? Roger, we have to get on this right away."

"Mrs. LaMarche, we need to be sure this is credible information," Officer Cruz said. "We have officers working on this right now. As soon as we know more, we'll get the word out, I promise. It may be best if you go home and get some rest. This is emotionally draining. You need to take care of yourself through this process."

"Mom, I think Officer Cruz is right," my sister Stephanie said. "Why don't we get something to eat and then go home? How does that sound to you, Roger?"

"I think Stephanie's right," Michelle added. "There's not much else we can do today. Roger, we're here for you, you know that, right? Dan can stay with the kids, and I can stay with you if that would help."

"I appreciate it, but I think I'll be okay," I said, knowing the last thing I needed was Michelle reminding me how horrible it was that my kids were missing.

"I'm going to be going Roger," Beckie says. "I promise you I'll be clean and sober. Watching you go through all this has really opened my eyes. Look, I'm sorry Abe is missing. I'm really sorry about Jenny. I saw her at a meeting a few months ago. We didn't really talk, but I heard she got involved with some bad guys."

I was surprised that Beckie had been going to the same meetings as Jenny. Neither of them said anything about it. I know Jenny knew I was concerned about Beckie. Why didn't she tell me she saw her at a meeting? Maybe some of the things Beckie heard would help the case.

"Beckie, I'm proud of you for getting sober," I said holding onto her shoulders. "Think about what Jenny said at meetings. Anything she shared may help us figure out who killed her and who has the kids."

Beckie looked into my eyes. It was the kind, thoughtful sister I had before the drugs. A tear trickled down her cheek, "Roger, I'm so sorry I've caused so much pain for our family. I want you to know that I will do anything, anything to get our relationship back to the way it was before I ever took my first hit."

Now Beckie is sobbing. I just put my arms around her and let her cry. As I held her, I thought about Jenny. If only Jenny could have held onto her sobriety. Then I started crying, too.

After we get ourselves together, Officer Cruz asked Beckie. "Do you think you'd be able to give us some information about these 'bad guys?' Maybe it could give us some insight into how Jenny died."

Beckie looked nervous, but she really rose to the occasion. I couldn't believe she was willing to talk to the police. The change in her surprised me.

"Mom, why don't you go with Michelle and Stephanie?" I asked. "I'm going to hang around here for a while and see if Beckie can be of any help." Mom went over to Beckie and gave her a hug. "I'm so proud of you. I know what you're going through is hard, but your family loves you."

Beckie hugged Mom and started crying again. "Mom, I'm so sorry that I caused you and Dad so much pain."

"That's all in the past," Mom said. "Now we just need to focus on getting Abe home and safe. It says a lot that you are here, honey. Roger, your whole family is here for you. Dad would be so proud to see how you stepped up, Beckie. Now just call me if either of you need anything. I love you both so much." Mom took a tissue from her purse and began wiping her eyes.

"Love you, too," Beckie said her voice filled with emotion.

Then Mom came up to me and hugged me. "I love you so much. You remember you are not alone. I'll see you back at home." She kissed my cheek and dapped her eyes again.

I couldn't remember the last time I heard my mother say this. I guess Abe's disappearance affected her more than I thought. "Thanks

Mom," I said, "that means a lot. I love you, too." Mom wiped the tear falling down my cheek with her tissue and walked toward the door with Stephanie and Michelle

"Love you," Stephanie said as she held back tears.

Michelle came up and gave me a big bear hug, "Oh Roger, I just…"

"Come on, Michelle," Stephanie said gently pulling my sobbing sister away. Stephanie gave me a quick hug and then the three of them left.

"Hey Roge, the four of us are going back to my house for a little while," Dave said. "Stop by if you need to talk or if you just want a cold beer."

"Yes, please come by," Robin added, giving me a hug. "Feel free to stay over if you'd like. We're a lot closer to the police station."

"Thanks, but I think I'm just going to stay around here for a bit until I hear something that can give me some answers."

"Well, you know where to find us if you need us. Come by any time. We'll probably be up for a while," Dave said.

"We're here for you, too," Fred added. "If you need anything, it's yours."

"Thanks. I don't know what I'd do without all of you," I told them, really meaning it. There was no way I could imagine going through this alone.

I grabbed a cup of coffee from the pot on the counter and looked up to see Detective Harrison.

"Mr. LaMarche, I just got the autopsy report from the coroner," he said. "If you come down to my office, I can share it with you."

"Thank you, Detective," I said, following him down the hall.

Once we got inside his office Detective Harrison took out the report and put on his glasses. "Ms. Crowley had three broken ribs, a broken nose, and a fractured clavicle when she died. She was beaten pretty severely, but her actual cause of death was suffocation."

CHAPTER 54

"So, these creeps who beat Jenny, they suffocated her?" I asked Detective Harrison.

"I don't know yet, Mr. LaMarche," Detective Harrison went on. "We got some information from your sister about some of the people she thought Ms. Crowley was associated with. One set of prints we found on Ms. Crowley matches the prints of one of those guys. We're looking for him now. There are other prints in the apartment, and we can assume they belong to Ms. Crowley and her children. Forensics is pretty sure whoever suffocated Ms. Crowley used a pillow they found on the couch. Some of the fibers from that pillow were found in Ms. Crowley's mouth and nostrils, but the prints on the pillow don't match the prints found on Ms. Crowley's body. The person who beat her may have had an accomplice."

"What about this woman who may have taken the kids?" I asked. "What do you know about her? Could she be the one who suffocated Jenny? Have you started looking for her?"

"We have some officers on this. It appears Mary White isn't at home. We do have the make and model of her car. We also saw that she made purchases with a credit card in Bangor, Maine on Friday afternoon. She also closed her bank account Friday morning and has a bank check for $253,000. I'm sure we'll be able to find her soon."

"The news media that was here was from New Hampshire and Boston. Can we add the Maine news stations to our list?" I asked.

"Already done, Mr. LaMarche. I've contacted news people at all three of the Maine stations. They're on their way now. I know they'd like to interview you to get some insight on the children."

"I'll do anything to help find Abe and July," I said. I looked up to see my sister Beckie coming down the hall. She looked awful; her face was flush. I could tell she'd been crying.

"Are you okay, Beckie? You don't look too good," I said. "Remember JD, that guy I went out with in high school, the one who got me hooked and ruined my life?' Beckie began. "They just brought him into the station. He's the one who beat up Jenny. His fingerprints were all over her. He just looked at me like I would be next, like he would have no problem beating the shit out of me. It creeped me out.

"Oh my god, Beckie, I'm so sorry. I'm sure it was terrifying seeing him. Are you sure he's the one who beat up Jenny?"

"He was bragging about it. He was screaming that he would beat her again. Apparently, she was keeping over $10,000 worth of H for him and it disappeared. He claims he didn't kill her, but he taught her a lesson. He said he was sure she wasn't dead because he wanted the drugs or the money. He told her he'd be back to pick it up."

"You mean, Jenny had heroin in her apartment that Abe could have taken? I can't believe it! How did I not know this? Was JD seeing Jenny? Did he take the kids?" I was panicked and angry. How could Jenny have put the kids in danger like this?

"Roge, I really don't think JD would hurt the kids. I know he's a piece of shit, but I don't think he'd have taken them. I mean, when I knew him, he had a little brother he was really close to. His parents weren't really there, and he took over the parent role as best he could. Maybe the kids started to see things and ran away.

"That was over ten years ago. He could have changed into an uncaring monster." I said. "How can you be sure he didn't take them."

"Something about the way he was talking, bragging about beating Jenny. I don't think he took them." Jenny assured me.

"Could they have gone to Mary White's because they were frightened? How do they know this woman? Where the heck are they?

CHAPTER 55

The Maine news stations showed up about an hour later. They were excited to hear that I was from Berwick and that Abe had roots in Maine. One of the reporters from WMTW Channel 8 seemed to take an added interest in the story. She explained that their station was doing a special called "The State of Addiction" and she believed that whatever had happened to Abe and July was clearly a result of Jenny being an addict. She told me she'd like to add this story to the special.

I told the reporter I'd do anything to make sure Abe and July are safe. If she thought putting them on this special would help, I was all in. She told me she was going to talk to the station manager and see if they could add some reporters to the story. She gave me some hope.

Once the reporters left Detective Harrison told me to go home and get some sleep. I wondered if that guy ever slept. I thought it was a good idea, but I really wanted to know more about this Mary White. I decided to drive over to her place and hopefully look around her house. I wasn't sure what I was looking for—my kids, I guess.

As I approached Appleton Street, I could see lots of police cars in front of Mary White's house. Apparently, they'd had the same idea as me.

I parked the truck and walked toward the house only to be stopped by a police officer. "Excuse me, sir," the officer said. "We're investigating a crime scene. I have to ask you to stay back."

"A crime scene?" I asked, taken aback. "Listen, my name is Roger LaMarche. You're trying to find my son Abe and his sister July. Maybe I can help you."

"Sir, the best thing you can do is let us complete our work. If we find anything, I'll give you a call," the officer said, handing me a card that read Officer Charles Goodwin.

"Officer Goodwin, I appreciate your help. I just feel so helpless. There has to be something I can do besides sit around and wait. I know Detective Harrison said this Mary White used a credit card in Bangor. Is someone following up with this? Can I go up to Bangor myself? Just let me know what to do to get my boy home!" I said, realizing I was losing it.

"I really can't imagine what you're going through," Officer Goodwin said, "but you have to trust us right now. We're checking out every lead. The Maine State Police have been alerted. Please believe me when I tell you the best thing you can do right now is go home. I promise we'll be in touch."

I've got too much energy to go home. It's only eight thirty. I feel like there's something I should be doing. This Mary White must have some kind of history or something. Maybe I can get some information about her online. Who knows—stranger things have happened.

"Officer, thank you for your help," I said. "I'll leave you to keep up the investigation."

As I was leaving, I decided to go over and talk to Rodney Smith, the man who told us he'd seen the kids. Maybe he knew something about Mary White that would help us understand why she took the kids—if she really did take them. He'd seemed like the kind of guy who would observe the goings-on in the neighborhood. As I approached his house, I noticed a light on, so I figured I'd just ring the bell.

I heard shuffling as someone came toward the door. It opened a crack and Rodney Smith peered out suspiciously. He looked like he might have been asleep in front of the TV. "Can I help you?" he asked rubbing his hand over his shiny bald head.

"I hope so," I say. "My name is Roger LaMarche. I talked to you earlier today with Officer Cruz about my missing children."

"Oh, yes, I remember now," he said his dark brown eyes staring down at me. "You were asking about them kids that been hanging around with Mary White."

"Yes, I'm their father. I'm out of my mind with worry. Are you sure you saw her drive away with them?"

"Yes, that's right, probably around nine o'clock on Friday morning. I was outside with my dog letting him do his business and she drove away. I waved to her, but she didn't seem to notice."

"Do you have any idea where she would have taken them, or why she may have taken them?" I asked.

"Well now, I did share this with the police, but I'll tell you cause you say you're their father. Ever since Bob and Jason died, Mary has not been happy. You can imagine what that'd be like," Mr. Smith said.

"Who are Bob and Jason?" I asked.

"Bob was her husband. He was a great guy. He and Mary used to come over with little Jason and visit with my wife Carol and our daughter Jackie. She and Jason were about the same age. Anyhow, Bob and Jason were killed in a horrible car accident, oh, probably thirty-five years ago." Rodney continued rubbing the white stubble on his brown chin. "Yup, thirty-five years, wow. Mary never seemed to recover from that. My wife Carol was real good about visiting her and all that, but Mary had a hard time watching Jackie grow up."

"Carol passed about four years ago. Cancer got her real good. I didn't see too much of Mary after that. Anyhow, them kids started showing up about a month ago. I'd watch Mary with them out the window. It's the first time I really saw her smile since the accident. She'd have that little fella out playing with Jason's old toys. The older girl would come and pick him up and they'd chat.

"I know Mary started cooking again. She's a real good cook. Sometimes my Carol would have her come for dinner and she would always bring something, cookies, a pie. Anyhow, she came over out of the blue the other day all smiles and hands me a big old apple pie. Then she starts telling me how she has these kids in her life now and she's found her purpose. I asked about the kids' momma, but Mary tells me the mother is sick so she's going to take care of them from now on."

As he said all this, red flags were going off in my head. "When did all this start?" I asked.

"Oh, I don't know exactly. She bring me that pie about a week ago. I think maybe just a few weeks," he said.

I started thinking about the last few times I saw Jenny. I know now that she'd been using, and probably heavily. I felt like such a bad father. Why hadn't July told me this? I'd really screwed up. If I'd only done something sooner, Jenny might still be alive.

"Mr. Smith, do you have any idea where Mary may have taken the kids? Would she have any reason to go to Maine?" I asked.

"Maine? I don't think so. Let me think" He paused and put on this look like he was trying to remember from a long time ago. "I believe Mary's family had a cabin in Maine. I think that's right. I don't think she's been there in quite a long time."

"Do you have any idea where in Maine?" I asked hopefully.

"Hmmm, I can't remember. I know she and Bob would go up there in the summer sometimes for a week or two, but that was long ago."

"Thanks a lot, Mr. Smith," I said. "Can I give you, my number? I mean, if you think of anything at all, please call me or tell the police. I just want to find my kids."

Mr. Smith took my number and then looked at me really seriously and said, "If Mary has those kids, you don't have to worry about them. Mary will keep them safe, and I know she'll feed them real good."

"Why would she take them? It doesn't make any sense to me. I mean, didn't she know she'd be arrested for kidnapping?" I asked.

Mr. Smith looked surprised and said slowly, "Well now, I think Mary's been the only one watching them kids. I certainly never seen you. Mary is good people; she'd never do anything to hurt them. She probably think she's saving them. Now if you love them kids like you say, why they been living with a drug addict mother in an unsafe place?"

Shame and guilt overtook me. This guy was right. Why had I been letting this go on? Could I have stopped it if I'd done something? It was too much.

"Thank you, have a good evening," was all I could manage to say.

CHAPTER 56

That night I couldn't help but think about what Mr. Smith had told me. *Why did I leave those kids alone with Jenny? I knew she was using. I should have pushed for a change. Should-haves get you nowhere. I promise when I get you kids back, you'll have a great life.*

I hoped he was right about Mary White keeping the kids safe. Maybe she was trying to save them. I didn't know, I just needed to find them.

I decided to check in on the job site before going over to the police station. I also wanted to run some things by Fred and Dave. I threw an old NSYNC CD into the player and started singing along to "God Must Have Spent A Little More Time on You." I was thinking about Jenny and how she'd laughed at me when she saw I had that CD. She'd laughed, but she'd known all the words too.

I can't believe this mess. Jenny, sweet, beautiful Jenny is dead. Our beautiful boy is missing. Oh Jenny, help me find him. I promise once I find him and July, I'll take care of both of them. I'll make sure they're together. They'll have good lives, I promise, Jenny. Help me out.

I realized I was crying. I also wondered if anyone had planned a service for her. I couldn't imagine Susan doing anything like that. I guessed that would land in my lap, too.

I arrived at the Maplewood police station around eight thirty and made my way to Detective Harrison's office. "Good morning, Mr. LaMarche. I hope you got some sleep," he said when I walked in.

"A little," I said. "I wanted to tell you some of the things Rodney Smith shared with me yesterday. He's sure Mary White has the kids. Also, the Channel 8 reporter wants to find the kids and use this case in a special they're doing on the opioid crisis."

"I also spoke with Rodney Smith and We believe Mary White does have Abe and July. We also believe they're somewhere in Maine. Her car was seen at the toll booth in Newport, Maine on Friday. The Maine State Police are on this, Mr. LaMarche. We have a copy of her New Hampshire driver's license and we've given it to the Maine state troopers. We also have troops at the border."

"The border?" I asked, panicking. "What do you mean? Do you think she would take them to Canada? Oh my God, if she takes them to Canada what recourse do we have? Can we contact the Canadian authorities?"

"Slow down, Mr. LaMarche. I don't know where your children are. Right now, it looks like they're with Mary White somewhere in Maine. No one's seen them at the border. We're just making sure, that's all. Now as far as the news reporter is concerned that's your call. Let me warn you, though, that sometimes these people can be a problem. Remember, their jobs are to sell stories. They have to make those stories as interesting as possible. I know your kids have been through a lot. You may want to hold off for a bit before subjecting them to a drug crisis story."

"Mr. Smith knows Mary White pretty well. He told me her family had a cabin somewhere in Maine," I suggested. "Are there any lakes up near that Newport exit? Maybe she took them there?"

"Maine is a big state, Mr. LaMarche," Detective Harrison said dismissively. "We're doing everything we can to locate the kids and help put Ms. Crowley's killer in jail for life. I know this is hard for you, but I promise we will find your kids.

I'll be in touch as soon as I hear anything. One more thing, we are done with Ms. Crowley's body. Do you have a funeral home you would like us to release it to?"

I didn't really have the energy to deal with Jenny's body, but who else did she have. "I guess, I could call O'Neil's, they're right in town. Can I talk to Jenny's sister and get back to you?'

It was strange knowing that Jenny's only relative was Susan. I knew I had to talk to her about Jenny's body. Jenny and I were close at one time, but not lately. I think Susan had to make some of this decision. I wondered what kind of state she'd be in when I got there. It was still early, so she might be okay.

When I pulled up in front of her place, I saw that not much had changed. Beer cans and cigarette butts littered the front yard. *Do I really want to do this?* I thought to myself. *Wouldn't it be easier if I just did it myself?* As I sat in my truck debating, Susan's son Dom came out of the house and over to my truck. It was hard to understand the kid, but I tried.

"Hi, Wogah, you going to talk to Mom?" he asked.

"Yup, how's she doing?"

"She not so good. Aunt Jenny's death got her cwying all da time. She been having lots of beer. She sweepin now. You want me to get her up?"

I looked at my watch: it was ten thirty.

"No, that's okay," I said. "I was just wondering if she'd set up a service for your Aunt Jenny."

"I don't fink so. I don't fink she did anyfing, but you can ask her. I bet she's up. Let me check," Dom said, and ran back in the house.

What am I doing here? I thought. *Obviously, this drunk person isn't capable of getting a funeral service together. Maybe I should just leave.*

As I was thinking, Susan came out of the house smoking a butt and carrying a beer. She looked like hell. It was hard to believe she was only thirty-five. "What the hell are you doing here so early?" she asked.

I got out of the truck and came over to where she was standing. *Man, she could use a shower.*

"Hi to you, too," I said. "Look, I was just wondering if you have any plans for Jenny?"

Susan looked at me like I was crazy, took a long drag of her cigarette, and said, "She's dead, Roger. Why would I be planning anything for her?"

I couldn't believe it. " The police asked me where they should send her body. Have you done anything about a funeral?"

"What the hell am I supposed to do? I ain't got no money. I don't know how to do that shit," Susan said, taking a gulp of beer.

"Well, I could help you. We could go to O'Neil's Funeral Home and talk to them. Do you know if Jenny wanted to be cremated?"

"I don't know if she wanted to be cremated. That wasn't a conversation we ever had. Look, I'm not any good with this stuff. Why don't you go down to O'Neil's and do what you think is best? Jenny's dead. Her kids are missing. I don't think she'd care if she's cremated or dropped in the ocean. Who cares what happens now?" As she said this she started crying.

"I don't know what would be best," I said. "Did she have a place that was special? A place you think she'd want to be forever?"

"My dad had this little fishing shanty in North Hampton between Rye and Hampton on the ocean. Jenny loved it there before she got screwed up with drugs. That's where she needs to be now," Susan said, surprisingly spot-on.

"That sounds wonderful," I told her. "I'll go down to O'Neil's and set it up. I think it makes sense for you, Dom, and me to do this together. Can you think of anyone else who should be with us?" I asked.

"Yeah, July and Abe need to be there. We aren't putting Jenny's ashes in the ocean at Northampton until her kids are back."

I felt like Susan had punched me in the gut. Of course, we had to wait for Abe and July. What was I doing? Why did Susan get this and I didn't.

"You're right Susan," I said. "It's just in my family we bury people the week they die."

"Well, Jenny was never in your family" Susan said " I know wherever the kids are, Jenny's with them. She'll lead you to them."

"I hope you're right," I said as I walked back to my truck.

CHAPTER 57

Setting up Jenny's final resting place was so much harder than I thought. I met with the funeral director and explained we would have a private service. He explained the cremation process and had me pick out an urn. That part was really hard. I thought of the Jenny I fell in love with and tried to find something that matched that image.

There was one beautiful urn that reminded me of the sea. The bottom looked like coral with small fish intertwined throughout. There were dolphins and mermaids on the top. It was so peaceful and happy. This was where Jenny needed to be. I had tears in my eyes as I explained this to the funeral director.

The next day I decided it would be best if I stayed away from the police station. Mom and the people from her church had been over every day helping any way they could, searching the internet and calling people. There was even one couple who'd been driving to lake communities and hanging up posters.

I was overwhelmed by the help. As the day went on, I grew more hopeful. I felt like something would happen, that we'd find the kids. I knew Jenny was helping me. I felt her presence.

Around noon I got a call from the police. Officer Cruz told me that Maddie Flynn had received an email from July. July had posted the email on Maddie's Gmail account. It said, *Hey Maddie, it's July.*

I'm alive and miss you soooo much. You wouldn't believe what's happened to me.

Officer Cruz wasn't sure where the email had come from. She believed it was really from July, which meant she was alive. If she was alive, then Abe must also be alive. July was close to Maddie, and I knew she'd write to her again.

"Did you ask Maddie to write back?" I asked "I mean, she should let July know how many people are looking for her. Tell Maddie to send her my phone number so July can reach out to me. Maybe I should go over to the school and talk to her."

"We've been in close contact with Maddie's guidance counselor," Officer Cruz answered. "Maddie did write back to July. We're hoping this will lead to something. In the meantime, we can only hope that someone's seen their pictures on the news."

CHAPTER 58

O n Thursday morning I got a call from Detective Harrison. He told me he was sure they'd found July. I jumped into my truck and hurried to the police station. I don't even remember the drive; I just know that suddenly I was running into his office.

"Mr. LaMarche, we received a call from Moosehead Lake Regional School in Maine this morning. A guidance counselor Charlotte Ellis, is sure they have a new student who's July. She's registered there as Julie White, and she's living with her grandmother, Mary White, in Rockwood. Ms. Ellis saw the report on the news. She says everything makes sense and she's positive this Julie is really July."

I can't put into words the emotions I felt just then. Relief I guess, but more than that.

"What about Abe, Detective?" I asked. "Did she say anything about Abe?"

"Well, Ms. Ellis knows July has a brother. She hasn't seen him, but July's talked about him in class. I take this as good news.

"It has to be Abe," I said elated." He's alive, right? This means they're both fine? I have to go there right now."

"There's one little glitch," Detective Harrison added, "and I hope it's just that. July didn't go to school today. The Rockwood police showed up at her house around ten o'clock this morning and no one was there. They went into the house and found a cat and it looks like wherever they went they'd be back. They're keeping an officer at the house waiting for their return."

"I'm on my way," I said immediately. "Thanks for everything, Detective."

"Now Mr. LaMarche," Detective Harrison began, "you're full of emotion right now. I don't think you should go on this trip alone. You should bring someone with you. It's about a five-hour drive."

"I'm bringing my mother, Detective. I'm going home to get her, and we'll drive to the Rockwood police station."

"The Maine police will extradite Mary White to New Hampshire," Detective Harrison said. "Those kids have been through a lot. They'll certainly be glad to see you."

"Thanks, Detective," I said. "I can't believe this nightmare is almost over."

As I walked out of the police station, I looked at the poster of the missing kids and shuddered. *I hope they're safe, I hope I find them.*

I got into my truck and headed off to get Mom. When I switched on the ignition "Call Me Maybe" was playing on WERZ. I took this as a good sign.

"I'm on my way, July. You keep Abe safe until I get there."

JULY

Trump pushes death penalty for some drug dealers

By <u>Dan Merica</u>, CNN
Updated 6:23 PM EDT, Mon March 19, 2018

CHAPTER 59

I don't really remember falling asleep, but I wake up with a start. It seems later that it should be. I run downstairs to look at the clock. It's 9:30.

"Oh my God, I'm late for school. How could you let me sleep so late?" I ask my "Grammy."

"Relax, Julie," Mrs. White says. "Jason and I have been having a great morning. We made you some waffles, and I'll cook up some bacon. I think you need to have a relaxing day—no worrying about school. The three of us are going on a moose hunt."

I start to get a little panicked remembering what Mrs. White did to Mom. Is she going to take me into the woods and shoot me, or just leave me to be attacked by a moose or a bear?

"Moose hunt, Julie, moose hunt," Abe starts singing as he dances around the kitchen.

The smell of bacon cooking stops my thoughts. I sit down at the table and give in to the taste of the light fluffy waffles swimming in delicious maple syrup. After the first bite I feel my body relax. It's amazing how food can make all my pain go away. I wonder if that's what drugs did to Mom? No thinking, just eat the waffles, savor the flavor, chew, swallow, stuff down fear, stuff down anger.

"What do you mean we're going on a moose hunt? Are we really going to kill a moose?" I ask, taking a bite out of a crisp piece of bacon.

Mrs. White laughs. "No, silly, I don't know how to shoot a gun. We're going to drive over to Kokadjo. That's a great place to see moose. I think we should bring a little picnic and enjoy Maine the way life should be. That's the state motto after all. Now finish up your breakfast and get dressed so we can get on the road. It'll take us about an hour to get there. Be sure to dress in layers, since you never know what the weather will do. I made some cookies while you were sleeping and we have chips, apples, and—let me see, what kind of sandwich should I pack for you?"

"Um, I don't know, I guess peanut butter is fine," I say, still swallowing the waffles.

"Well, peanut butter it is. Do you want strawberry jam, grape jelly, or blueberry jelly?' Mrs. White asks.

Suddenly I get this image of Mom and I making strawberry jam the summer Roger came to live with us. We spent the day at a farm picking strawberries. I think I ate more strawberries than I picked. Mom told me she used to make strawberry jam with her mom when she was little. I can still smell the strawberries boiling in the pan. I bet we made at least ten jars.

"Julie, what kind of jelly do you want?" Mrs. White asks me again.

I look into the face of my mother's killer. The woman who thinks she's saving me. I say to her in a tone that I hope hurts, "You know, Mrs. White, I used to make strawberry jam with my mother. She wasn't a bad person. You never knew her." I throw my plate into the sink and run upstairs.

"Sissy, no cry," Abe calls after me.

"Not Sissy, Jason. That is not Sissy," Mrs. White says in a harsh tone that stops me in my tracks.

I run back downstairs and grab my brother before she could force him into his room or worse. "Abe, you are Abe, and I am Sissy," I tell him.

Abe gets really freaked out. "I Jason, no Abe," he says, crying.

I begin crying too and just grab him tight, though he struggles to get away.

Then Mrs. White comes into my room and acts like everything is fine. "Okay you two," she says, ignoring my story about Mom and the jam. "The car is all packed, so let's go. There are a lot of moose to see."

Now what do I do? I hate this feeling. How can I forget this loving grandmother is the woman who killed my mother? . If she's pretending to be my grandmother, shouldn't she know something about Mom? I just want her to see how much she's hurt me. I want to hurt her too.

I start saying words I know will make her angry, and I don't care. "You know, Mrs. White, if you're pretending to be my grandmother shouldn't I tell you some things about my mother, your 'daughter' that you killed? Don't you want to know what she was like before you sucked the life out of her? My mother, *Abe's* mother, the kind, funny, talented artist? She wasn't just the woman you saw the night you killed her. Don't you want to know about the person whose life you took?" I look at her as I say this, daring her to hurt me.

What Mrs. White does next creeps me out a little. She doesn't get mad; she just walks over to my bed and hugs me. "Your mother must have been wonderful at some point because you are an amazing girl," she says. "I told you God sent me a strong message that I had to do what was best for you, and yes, Julie, helping your mother out of her pain and giving you a new start on life was part of his plan."

She kisses the top of my head. "Now you get dressed. We're going to have a wonderful day."

I decide to just go with it. I mean, what choice do I have? Mrs. White is in charge. There's nothing I can do. I could stay in my room, or I could run away, but where would I go? If I went back to Maplewood, who would take care of me? Mom is dead. I can't picture Aunt Susan opening her drunken arms to me. Roger would take Abe, but I wonder if he'd take me. He was there for me once, and he knows how attached Abe and I are. Maybe he would, but if he didn't, what would happen then?

I dress in layers, since Mrs. White's right about never knowing what the weather will be like up here. I walk downstairs and see Abe in an adorable outfit. He has on jeans, a flannel shirt, and a moose hat. I have to scoop him up; he's too cute.

"Well, that's better," Mrs. White says, inspecting my outfit. "You're both going to love this place, I promise. Even if we don't see any moose, the drive is beautiful. We can have a nice picnic and enjoy the scenery. It's an absolutely beautiful day."

As I walk outside, I feel the rays of the sun that make it seem warmer than sixty-two degrees. I don't know if I need all these layers. I buckle Abe into his car seat while Mrs. White puts the rest of our things in the trunk. Maybe this will be a good day after all.

As we begin the drive Mrs. White starts telling us a story about when she was a girl. Her dad took her to the place we're going to. I guess they saw lots of moose. One even came so close to their car that Mrs. White was able to touch it. She talks on and on, and Abe is laughing because she makes funny sounds when she tells us about the moose. I'm not really sure how she does it. I feel like she's trying too hard to get me to trust her, and I don't think I can. I mean, who could trust the person who killed her mother?

I take out *Sea of Monsters*, the book I'm reading now. Percy meets his brother, Tyson, who's a baby cyclops. Even though Percy has a tricky time, he wasn't abandoned by his parents. Sure, his father, the god of the sea, is absent quite a bit, but his mother is still in the picture—no crazy neighbors killed her.

After we've been driving for a while, Mrs. White starts yelling, but it's a happy yell, not an angry one. "Oh my, look, Jason, Julie, a moose! Right in front of us, a big bull moose, oh my, wow! Can you see it?"

I have to admit, it's pretty awesome. It's about a hundred yards in front of us. This is the first time I've ever seen a moose. It's so much bigger than I realized. I thought they were the same size as deer, but the moose is much bigger than Mrs. White's car. Its antlers are massive. I wouldn't want to be headbutted by them. . It's hard for Abe to see it from his car seat, so I tell this to Mrs. White.

"Oh Julie, you're such a great sister," Mrs. White says, pulling over. "Of course, we want Jason to see. We can get a better view from the side of the road anyway."

Mrs. White is so excited to show Abe the moose and as she unbuckles him, she tells him there's a big surprise waiting. The moose looks up as Mrs. White takes Abe out of his car seat and saunters into the woods. I don't know if Abe even saw it.

But what Abe does see really shakes Mrs. White. A white truck the same as Roger's drives by, and Abe starts clapping and yelling, "Daddy truck, Daddy truck, Daddy, yay, Daddy!"

Mrs. White looks like she's seen a ghost. She quickly puts Abe back in his car seat, turns the car around, and starts driving away from our moose hunt. "That can't be, Jason, there is no Daddy. You hear me, no Daddy!" She screams this as she drives faster.

Abe looks like he's going to cry again. I take his little hand and whisper, "Yes Abe, Daddy's truck."

"Daddy's truck," he whispers back.

Mrs. White is freaking out again. "God promised me you would be my children. I sacrificed so, so much. No one will take you from me! No one! Do you hear me, Jason?!"

Abe's little lip starts to quiver. "Daddy, Daddy," he cries.

"Don't worry little guy," I promise him. "We'll find Daddy."

CHAPTER 60

The more Abe cries and screams for Daddy, the crazier Mrs. White becomes. She's driving like she's in the Daytona 500. I try to calm Abe down by singing softly to him, but you can see he finally understands "Grammy" isn't going to care for him the way his daddy did.

Roger was crazy about Abe. You could see it when he came to pick him up. Abe would run to Roger and Roger would twirl him around. He'd always tell him what they were going to do that weekend, and Abe couldn't wait to leave. I can't really blame him.

"Julie, you must help me. Jason cannot keep saying 'Daddy.'" She speaks firmly to Abe. "Jason, no Daddy! Daddy is gone. There is no more Daddy! Oh my, stop him, Julie! NO MORE DADDY! Do you hear me? There is no Daddy, there is just Grammy now! Stop this, Jason. You are mine! I will not have you saying 'Daddy!'" she screams.

Abe is inconsolable, "Sissy, Daddy's truck," he sobs. "Daddy, Sissy, where Daddy?"

"It's okay, Abe. We'll find Daddy, don't worry," I promise. I need to get both him and Mrs. White to calm down.

"Don't you tell him we'll find Daddy, Julie," Mrs. White screams. "We will not find Daddy! There is no Daddy!"

The more agitated Mrs. White becomes the more erratically she drives. I start to get scared.

"Grammy, please be careful. You're driving awfully fast," I tell her, trying to sound calm.

Instead of slowing down, she drives faster and screams, "I have saved you children! Do you know what your lives would be like if I hadn't saved you? You probably would have been sold into a slave trade by some drug dealers. Your lives will be so much better with me. This 'Daddy' isn't going to help you. Believe me, your life is going to be great!"

Right then I hear a *wee oo wee oo* sound and see the flashing lights of a police car following us. I get really scared.

Mrs. White doesn't slow down or stop; she just drives faster. I'm not sure if she knows the police car is behind us. I don't know what to do. Mrs. White's getting crazier, and I'm afraid we'll crash or something.

"Grammy, there's a police officer behind us. I think you need to pull over," I say.

"No one is taking you from me. Do you hear me?" Mrs. White keeps screaming and crying now as she drives faster. "No Daddy, no police officer. You are mine. God promised if I put that pillow over your mother's face, you would be safe. He promised you would be mine and I will keep you safe!"

Abe is crying, too. "Daddy, no Grammy, Daddy." He keeps crying this over and over.

Suddenly Mrs. White pulls off the main road and steers the Toyota onto a bumpy dirt path. She has to slow down, but she doesn't. I make sure Abe's car seat is buckled tightly. I don't really know how to pray, but I decide now's the time to start. The police officer is still behind us with lights flashing.

Suddenly, right in front of us is a moose.

CHAPTER 61

I'm terrified. I don't know if Mrs. White will stop or plow into the moose. If she hits the moose, we're all dead.

"Please, Grammy, stop! STOP!" I yell as loud as I can.

I think the moose must have heard me because he runs out of the way.

Mrs. White just keeps driving down this dirt path. The police car keeps following us. I knew if Mrs. White doesn't stop there's a good chance, we'll all be dead. You can't drive sixty miles an hour down a dirt road in a Toyota and be safe.

I look out the back window and see the police officer close behind. I want to yell something to him, anything. He's on his radio and keeping an eye on us. I don't know how far this trail goes, and I don't know if Mrs. White has any idea what she's doing. She continues her ranting about how she'll keep us safe, safe, safe.

I decide I need to try and make Mrs. White see that right now we're not safe, safe, safe, but I have to be careful because she's so crazy. "Grammy, I love you!" I start, hoping to break her from her tirade. "Please listen, I love you! I will always love you. You saved me from my horrible life. I want to continue living. You said you'll keep us safe, but right now we're not safe. I'm afraid you're going to crash the car. Please stop. I LOVE YOU! Please, please stop!"

It works. "Oh Julie, you do love me," Mrs. White says. "How I dreamed of this day."

She slows the car way down and acts like there isn't a police car on our tail. "Oh, my Jason and Julie, look right out the window. It's a mother moose and her two babies. We must get out and see them. I'm so, so happy. Look, it's just like I'm the mother moose and the two calves are you and little Jason."

ROGER

Nearly One in Three People Know Someone
Addicted to Opioids; More than Half of Millennials
believe it is Easy to Get Illegal Opioids

May 06, 2018

CHAPTER 62

As I was driving to pick up Mom, I got a call from Officer Cruz.

"Roger, Detective Harrison wants you to know they found Mrs. White driving on Route 6 near Greenville, Maine. The police are in pursuit. They believe the kids are in the car. Detective Harrison told the Maine State Police you'd meet them at the Greenville Police Department."

"Are the kids safe, Officer?" I asked, panicking. "What do you mean when you say the police are in pursuit?"

"The police are following Mrs. White at a safe distance trying to get her to pull over," Officer Cruz assured me. "By the time you get there, I know they'll be in police custody. No need to worry, Roger, we've found your kids."

No need to worry, she says—all I've done is worry. "Thank you, Officer. I should be there by four o'clock."

I hung up the phone and wondered if I should stop to get Mom. I had to tell her about the kids, and I had to convince her that July is really her granddaughter. Five hours in the car should do it, I hoped.

I called her after I hung up with Officer Cruz. "Mom, they found the kids. They're in Greenville, Maine. I'm going to pick them up. I really hope you'll come with me. I need you, Mom. I need to stay sane and safe on the way," I said.

"I'll throw together a few sandwiches and meet you in the driveway," she said. "Oh Roger, this is such great news. I'm so, so happy. I can't wait to hug Abe. I've also been thinking about July, and I've been praying so hard. I'll be ready in less than five minutes."

When I pulled up in front of the house Mom was waiting in the driveway with a cooler and a bag. She literally jumped into the truck, hugged me, and said, "Let's go, time's a wastin'."

After a few minutes, Mom started speaking. "I've been thinking and praying," she said. "Father Dube has really helped me understand that you must adopt July."

I just stared at her. I couldn't believe the change.

"Now just hear me out, Roger," she said. "That girl is all alone in the world. When Abe's with us all he talks about is Sissy. We can't separate them after all they've been through. I know this will be hard, but I'm here for you and so are your sisters—all of them."

I didn't even know how to begin, "Oh Mom, I just... of course I'm adopting July. I'm so overwhelmed by all your support, I don't even know what to say."

"When you were with Abe's mother, I wasn't happy. I don't have to tell you that, but Roger, little Abe is such a joy. Knowing he was in danger, ohhh, I just can't," she said, beginning to get choked up. "I had a strong feeling that if July was with him, he'd be safe. I started to think of all that little girl has been through. I promised God that if Abe was returned to us safely, I'd be sure that July would have a wonderful life. I'll do everything I can for her."

"I can't tell you how much your support means," I tell her. "I've been beating myself up for leaving Abe and July with Jenny. Why didn't I see what was happening? I sometimes think I knew what was going on and just ignored it. Oh Mom, I have so much I want to do for both kids. I just can't wait to find them."

JULY

Mental Health and Opioid Dependence: How Are They Connected?

Medically reviewed by Timothy J. Legg, Ph.D., CRNP — Written by Stephanie Watson — Updated on October 16, 2019

CHAPTER 63

The moose looked so peaceful. They're in a little field munching on grass. Mrs. White is just getting out of the car to take Abe out of his car seat when I hear:

"Put your hands on top of your head, now."

It's the voice of the police officer who's been following us for the last twenty minutes. I jump out of the car, not sure what I'm going to do. Suddenly, I realize I don't want anything bad to happen to Mrs. White.

"Officer, please don't hurt her. She was just trying to show us a moose," I say.

"It's okay, Julie. We'll get through this," Mrs. White assures me with her hands on top her head.

The police officer begins saying those things you hear police say on TV. "You have the right to remain silent...."

I start to cry. What does this mean? If Mrs. White is arrested, what will happen to us? I realize Abe is still in the car. He's still crying for Daddy. I walk over to let him out of his car seat.

"Policeman, hi Policeman," Abe says. He doesn't seem to realize "Grammy" is being arrested.

The police officer puts handcuffs on Mrs. White and puts her in the back of the police car. When he's finished, he comes over to talk to us. Smiling, he squats down to my level and says, "You must be July and Abe."

I'm not sure what to say, but Abe says, "No Abe, Jason."

The police officer looks a little confused. "I'm July Krativitz and this is my brother Abe LaMarche," I say.

"My name is Officer Williams. We have been in contact with the Maplewood, New Hampshire police. They let us know Abe's father is on his way to pick you up. We have a report that says you've been kidnapped by Mrs. White. Is this correct?

"I think she was trying to save us, Officer. We had a tricky life back in Maplewood," I say. "For a while, at least, Mrs. White seemed to be the only person to care about us." I realize that for a long time no one cared about me. Mrs. White may be crazy, but she genuinely cared for me. I can feel tears and try to push them back.

"I'm glad we found you. Another police officer, Officer Hopkins, is on her way to pick you up and bring you to Greenville Police Station. I'm going to take Mrs. White there too," Officer Williams says.

"Why can't we come with you?" I ask. "I'm worried about Grammy. I mean, yeah, she did kidnap us, but she never hurt us. Well, she did hurt…" I try to speak, but I can't say it. I just start crying.

"It's okay July—it's okay. We'll make sure both of you are safe," Officer Williams says.

"No cry, Sissy. No cry," Abe says, patting my back.

This just makes me cry more. I start thinking about everything that's happened to me these past few days. I have so many emotions. Relief that Abe's calling me Sissy and we're no longer with Mrs. White. At the same time, I'm scared about what'll happen to me and Mrs. White. I know I should be angry with her but right now, I'm don't want anything bad to happen to her. I don't think she wanted to hurt us. Then I think about what she did to Mom, and I hate her. I'm overwhelmed and confused.

Soon another police car and a tow truck drive down the dirt path. Mrs. White is sitting in the back of the police car looking straight ahead. I want to go over and tell her so many things, but I just keep crying.

Officer Hopkins comes over to us. She's really kind. She reminds me of Ms. Paulson, my language arts teacher in Maplewood. She has the same haircut, short on one side and longer on the other, and the same brown eyes. I trust her right away for some reason.

"Hi July, Abe. I'm Officer Hopkins. You're going to come with me. We're going to the Greenville Police Station to wait for your father," she says.

I let her take us over to her cruiser, and I'm surprised to see that there's a car seat in the back. "Do you hear that, Abe?" I say. "Daddy's coming. "

I'm not sure what to think. Roger's coming for Abe, but what about me? I don't even remember my father. I guess this is when I'll have to go to a foster home. I sure hope it's better than the one April had to go to. I watch Officer Hopkins putting Abe in his car seat and start crying again. How am I going to leave Abe? I haven't really processed this.

"I spoke to Officer Cruz in Maplewood," Officer Hopkins says. "She told me your dad is on his way. He should be here in just a few more hours."

I decide I need to bring this up. "Um, Officer Hopkins, Roger isn't my father. Does this mean I'll have to go to a foster home?" I need to know. I have to get myself ready.

"I'm sorry, July, I can only tell you what Officer Cruz told me. She said to tell July and Abe that their father is coming, and he can't wait to see them You've been through so much, sweetie, and I know there are many people who are praying for you. As a matter of fact, a few of them are waiting for you at the station."

I try to think of who would be waiting for me. I mean, I didn't really get to know a lot of people in Maplewood. I think of the few short days we've been here in Greenville, but they feel like weeks. I start to remember what brought us here and what Mrs. White confessed to me about Mom. It makes me really, really angry.

"Officer Hopkins, you know that Mrs. White killed my mother, right?" I ask.

"Oh July, I'm so sorry," Officer Hopkins tells me. No, I didn't know that. Would it be okay if I gave you a hug?"

I can't speak, so I nod my head, yes. As tears flow down my face.

Officer Hopkins hugs me and says, "Let it out, It's okay. You're safe now." She hugs me while I cry so much, I start to hiccup. Once I'm able to get myself together, Officer Hopkins hands me a tissue she's pulled from a small tissue package in her pocket. " I have no idea what happened to your mother, " Officer Hopkins says quietly, putting her hand on my shoulder, "When we get back to the station would you tell that to Detective Williams? Please understand that whatever you have to say is very important."

I nod my head again and climb in the backseat of the cruiser with Abe. "No cry Sissy, no cry," he says. I wonder what's going on in his head.

We pull up to the Greenville police station and I see Mrs. White being taken inside.

"Bye- bye Grammy," Abe says.

"Yup, bye-bye Grammy," I say.

We walk into the station, and I see Ms. Ellis. She's with Bryce and someone I'm guessing is his father. All of them come over without saying anything. Ms. Ellis gives me a hug and tells me she'll stay with me until Roger shows up. "I called Bryce's dad when I found out what was really going on," she says.

"My name is really July," I say.

"Hi July," Bryce says.

"I'm overwhelmed by all of this," is all I can manage to say.

"Julie—I mean, July—I had no idea you were kidnapped," Bryce says. "Why didn't you tell me? I could have helped you."

I don't say anything, but I start to cry again.

"I'm sorry, I didn't mean to make you cry," Bryce says.

"It's OK, July," the man next to Bryce says. "I'm Bryce's father, but you can call me Russ. When Ms. Ellis called us, I stopped by your place and tried to figure out what you wanted to bring home. There's so much stuff there, including a cat. If you let me know what you want to bring, I can get it together for you."

"Um, I don't know what we really have," I say. "I mean, sure, there's Annie the cat, but she's really Mrs. White's cat."

"Annie, Annie," Abe says.

"I guess we should take Annie," I say. "I mean she can't just be alone." As I say this, I start thinking about all the things Mrs. White bought for us and I start to get overwhelmed again. I have all the Percy Jackson books, new clothes, and new shoes. I can't believe all the things Mrs. White did for us, but I also remember what I had to give up in exchange for all of it: my mom.

"I think we should just take Annie," I say more firmly. "Ms. Ellis, there are clothes and books and things at the house that I don't want. Can you be sure that they go to someone who needs them. Maybe Sarah would want the Percy Jackson books? You might know someone who could use my clothes. I don't want them."

"Oh July, I most certainly will be sure your things go to someone who needs them," Ms. Ellis says. "But are you sure? We don't have to do anything unless it's okay with you."

"Yeah, I'm sure," I say again to Ms. Ellis. "There are lots of things that I need to leave here. I also need you to know that my mother really is dead." As I say this, I start to get teary again. "Mrs. White, my so-called grandmother, killed her. She told me about it like it was perfectly fine."

"July, would you be willing to tell that to Detective Williams?" Officer Hopkins asks.

"I'll be with you the entire time," Ms. Ellis says. "You're not alone, July. We'll all be with you. You're such a brave person, but if you don't want to say anything, that's okay too. It's your call, so just remember that."

"We'll stay with Abe," Bryce says.

. "It's still weird calling you July. I like it, I just—I don't know. Anyway, Dad and I can hang out with Abe, right Dad?"

"July, you do what you want," Russ tells me. "Talk to the detective, wait for your dad, whatever."

I look at these people who don't really know me, but that I know would keep me safe without killing my mom. "I'm ready to talk to the detective," I tell Officer Hopkins.

"I'll come with you," Ms. Ellis says in a way that lets me know I can trust her. "I don't want you to be alone. Please know that I'm here to help and support you."

"Go ahead, July, we'll watch Abe," Bryce says. "You got this."

"Thanks, Ms. Ellis, I'd really like it if you could be with me," I say. "And thanks, Bryce, for watching Abe. He really likes trucks."

"He'll be fine," Bryce says. "Take your time. Come on, Abe, let's go look at the police cars."

Ms. Ellis and I walk to Detective Williams's office. The door is open, and Officer Hopkins is inside. "Thank you so much for coming," she says. "Detective Williams, this is July Krativitz, the girl I was telling you about, and this is Ms. Ellis, a guidance counselor from Moosehead Lake Regional School."

Detective Williams shakes our hands. "Officer Hopkins tells me you have something you'd like to tell me about Mrs. White and your mother."

"Take your time, July," Ms. Ellis says. "I'm right here for you."

"Okay, well, Mrs. White told me that she killed my mother," I tell Detective Williams.

"July," Detective Williams says, "I need you to think very hard. Are those the words Mrs. White said, 'I killed your mother?'"

"Well, not really. She didn't say 'I killed your mother.' She told me God told her to put my mother out of her misery. She told me if Mom was dead, we would be safe with her, and our lives would be better."

"Thank you for telling me that, July. I need you to understand that when this case goes to trial, you'll probably have to testify. Do you know what that means?" Detective William asks.

"I think so," I say. "I just know Mrs. White killed Mom. I asked her why she did it and she told me God wanted her to keep Abe and me safe. She wanted to keep Abe and me as her kids."

"Okay, July. You did a great job," Detective Williams says. "I'm going to share this with the Maplewood police. I'm sure they'll contact you. Officer Hopkins told me your father was coming, and he should be here soon."

"You did a great job," Ms. Ellis tells me. "I know this is hard for you. There's a really great ice cream store down the street--would you like to go? My treat. I'm sure Abe would like something too."

I'd love anything to eat right now, especially something sweet. "That sounds wonderful. We haven't really had anything to eat since breakfast."

"Oh dear, you must be starving. Maybe you'd rather have pizza?" Ms. Ellis says.

"Pizza would be great," I say.

As we leave Detective Williams's office, I look down the hall and see Mrs. White sitting on a bench, still in handcuffs. She doesn't see me. It's really hard to look at her. I suddenly feel so guilty about what I said to Detective Williams. I mean, everything I said was true, but because of what I said Mrs. White will go to jail for a long time. I think she did what she did to Mom and us because she really cares. I know that sounds really messed up, but it's what I feel like.

"Julie—I mean, July, are you okay?" Ms. Ellis asks.

I just point toward Mrs. White. I try to say something, but I can't find the words.

Ms. Ellis seems to know what I'm going through, because she says "You must have some conflicting feelings about Mrs. White. She did do some nice things for you. But you also have to remember the things she did that were wrong. She had no right to take you and Abe and change your names. What she did to your mother was horrible. Don't doubt yourself, July."

I start crying again. Ms. Ellis wraps me in a hug, and it feels so good.

"Let it out, July. You've been through so much. This nightmare you've been living will be over soon."

I cry for what seems like hours, until there are no tears left. I look up and notice that Mrs. White is gone from the bench. I'm not sure where she went, and I don't really care.

Abe is playing with Bryce and Russ when I come back. They've found some trucks and are zooming around on the floor. Abe is so happy. I think about what he was doing just a few hours ago, crying for his daddy and trapped in a car with a crazy woman. He seems to have forgotten all that. "We were going to get some pizza. Would you like to join us?" Ms. Ellis asks Bryce and his father.

"It's all right," Russ says. "As long as you and Abe are safe, I think we can be going."

I suddenly realize I'll probably never see Bryce again. I walk over and just give him a hug. It isn't weird at all; it seems natural, like we've been friends for more than just a week. "Thanks for everything," I say.

"When you get back to Maplewood, send me an email. It would be good to stay in touch." Bryce says, going over to the counter to write down his email address. As he hands it to me, he says, "If you ever need to talk, reach out. Losing your mom is a big deal. It never gets easier, just different."

"Thanks, Bryce. I'm really glad I met you," I say.

Bryce and his father wave goodbye and walk out the door. Going back to Maplewood is starting to feel real. I'm not sure how I feel about leaving Moosehead. The reason I came is so convoluted, but I really did like what I discovered here. It's a beautiful place and the people are caring. I loved the school; having nine kids in your class is really cool.

"Come on kids, pizza's waiting," Ms. Ellis says, walking out the police station door.

I grab Abe's hand and start walking toward the pizza shop with Ms. Ellis. As we're walking, I think I see Sarah, the girl from my grief support group. I still feel like I need to talk to her about her dad's death.

"I've been thinking a lot about Sarah, the girl from our group," I tell Ms. Ellis. "I'm worried that she's too ashamed to really share what's going on with her."

"What do you mean?" Ms. Ellis asks.

"Well, she didn't share how her dad died like the other kids did. She was so quiet and uncomfortable when the others were talking. Having a parent who's a drug addict is shameful. Your parents aren't supposed to be drug addicts. That's the part that's hard to share with people. I know because I tried to hide this part from everyone too. It's fine for a parent to die in a car crash or have cancer, but it's not okay if your parent dies from a drug overdose. I think that could be a real problem for Sarah."

"You're right, July, having your parent die of a drug overdose is difficult for most kids to talk about," Ms. Ellis says. "" I can't tell you what happened to Sarah's dad but I wish you could share those insights with her. I think she could use someone like you in her life. I hope she can get to a point where she feels comfortable talking about what happened."

"Yeah," I say. "Maybe if I got to know her a little bit better, I could share what was going on with my mom. Maybe then she'd see that she isn't the only one."

"I guess we have to do a better job helping kids feel comfortable sharing," Ms. Ellis says. "There are a lot of kids whose parents have problems with drugs. It's a crisis in our country right now. I'm sure when you get back to Maplewood, you'll realize you're not the only one who's had a parent with a drug problem."

"I guess you're right," I say. "I'd like to meet some other kids who had a mom like mine. I always thought I was the only one. It was really hard trying to concentrate in class knowing Abe was alone with Mom. I mean, I worried that Mom would be out of it or sleeping and Abe would find her drugs and eat them. There were times I worried I'd come home to find both of them dead."

"Oh, how horrible," Ms. Ellis says. "I know your guidance counselor, Mrs. Masterson. I worked with her when I was at UNH, and I'm sure she knows a support group you could join. I can call her and let her know."

I can't really picture Ms. Ellis being friends with Mrs. Masterson. I mean, Mrs. Masterson seems pretty clueless about what life is like now. She's older, like Mrs. White's age. She seems to spend most of the time with the student council kids doing community service. I don't think she even knows or cares who I am, I can't talk to her the way I can with Ms. Ellis.

"Mrs. Masterson isn't like you, Ms. Ellis. She's not someone I can open up to."

Ms. Ellis just smiles. I don't think she knows what to say. We get to the pizza place and find a booth. Ms. Ellis orders our pizza and hands a juice box to Abe and lemonade to me. Abe looks out the window, there's a woman walking two dogs. " Goggie,"he says. Ms.

Ellis and I giggle at the cuteness of his speech. As our pizza is placed on the table, Abe continues looking out the window, "Daddy, truck Sissy," he yells clapping his hands, " Daddy truck."

As I look up, I see it really is Roger's truck.

ROGER

A generation of heroin orphans

By <u>Deborah Feyerick</u>, CNN
Updated 9:03 AM EDT, Mon May 1, 2017

CHAPTER 64

It was so surreal driving with Mom to pick up the kids. She shared so much with me. We talked about Jenny and Beckie's problems with drugs. I guess I never realized how difficult Beckie's drug addiction was for both my parents. My mom was convinced it contributed to my father's death. I can't believe how much money they spent trying to get her help. I guess you do anything for your kids.

When I told Mom that the police thought Jenny was involved with JD before she died, she told me she hoped they locked him up for a long time. She had tears in her eyes when she looked over at me. "That JD ruined your sister and killed Abe's mother. I hope he rots in jail."

I certainly agreed with her on that. It was hard to watch these two amazing women, Jenny, and Beckie, destroy their lives because they were addicted to drugs. Hopefully it wasn't too late for Beckie too.

"You know," my mom said, "when I was talking to your sisters about July, Beckie was the first one who said that we had to do whatever we can to help that little girl. I really think if July is in Becky's life it will help her stay clean."

I thought about this. I didn't know if I wanted July to be around Beckie, since July's seen so many problems with drugs already. I didn't know if I could trust my sister to be with her, but I didn't share this with my mother.

"July's has been through so much," I said. "I think it'll take her a while before she feels safe. I also have to figure out where we're all going to live."

"What do you mean? You'll live with me. I have plenty of space and I already have a room and toys for Abe. July can sleep in Michelle and Beckie's old room. Oh my, I feel horrible, I didn't get July anything—I mean, I packed books and toys for Abe, but I really want her to know she's welcome."

"I'm sure you can take her shopping when we're home," I told her. "I was just thinking that I'd get a place in Maplewood so July wouldn't have to change schools."

"I'm sure July could adjust to school in Berwick. It might be good for her to have a fresh start. I know this won't be easy for any of us, but we have to try. I just feel horrible about how unwelcoming I was when you first got together with July's mother."

"Her name was Jenny, Mom," I said.

"Okay, with Jenny," she said in a tone that let me know she'd never accept her as an important person in my life. "It's just so hard for me to put my finger on it. I wanted everything to be perfect for you. You've always gone after girls who need fixing. Remember that girlfriend you had in high school, Marissa? I never met a girl so needy. Jenny reminded me of her, and she already had a child. I knew she would be the kind of woman to hurt you but that's all in the past. These last few days with Abe gone missing, not knowing what was happening, I did a lot of thinking and praying. I know helping July is the right thing to do." As Mom told me all this, I felt like she was trying to convince herself more than me.

"I can't tell you how much having you here and wanting to help July and Abe means to me. I mean, they've been through so much. You've also been through so much with Beckie and Michelle and her kids. Are you sure you're up for this?" I asked, wondering if she'd thought it through.

Mom turned to me and held onto my arm letting me know she was serious. "When your dad and I went to counseling with Beckie the first time she was in rehab, we had to learn what one day at a time means. I'm not very good at it, and sometimes I forget, but this is something we have to do. That little girl will need stability, help, support, and counseling. I'm sure about this. We'll have some rules in our house, but the biggest rule will be honesty and building trust. Father Dube gave me the name of some counselors we could meet with when we're all ready. I think this will be good for you, Roger. There are parenting groups and grief support groups, all kinds of things."

As my mother was talking, I started to get nervous. Of course Abe and July would live with me, but it wasn't going to be easy. I was excited to see that Mom wanted to help me, but at the same time I wondered if it'd be too much. I thought about finding my own place and just getting Mom's help when I needed it.

I'd never been up to Moosehead Lake, and as we got off 95 and onto Route 5, I understood how rural the place really is. There was literally nothing there, just a few houses and a cow here or there. We drove for another hour and finally I saw the sign that said *Welcome to Greenville, Maine.*

My GPS took us to the police station. Mom and I jumped out of the truck and ran inside. I was so anxious to see Abe and July that I forgot to shut my door. Mom just grabbed my arm, looked into my eyes, and said, "It's going to be okay, Roger."

"I just realized that Abe and July might not know Jenny's dead," I said, getting teary. "How am I going to tell them?"

"I'm with you," Mom said, giving me a hug. "You love those kids. It'll be hard, but they have you and you have me. Now let's go bring them home."

We walked into the station and over to the desk. I explained to the officer that my name was Roger LaMarche, and I was here to pick up my kids. He asked for an ID, then took me and Mom to a little room and asked us to wait.

Soon a detective came in without Abe or July. I got a little panicky then, so I stood up and asked, "Where are the kids? Are they okay?"

"I'm Detective Williams," he said. "And I'm sorry, ma'am, I don't know your name."

"I'm Roger's mother," Mom told him. "Where are Abe and July?"

Detective Williams sat down, which made me a little nervous. "Abe and July are safe," he said. "They're at the pizza place down the street with a guidance counselor from the school July was going to."

"July was at school. Why wouldn't she tell the people at school what happened?" I asked.

"Mr. LaMarche, July is a very brave girl. She's experienced many traumas. She told me Mary White confessed to her that she killed her mother." Detective Williams stated this very matter-of-factly.

This freaked me out. "What do mean? July knows her mother is dead. Oh my God, this is awful. How did she handle it?"

Detective Williams continued speaking. "I just want to make you aware that July's agreed to testify against Mary White. I've given her statement to the Rockingham County District Attorney's Office."

"What do you mean?" I asked. "She's been through so much. Is this really necessary?" I realized then that I just needed to see July and let her know I was here for her. Her life had been so hard, and this piece may have been too much.

"Listen, Detective," I said. "I want this woman to go to prison for a very long time, but right now I just need to see my kids."

"I understand, Mr. LaMarche," Detective Williams said. "I just wanted you to be aware of what was happening. I asked Ms. Ellis to bring the children back when they're done with their pizza."

"Well, Detective, I want to see them now," I said. "I'll meet them at the pizza place. Just tell me where it is."

"It's at the end of the street, Detective Williams said. "I'll grab a car and come with you to make sure the kids are safe with you. Call me if you have questions, or if there's anything more, we can help with."

"I'm just anxious to see the children," Mom said. "Please, can we go now?"

"I'll lead the way," Detective Williams said.

JULY

Loving and losing an addict

By Barbara Theodosiou
Updated 10:50 AM EST, Wed December 23, 2015, CNN

CHAPTER 65

Seeing Roger's truck makes me so nervous. I know now that my life is about to change forever. Ms. Ellis puts her arm around me; I guess my fear was showing on my face.

"July, I know I've only known you for a little while, but what I do know is that you're brave, amazing, smart, and a survivor. I know you're nervous, but believe me, there are people in your corner. I'll help you as much as I can—I promise," Ms. Ellis says.

I don't know what to say. I'm not sure I believe what Ms. Ellis is telling me. I glance over at Abe, who's happily eating his cheese pizza. I wonder if he has any idea what we've been through. He's so innocent. He looks up at me with his big, beautiful eyes and smiles. "Pizza good, Sissy," he says, trying to push a piece into my mouth.

I give him a big hug and start tickling him.

"Stop, Sissy, stop," he says, laughing. Suddenly, he leaps from his chair. "Daddy, Daddy!" he yells, running to Roger.

Roger, his mother, and Detective Williams are walking into the pizza place. I get a weird butterfly feeling in my stomach. I'm not sure what's going to happen.

.

"Oh July, you're safe," Mrs. LaMarche says, grabbing me in a tight hug and not letting go. "I'm so sorry I didn't see how wonderful you really are. All that's going to change from now on. I want you to call me Memere. Abe is so, so lucky to have you as his sister."

I don't know what to say. I mean, I just had one strange grandmother experience. Roger's mother never really treated me like I was special. Her grandkids call her Memere; I call her Mrs. LaMarche. She never really seemed to like me. I guess I only really saw her that one time I went to her house for Christmas. She had lots of gifts for the other kids, but all she gave me was a pair of mittens. She never invited me over or anything like that. I'm suddenly confused and more nervous.

I look over at Roger. He's crying a lot, and it looks like he's going to squeeze Abe to death. He finally gives Abe to his mother and gives me a big hug.

"July, there are so many things I need to tell you, but the first is that you're safe now. You're coming home with Abe and me. I promise that from now on you'll truly be safe. I'm so, so sorry that you had to go through everything you went through." As he says all this he's sobbing like a baby, so it's pretty hard to understand him.

Roger finally gets himself together. "July, I abandoned you when I left after Abe was born. I understood that your mother had a problem with drugs, but I just pretended you were fine. That's something I will regret for the rest of my life. You were, and still are, way too young to have gone through what you did. I knew deep down it was wrong to leave you and Abe with your mother. I don't know how you can possibly learn to trust me, but I think we should try. Are you okay with that?"

I look over at Ms. Ellis; she's smiling and has tears in her eyes too, like this is a happy reunion scene. I don't know how to feel or what to say.

"Roger, is Mom really dead?" I ask.

He looks at me with this really kind expression. I see the Roger who used to wake me up in the morning and make me breakfast. The Roger who took me to the bus stop. The Roger who likes to sing pop songs. I remember all the things he'd do to make me feel safe when he lived with Mom and me.

"Yes, Princess, your Mom died the day you went missing. I'm so sorry," he says again, wrapping me in a hug and kissing the top of my head.

Now it's my turn to cry. I guess I still had a little bit of hope that maybe Mom was alive and could get better. "I guess I was hoping Mrs. White was lying," I sob. "I can't believe she really killed Mom."

"No cry Sissy," Abe says, coming over to me.

"It's okay, Abe," Mrs. LaMarche says, and I feel her hand on my back too. "Sissy needs to cry. She can cry all she wants. July, you're so brave, and this is so much to go through. Roger and I have made a cozy bedroom for you at my house. Abe already has a room there. Tomorrow, or whenever you're up to it, we can go shopping for things you'll need."

"Oh Mrs. LaMarche, I don't know if I can go shopping," I say. "Mrs. White bought me lots of things. I told Ms. Ellis to donate most of it. I don't want to remember that this woman who bought me those things is the same woman who killed my mother."

"Of course," she says. "I don't want to put any pressure on you. We'll go through this together. It's going to take both of us time to trust and get to know each other, and time certainly is something we have a lot of. I know you've been calling me Mrs. LaMarche for a while, but I really would like it if you could call me Memere. If that's too hard you can call me Viv. I just want you to feel at home and comfortable." As she says this, I know she means it.

"July, it looks like you're going to be okay," Ms. Ellis says. "You certainly have people who care for you. I don't think you have to worry about going to a foster home."

"Oh, July, I would never, ever let that happen to you," Roger says. "Abe needs his sister and so do I. Are you ready to go?"

I look at Ms. Ellis and start to think of all I've been through in the last week, or even the last two years. Am I ready to go? I have no idea, but I'd like to try.

"I think I am, Roger."

ROGER

*The US Opioid Crisis Is Pulling Families Under at an
Alarming Rate, and We Need to Take Action*

August 3, 2020*by* <u>MURPHY MORONEY</u> *Popsugar*

CHAPTER 66

I couldn't believe how much July and Abe had grown. Or maybe they hadn't—they just seemed older. Maybe it was all they'd been through, or maybe I just hadn't spent enough time really looking. I was so consumed with Jenny that I neglected the kids. I really didn't know how I could make it up to them, but I knew I had to try.

"Thank you, Ms. Ellis, for all your help," I said.

"Call me Charlotte," she said. "July is something. I hope you'll stay in touch, July. You have my email, right?"

"I'll make sure she does," I said.

"Mr. LaMarche, I believe the New Hampshire's District Attorney's office will be in touch with you," Officer Williams said. "Please don't hesitate to call me with any questions."

"Thank you. I know getting through this is going to be hard, but I'm certainly up to the challenge," I said, giving July a reassuring hug.

When I was putting Abe up into his car seat I said, "Up you go, Abe."

He said, "I no Abe, I Jason." I look at him puzzled. Did he forget his name? Is there something else going on?

"You are Abe," I said. "You are my Abe."

"Grammy say no Abe, Jason," he said to me.

July stepped in and grabbed Abe in a tight hug as she continued putting him in his car seat. "You are Abe. No more Jason. No more

Grammy. Grammy is all gone. Abe, Daddy, Memere, and Sissy are here. We're going to Memere's house to stay."

"Sissy, come too, Memere?" Abe asked.

"Yes, she is," Mom said. "She's always going to be at Memere's with you."

"Sissy at Mommy's house," Abe says.

I could feel the tension from everyone, but July was the one to speak up. "No more Grammy or Grammy's house," she said calmly. "No more Mommy or Mommy's house, just Daddy, Memere, Abe, and Sissy."

"Sissy, no Julie, Sissy," Abe said.

"That's right Abe, no more Julie," July said, kissing Abe and going around to her side of the car. "I will never, ever be Julie again, and you will never be Jason."

I felt the hesitation in July as she climbed into the truck. I wanted to reassure her, but I didn't know how. I wanted her to tell me everything that had happened to get them to Greenville. I wanted to know what her life was like with her mother before she died. I knew I might never know the answers, but I also understood that July would tell me all this in her own time, someday.

JULY

Anger, Hope from Families and Survivors of Opioid Crisis

By CARLA K. JOHNSON March 26, 2019 AP NEWS

CHAPTER 67

?

The drive back to Berwick seems really long. I don't remember it taking that long to get up to Moosehead. Abe falls asleep and so does Mrs. LaMarche. I'm happy that Roger plays his NSYNC CD and doesn't force me to talk about what happened. I just don't want to relive anything. I just want to be quiet.

Soon I realize both Roger and I are singing "A Little More Time on You." This just makes me start laughing—like, really hard.

"Is my singing really that bad?" he jokes. "Come on, I thought you were my girl"

"I don't know," I say, chuckling. "I just forgot about this part of you. I also remember that my guidance counselor told me that sometimes our emotions are confused, and we laugh when we think we should cry. I'm not sure why I'm laughing, but my bet is that it's because you really wish you were in a boy band."

"I really have missed you, July," he says teasingly before he goes back to singing off key.

I can't believe how easy our banter is. It's not forced. It's just silly. I hope this is how life will be. I know it won't always be like this, but I'm glad he knows this is what I need.

When we get back to the house Mrs. LaMarche shows me all around. Maybe she doesn't remember that I've been in her house before. She wants me to be sure I don't feel like a guest. She brings me up to my room and I notice some of my mom's paintings on the walls. I get a little teary.

Then Roger and Abe come in. "I really want you to have part of your Mom with you July," Roger says, full of emotion. "There were so many parts of her that were amazing. Her art was just one of those pieces. When I look in your eyes, I see all the parts of her that were good."

"When you're home, remember it's okay to talk about your mother," Mrs. LaMarche says. Don't be afraid to tell us your feelings. We're here to help you."

I'm overwhelmed and not sure what to say, so I say nothing. I walk over to one of the paintings. It's a beach scene outside of my grandfather's fish house. I know this place well; it's where I was the happiest with Mom.

Roger comes over and puts his hands on my shoulders. "July, I talked to Aunt Susan. We had your mother cremated. We want to bring her ashes to your grandfather's fish house and have a small ceremony. I'd be really happy if you could read something."

"I know just the right poem to read," I tell him, "but it's in my journal at Maplewood Middle School."

"In that case, I'll call the principal and see if I can pick it up on my way home from work tomorrow," he says. "You and I also have to talk about school. Now that you're living in Berwick, you'll most likely need to change schools. How do you feel about this?"

"I guess it would be good to start over, but I'll really miss Maddie," I say, suddenly realizing that I really need to see her.

"I talked to Maddie while you were missing," Roger says. "She really wants to see you too, and she's always welcome here. Friends like Maddie are friends for life. Maybe you'd even like her to come to your mother's service?"

"Thanks, Roger, that would be great," I say.

"Do you have her number? You could call her now from my phone."

"Can I send her a text?" I ask. I don't know—for some reason, talking on the phone right now seems weird. "Would it be okay if I met her tomorrow?"

"Tell you what," Roger says, "you text her and see if she can meet you tomorrow after school. I'll take you there to find your book and check in with the teachers. How does that sound?"

"I'm not sure. I mean, I don't want all kinds of people feeling bad for me or looking at me weird because my mother's dead, and I really don't want to see Mr. Win," I say, thinking how weird and awkward he'd be.

"That's fine," Roger says. "You text Maddie and tell her about your mother's service on Saturday. Here's my cell."

"Thanks," I say as Roger leaves. I know Maddie's number by heart, so I go into messaging and type it in.

Rogl: Hey Maddie, It's July. I'm living with Roger now

Maddief: OMG Is it really you?

Rogl: It's really me. How are things with Nate?

Maddief: Never mind how r u?

Rogl: Oh, Maddie I miss you so much.

Maddief: I miss you 2. When can we get together? I want to see Abe.

Rogl: Roger says I can see you anytime. We're having a service for my mother on Saturday. Can you come? Also, can you get my writing journal from Ms. Paulson? Roger was going to go to school to get it, but I don't really want him reading it. If you get it, I could come over and pick it up.

Maddief: Done deal. I miss you sooooo much. I can't wait to see you and tell you everything.

Rogl: Text Roger and let us know when to meet you. See you soon.

Maddie: Bye

I walk downstairs to give Roger his phone. Abe is sitting with him in a big reclining chair, holding his teddy bear. He's almost asleep. Abe looks so content. His eyes keep closing and so do Roger's. I don't ever remember seeing Abe like this with Mom. It must have been really hard for him to go from Mom's to Roger's every week.

I decide I need to take a picture. I guess I just want to keep this moment, the moment that Abe is truly where he's supposed to be. I wonder if I'll ever feel like that.

I feel a hand on my shoulder, then turn around to see Mrs. LaMarche. "It almost killed Roger when you and Abe went missing. He just kept saying over and over, 'If July's with him, she'll make sure he's safe. I know she'll keep him safe.' I hope you know how much you mean to him I hope in time you'll come to trust us as your true family."

I look over at my brother and Roger, peaceful and content. I turn to Mrs. LaMarche and try out the grandmother name, "Yes, Memere, I really hope so too," then reach out and give her a hug.

It feels like maybe, just maybe, things will work out.

CHAPTER 68

On Saturday, Roger, Memere, Aunt Susan, Dom, Maddie, Abe, and I go down to North Hampton to leave Mom's ashes by the sea. Roger had Mom's ashes placed in a beautiful urn that looks like the ocean. I know Mom would really love it.

When we get to the front of the fish house that used to belong to my grandfather, Aunt Susan tells us to get into a circle and hold hands. She asks us to close our eyes and think of a favorite memory of Mom. Everyone's eyes are closed. The only sounds you can hear are the gulls cawing and the waves crashing to shore. It's a sunny day and the wind is calm, which is good if we have to throw ashes into the ocean. When I close my eyes and feel the warmth of the sun on my face, I can hear my mother's voice: "You're the best thing that's ever happened to me, July. Don't ever forget how amazing you are."

I open my eyes and see Mom laughing and splashing in the water. "I'm okay now, July. Your life is just beginning. Roger's a great guy, and I know the day he entered my life was a blessing. Tell your brother about the times you and I went down to the sea. Teach him how to build sandcastles and paint. I love you, my summer girl."

I don't think other people see or hear Mom. I finally hear Roger's voice saying, "July you have a poem that you want to read, right?"

I open my journal and look at the poem, the one Ms. Paulson thought was so amazing, the poem I wrote about Mom. I think this is the right place and time to share it.

The Sea
by July Krativitz

Sitting beside the sea
Listening to the waves
Feeling the sunshine on my face
This is a memory that I keep with me.
       Mom
Laughing, splashing, twirling me in the air.
Smelling the salt, tasting the sea.
Mom points to a crab
We watch as he digs himself into a protective hole.
Is that what you've done
       Mom?
Are these drugs your protective hole?
Why have you disappeared?
I want to go back to the sea with you.
I want to see you free.

When I finish reading everyone has tears in their eyes. Roger hands us all some of Mom's ashes. "It's time for Jenny to be free," he says, throwing her ashes into the sea.

As I let go of Mom's ashes and watch them dance on the waves, I know this is really goodbye. She's really gone now. I wonder what would have happened if Mom had never tried those horrible drugs. But that's not the life I'm supposed to have. I look over at Abe jumping over the cold waves, not really understanding that we're saying goodbye to his mother. *Don't worry, Mom, we'll be okay*, I think. I run over and twirl Abe around in the waves just like Mom used to do to me.

* * *

A few weeks after Mom's burial I receive a subpoena to testify at Mrs. White's trial. Roger and Memere keep telling me they'll be with me every step of the way, but I'm not sure how I'm supposed to feel about this whole thing. I know Mrs. White killed Mom. I also know she believed that by killing Mom she was saving Abe and me, but she never asked me if we needed saving. Her whole talking to God about this still freaks me out.

Memere takes me shopping before the trial, just the two of us. She tells me it'll be a girl's day. We go to Kohls, and she lets me pick out jeans and shirts for school, but she also helps me pick out a couple of dresses for the trial. She tells me she wants me to feel confident, but also look like I'm twelve. I'm not really sure what that's supposed to mean.

I end up getting a navy-blue pleated skirt, a white blouse, a red cardigan, and a simple pink dress with little white and yellow daisies on it. We also buy some pairs of new shoes. Memere oohs and ahhs as I try on each outfit. It's actually pretty fun.

We go out to lunch at Panera. Once we get our food, Memere pulls out this little wrapped box. She's teary-eyed as she says, "July, this is for you. I hope you'll keep it close to you. Remember that you're an important part of our family."

I open the little box and inside is a gold chain with a beautiful locket. I open the locket and on one side is a picture of Mom, Roger, and me, and on the other side is a picture of Memere, Roger, Abe, and me.

I don't even know what to say. I just keep looking at the pictures. I can feel tears flowing down my cheeks, and I look up to see Memere crying too.

"Do you want some help putting it on?" Memere asks.

"Yes, please," I say. "It's so beautiful, I don't even know what to say."

"You don't have to say anything," Memere says as she holds on to my hand. "It's important to me—to us—that you remember where you come from. We'll always be here for you no matter what. The next few days may be challenging, and I know you'll be feeling many different feelings, but remember who's in your locket. We'll always be there for you."

When we get back home, I notice a few cars in front of the house. I look over at Memere. She just smiles and says, "Hmm, I guess we should see who's here."

As I walk into the house, I notice Roger's sisters and all of their kids. Roger's holding Abe. He walks up to me and hands me an envelope. "Go ahead, open it," Roger says. "But you have to be really honest with me. I hope your answer will be yes."

I open the envelope and take out a legal-looking document. It's a petition to the court for Roger to be my legal guardian. As I'm reading it I get a chill. I would really be Roger's daughter. I'd never have to go to a foster home. As I look around at my new family, I know there's no place I'd rather be.

I look up at Roger and give him a giant hug. "Does this mean I can call you Dad?" I ask.

"I hope so, July," he says, kissing the top of my head.

CHAPTER 69

I put on my navy-blue skirt, white blouse, and red cardigan. I look at myself in the mirror and decide I need to put my hair in a ponytail. As I pick up the hairbrush, I realize my hand is shaking. My stomach is jumping around, and my hands are sweaty. I don't know if I can really do this.

There's a knock on my bedroom door; it's Memere. "You look perfect, July. Do you want me to help you with your locket?"

I can't believe I almost forgot to put it on. "That would be great, Memere. I don't know why I'm so nervous."

"Oh honey," Memere says, wrapping me in a hug. "What you're about to do is very hard, even for an adult. When you're on the witness stand, look right at me or your dad. Don't look at Mrs. White. You answer the questions truthfully. Take deep breaths. When this is over, we'll go out for a nice lunch anyplace you want."

The last thing I want to do is think about food. It's usually the only thing I can think of when I'm nervous.

We walk down the stairs and I see Abe playing with Dad. I look at this happy scene and suddenly realize that this would never have happened if Mrs. White had gotten her way.

"Sissy!" Abe says, leaping up and giving me a hug. "Play truck, play truck."

"Wow, you look great," Dad says. "How are you doing?" He sounds very concerned.

He looks great, too. He's dressed in a navy-blue suit. I don't think I've ever seen him in anything but blue jeans.

"I'm nervous, but I think I'll be okay as long as you're there," I say.

Memere's friend Mrs. Brady comes in. She's going to watch Abe while we're at the courthouse. "Abe, I just left the library and found so many books we can read," she says. "Say bye to Daddy, Sissy, and Memere." Abe grabs some of the books, ignoring everything else Mrs. Brady said.

"Good luck, July, I can be here as long as you need me," Mrs. Brady tells me before turning to my dad. "Abe and I will be fine, Roger. You just take care of your daughter."

We climb into the truck. Dad puts in NSYNC, of course, and he starts singing in his silly off-key way trying to make me laugh. When I smile at him, he stops singing and says, "I'm so proud of you, July, and I know your mother is too. I don't know too many kids who could have done what you've done. No matter what happens today, I have your back."

"So, do I," Memere adds.

It doesn't take very long to get to the courthouse. Roger parks the truck and I notice that I'm holding his hand as we walk inside. A very professionally dressed woman meets us as we enter. "Hello, I'm Hannah Carter, the district attorney," she says. "And you must be July."

I shake her hand and try to say "Hi," but my mouth is too dry, like my tongue is stuck to the roof of my mouth, so it comes out as less than a whisper.

Roger steps in. "I'm Roger, July's father, and this is my mother, Vivian LaMarche."

Ms. Carter shakes their hands too. "Nice to meet you. I wanted to go over some of the questions I'm going to ask you, July. I know this will be difficult, but I want you to just focus on me. Whenever you're nervous, just look at me. How does that sound?"

"My dad and grandmother said I could just look at them," I say.

"That would be fine too. Basically, I'm going to ask you to tell us when you realized you'd been kidnapped. I'll also ask you about when Mrs. White told you that she'd killed your mother. I'll ask you to tell the court everything you remember her saying. Do you think you can do this?"

"I'm really nervous," I admit. "I mean, if I tell the court everything Mrs. White did, what will happen to her?"

"Well, that's up to the jury and the judge," Mrs. Carter says. "You just need to tell the truth."

"Remember, July, you did nothing wrong," Dad adds. "Mrs. White should never have taken your mother's life or kidnapped you and Abe."

I look at Dad, who just a short while ago was still Roger. If Mrs. White hadn't done what she'd done, who would I be with now? Would Roger still have adopted me? I don't want to think about this.

"Okay, Ms. Carter, I'm ready," I say.

"Please call me Hannah," she says. "Remember, Mrs. White's lawyer is also going to ask you questions. I don't know what she'll ask, but if it sounds like something I don't like, I'll say, 'Objection.' How does that sound?"

It sounds scary, but I say, "Okay, I guess."

"Good. In that case I'm going to tell the bailiff and judge that you're here. Why don't you all wait out here until you're called in," she tells us more than asks us as she disappears into the courtroom.

"Would you like anything?" Memere asks. "I noticed a soda machine and a snack machine as I came in."

"Water would be great," I say.

Memere leaves and Dad comes over and gives me a hug, then kisses the top of my head. "I'm right here," he says reassuringly. "You'll be okay."

I'm not sure why I pick this time to ask, but I do. "Roger—I mean, Dad—if Mom was still alive, and you knew she was still using, would you have taken Abe?"

"Wow, that's a heavy question," he says, thinking. "I guess that was my thought on Friday before I found her. Why do you ask?"

"I don't know. I guess, I'm glad you're my dad now and everything, but would you have left me with Mom knowing she was using?" I don't know why I ask this. I mean, what was he supposed to do?

"Oh July," Dad says. "I was worried your mother was using again, and I knew I couldn't leave Abe in that situation. Honestly—I mean, really honestly—I'm not sure what would have happened to you. I hope I would have taken you with me. In fact, I know that right this very second. I'm so proud to have you as my daughter. I know it's impossible to what-if, but I often wonder how different our lives would be now if your mother had never used drugs."

"Me too," I say as Memere comes back with the water.

"You two look like you just had a deep conversation," Memere says.

"We were just what-iffing," Dad says. "Something you should probably never do."

"Oh no, never what-if," Memere says, hugging me away from Dad. "It'll make you crazy. At this point in my life I realize everything that happens is part of a great plan that we can't really understand. I'm happy that you're part of our family, July. I know that if things had turned out differently you might not be, and I would have missed out on a wonderful granddaughter."

"July Krativitz," the bailiff calls, "it's time for you to testify."

"I can't wait to be July LaMarche," I tell Dad and Memere.

"It'll be really soon, I promise," Dad says.

"I know you can do this," Memere says. "Remember all those horrible things Mrs. White did to you and Abe. We'll be right here for you."

"Just keep your eyes on us," Dad adds.

We walk into the courtroom, and I see Mrs. White sitting at the front table. There's no way I can pretend she's not there. I walk to the seat next to the judge. The bailiff asks me to raise my hand and swear that I will tell the whole truth. The whole time I'm doing this, I look at Mrs. White. I can't help myself.

She's smiling at me and mouthing "*I love you, Julie.* "I then start to remember all the things she told me. I had to sign that contract. I watched as she punished Abe for calling me Sissy. I remembered the night she told me she killed my mother.

Then I look past her and see Memere and the man who's now my dad, who was tortured as much as I was during that time. His eyes tell me he loves me. Sitting next to him is my grandmother, this woman who truly loves her son and my brother. I know it'll take time, but she and I will get there. Our relationship is respectful. We're learning to trust each other. I never really trusted Mrs. White. I thought I did, and I thought she would keep me safe, but now that I'm part of the LaMarche family I know that I really am safe.

Soon I realize that Ms. Carter is asking me questions. "July, please tell the court your name."

"July Louise Krativitz," I say.

"How do you know the defendant?" Mrs. Carter asks.

"She was my neighbor," I answer, looking at Dad. He and Memere are sitting on the right of the courtroom, so I can look at them and not at Mrs. White. I notice that Stephanie and Beckie are also in the courtroom, and so is Ms. Ellis. I can't believe she came all the way from Greenville.

"Can you tell the court about the day Mrs. White kidnapped you?" Ms. Carter asks.

"Objection," Mrs. White's lawyer says.

"Tell us about going to Moosehead with Mrs. White," Ms. Carter says.

I think about this, about everything that's changed. I'm not sure how much I should say. I just start at the beginning. I look at all the people who are there for me and know I can do this.

"Well, I was really afraid because my mother was really beaten up. I ran to Mrs. White's house because she was watching my brother. I told her that my mother was really beaten up. She went over to see what was happening with my mom. When she came back, she told us we were staying at her house. The next day she told us she thought it would be a good idea for us to go away for a while. We went to her family's house at Moosehead Lake."

"When did you come to believe you would be staying at Moosehead?' Ms. Carter asks.

"Objection," Mrs. White's lawyer says.

"July, at some point did Mrs. White tell you that you were home?" Ms. Carter asks.

"Yes," I say. "I didn't understand why Mrs. White would be toilet training Abe, my brother, if we were only going to be there for a few days. Mrs. White told me that we were home, and that God had told her to keep us safe."

"When you were with Mrs. White, did she ever tell you that you or your brother should change your name?" Ms. Carter asks.

"Well, Mrs. White had me sign a contract saying that my name was Julie White, and she told me Abe would be called Jason because he was her son."

"Objection," says Mrs. White's lawyer.

"July please explain what you mean when Mrs. White said that Jason was her son," Ms. Carter says.

"Mrs. White told me that Abe was Jason. She truly believed Abe was her son Jason. She was screaming about it and everything. It was really creepy," I say.

"Objection," yells Mrs. White's lawyer.

"Overruled," says the judge.

"July, there was one night when Mrs. White explained to you what happened to your mother. Will you please share this with the court?" Ms. Carter says.

This is the part I really don't want to talk about. I take a deep breath and try to remember what Mrs. White said.

"Take your time, July," Ms. Carter says.

"Mrs. White told me that God told her she needed to kill Mom so she could save us," I say.

"Objection," Mrs. White's lawyer yells.

All of a sudden Mrs. White stands up and starts yelling in that stern voice that I came to dread. "Julie, you know what God told me! I was to put your mother out of her misery to save you and little Jason! God told me to save you!"

"Order, order!" the judge yells, but Mrs. White just continues. "I LOVE YOU JULIE! YOU LOVE ME! YOU TOLD ME THIS! YOU ARE SUPPOSED TO BE WITH ME! GOD PROMISED ME IF I JUST KILLED THAT BIRD OF A MOTHER ,YOU WOULD BE MINE! LITTLE JASON IS MY SON! YOU STAY

AWAY FROM HIM, YOU HEAR ME?!" Mrs. White is screaming at my family.

The judge has the bailiff take Mrs. White away. He tells me I'm dismissed. I run to my dad, and he just hugs me. Soon I realize so many people are hugging me, Memere, Stephanie, Beckie, and Ms. Ellis. I think this nightmare may be over.

CHAPTER 70

Dad came into my room later that day. He told me that Mrs. White was put in a special place for people who are criminally insane, and we wouldn't have to worry about her anymore. He also told me he'd heard from his lawyer about my adoption. It looks like I'll be his official daughter on July first. As he told me this he said, holding back tears, "I can't help but think your mother had something to do with this. You know that July was her favorite month."

"Does this mean that on July first I'll really be July LaMarche?" I ask.

"Legally, you'll be my daughter on July first, but I hope you know you've really been my daughter for much longer. The first time I saw you, I knew you were something special," Dad says.

"You know, Dad, the day we threw Mom's ashes in the ocean, she told me you were a really good guy. She told me it was a blessing when you came into our lives. For so many reasons, I know Mom got this right."

"Your mom was a really smart woman, but I think the way you came into my life was a blessing," Dad says. "Come into my room—I want to share one of the happiest days of my life with you."

I follow him into the bedroom and he points above his bed. "Look," he says.

Hanging above his bed is the picture Mom painted for him the day she told him she was having a baby.

"That day is one I'll never forget," he says as he hugs me, "and you, July, were a big part of it. I wish Jenny were alive to see me adopting you. I know this is going to be another of my happiest days."

"You know, Dad," I say, looking up into his eyes, "Mom is always with us. Who do you think made sure you would find us and keep me safe, safe, safe?"

"I do still hear her voice, and I know she'll be protecting us for a long time," Dad says.

I go back into my room and look at the picture Mom painted of the old lighthouse in New Castle. I know you're happy, Mom, and I know I am, too. I guess we can both rest easy now. Enjoy heaven. I hope you're painting by the sea.

ACKNOWLEDGEMENTS

I would like to give special thanks to my husband, Tom, who always believes I'm capable of anything.

Thanks also to my sister, Judi Paradis, who left us too soon. I miss her positive encouragement. Comparing my writing to Katherine Patterson meets Stephen King kept me going. I know I'll always hear her voice when I'm writing.

Thanks to Joe Panzica, who continues to be my sounding board and refuses to let me stop writing.

Thank you to my editor, Ian Rogers, for pushing me to do my best.

Thanks also to my sisters Lee Paradis, Michelle Hamblin, Jill French, Renee Krikorian, my brother Jack Paradis, and my many nieces and nephews. We are so fortunate to have each other.

Thanks to my daughters Megan Mack, Kate Hopkins, and Morgan Turner; their amazing spouses, Trevor, Shawn, and Russ; and the joys of my life, my grandchildren: Bryce, Ivy, Claire, Emma, Coraline, and Oonabelle. Remember, it doesn't matter how old you are, you can always accomplish a dream with hope and perseverance.

I would like to thank all the students in my Period Five class from 2018-2019: Meaghan, Molly, Lia, Aubrianna, Alex, Kaylin, Evan, Erin, Emma, Gracie, Braxton, Samantha, Samantha, Layla, Annie. Thanks also to David, Treston, Lin, Amber, Charlotte, and so many of my other students from Dover Middle School. Your help and encouragement made this possible.

There are so many friends who encouraged me as I continued to find my voice. Thank you for reading and telling me, yes you can: Gail and Richard Kushner, Joanne Mercier, Joanne Morin, Cherie Corbett, Cori White, Laurie Johnson, Linda Stimson, Deb Dube and Jessica Goldman.

Thanks to my colleagues and friends from Dover Middle School who know July, especially Jess Clark, Alison Ritrosky, Lesley Allen, and Deb Hackett.

Special thanks to my cheerleaders, Denise Copley and Margaret McDermott—life is always better with friends.

I would also like to express my gratitude to my niece, Scarlett Krikorian, and my sister, Lee Paradis, for the cover artwork and design.

Milton Keynes UK
Ingram Content Group UK Ltd.
UKHW032020240823
427459UK00004B/76